"Guess Who?"

"Oh, what the hell is this?" Marie demanded . . . Then she paused and cautiously felt the large, tapered hands, covered with smooth scales, that lay over her eyes. In the next instant she exploded out of the dragon's light grasp and leaped into Dr. Barker's arms. Of course, he was not at all prepared to catch her, and she was a tall girl in the first place. The result of that most ill-considered move was that she bowled him over and the pair crashed to the floor in a sprawl of arms and legs.

Vajerral, drawn to the sound of the mishap, grabbed the back of the recliner and pulled herself up to the limit of her long neck, and found herself almost eye to eye with Jenny. The girl screamed, and the dragonet replied in kind. Unfortunately she was undecided about screaming and breathing flames, and the result was a rather feeble mixture of both. Allan entered the room at a run.

"Your sister?" the sorceress asked complacently, indicating the tangled mass of bodies between them.

It was at that fortuitous moment that the pizza arrived.

MAKE WAY FOR DRAGONS!

THORARINN GUNNARSSON

ACE BOOKS, NEW YORK

MAKE WAY FOR DRAGONS!

• Part One •

The Way Between the Worlds

THE RIFT WAS thrust wide with a brilliant flash of light at the point of actual breakage. A circle of fire raced outward across that sheet of icy blackness, eating away the barrier between the worlds. An icy wind poured out through the steadily expanding opening. It swept outward in unseen waves across the dry grass of the clearing where the rift hung suspended a hundred feet up, bending the winter-barren branches of mountain hardwoods.

The edges of the rift were still burning and peeling away as a form dark and deadly shot through that long, black tunnel from beyond. A shape that was vast, menacing and ghostly. It hurtled out into the night of the new world, and the dark mists that had clung to its form fell away, revealing a reality that was even more deadly and terrible to behold. A draconic form, fully sixty feet from fanged snout to armored tail and a hundred across his powerful leathern wings, Vorgulremik erupted into the cold night air screaming his rage and defiance in a voice that shook the mountains. Steel dragon and sorcerer of the Dark Magic, he should have feared nothing that hunted the many worlds. And yet fear for his very existence had driven him to seek this last, desperate escape by fleeing into an unknown world.

Vorgulremik screamed again as he arched his back and cupped his vast wings to lift himself above the trees as he raced away toward the distant heights, trailing wisps of magic mist that were black even against the cloudless night sky. All dragons were natural gliders, using their wings only for lift as they relied upon levitation to propel them swiftly and effortlessly through the sky. Such was a part of a dragon's native magic, not unlike its fiery breath or its ability to see without light.

Vorgulremik was no exception, as great and powerful as he was. He was also near the end of his natural strength from an hour's running fight and from the supreme effort of opening the rift, something few workers of magic could accomplish at the best of times. For now he fled blindly into the darkness, not even pausing to seal the Way. It was too late for that.

Moments later a second dark form shot through the rift. Small, silent and swift, this dragon was determined to have an end to this contest. It seemed inconceivable that the mighty Vorgulremik should have been fleeing for his very life from this tiny sorceress. Dalvenjah was just under nine feet, two thirds of that graceful neck and long sweeping tail, and only twelve across her sharply tapered wings. She weighed barely two hundred and fifty pounds to the steel dragon's five tons. But she was fully his equal in her command of magic, and perhaps soon to prove herself the better. She also possessed the advantages of speed and quick responses that were a part of her smaller, lighter form. Unnoticed for the moment, an even smaller winged shape rushed through the Way behind her. The tiny dragon paused for a quick look, then darted away for the shelter of the nearest trees.

The golden dragon found her prey quickly and the chase began. This fight was to the death, wherever it led or however long it lasted. Dalvenjah had determined that, although outward appearances did not argue that she could win. Vorgulremik was completely encased in an impenetrable shell of steel-hard plating, from which his kind derived their name. Each of his powerful claws bore swordlike talons capable of rending iron as easily as leather, while the length of his spine from head to tail-tip bore a protective ridge of knife-edged plates. His jaws—

powerful enough to snap Dalvenjah's head from her neck, should he be lucky enough to catch her—were armed with sharp fangs as long as Dalvenjah's forearm. His massive head was crowned with a pair of forward-facing ramming horns that glittered with the same metallic sheen as the rest of his armor.

Dalvenjah, by contrast, had no natural weapons except for fangs that could never penetrate his hard scales and a pair of small, almost fragile-looking horns above and behind each of her large jewel eyes. She was softly scaled, a gleaming gold, although her scales were proof against the worst flames. She was a Veridan, a trained warrior-sorceress, although the sword and knives in her harness were useless against the steel dragon's tough scales. But her fiery breath was just as hot and she could match him for range. Her magic equalled his, and her fury was daunting. He was running in fear for his life from her, doubting his ability to win this battle.

She found him easily enough, rushing low over the trees not a quarter of a mile away. There were no clouds in the clear night sky into which he could disappear, and he was too big to fly beneath the trees. There was nowhere for Vorgulremik to hide, and he realized this. His ploy of escaping into another world had not worked, for she had followed him. And as long as they were in the same world, he could not run far enough to hide his magic from her. He had no choice but to fight.

Dalvenjah was not surprised when she saw him circle wide as he turned back to attack. She had made this fight unavoidable, for she had no more choice in this matter than he did. She had not expected him to open a rift to escape her, but she was not about to leave him to plunder and terrorize a new, defenseless world. She had a duty as a Veridan, a sorceress of the highest order, to protect all life, and it was in a way her fault that he was here. Locked into a battle that neither could afford to flee, the two contestants began to move toward each other for the final contest.

Dalvenjah glanced about at this new world while she could and tried to reckon her advantages. She would have guessed that he would have retreated into some world he knew, but he had opened a rift at random in his haste and fear. These high, forested mountains were far more like her own home than his. This wild, rugged land was full of places where she could hide that he could not, and the biting winter cold would work against him. Nor did there seem to be any danger that she could be distracted trying to protect innocent victims, as Derjadhan had been fatally distracted in his own fight with this evil beast only two weeks earlier. No, coming here had been nothing but a mistake for her enemy.

Vorgulremik turned sharply to cut back but paused in flight to hover by lift magic, his wings beating slowly for balance. "Dalvenjah Foxfire!"

"What would you say to me, Vorgulremik Bluesmoke?" She arched her long neck to call back.

"Do not make this unavoidable, Mindijarah!"

"You have made this unavoidable!" she screamed back at him, desperation and pain shading her voice. "You owe me a life, and there is only one way that you can repay that."

The steel dragon arched over and began to rush forward, a headlong attack that Dalvenjah recognized immediately as a feint. Vorgulremik was too far spent to fight an offensive battle; he needed to hold his own, forcing her to come to him. Speed, quickness and endurance were all her advantages just now, and they both knew it. Still, the primary rule was that a steel dragon was as unpredictable as a golden dragon was swift and crafty. Vorgulremik hurtled on, the wind whistling over his knife-edged spines, while Dalvenjah held back and waited for him to come.

The two dragons met head-on in flight above the silent forest, and it almost seemed that Vorgulremik was not going to dodge. At the very last moment Dalvenjah saw the bunching of the shoulders of his wings and knew that he would hurtle himself sharply upward and to her left. But she was the quicker, using a powerful thrust of her own lift-magic to send her circling close around his long neck and above his head. The tail-snap at his vulnerable eye missed, but the blow to his face was nearly enough to stun him. Vorgulremik flinched and almost lost his balance in his weakened state, falling a short distance before he was able to correct. His right wing dipped low to rake through the trees, breaking branches but doing him no harm.

Dalvenjah circled back quickly, but Vorgulremik had already seen the futility of that particular approach and climbed into the upper reaches. He could not fight according to her terms, with quick darts and dodges; he needed room to run and turn, both to protect himself and to attack. Dalvenjah circled him in an almost teasing manner at a safe distance, having already seen that he was careful not to wander too far from the rift. He wanted to keep it at hand as a safe retreat back to where he had started, should he again find himself unable to either win this battle or escape.

Dalvenjah turned to dart in suddenly from behind, her sleek form trailing ribbons of blue mist as she shot like an arrow at her prey. So swift was her attack that Vorgulremik almost failed to notice her until it was too late, jerking himself around to avoid her rush. He snapped at her small form as she darted past just below his armored belly. She muttered to herself the words of the power that she would command, and the steel dragon felt his lift-magic fail him at the very moment that he was relying upon it entirely. He fell tumbling from the air nearly into the treetops before he was able to bring himself under control. He climbed laboriously with long, powerful strokes of his unaided wings, striving to regain some height before she could come at him again.

Dalvenjah harassed him again and again with that simple trick and several others, keeping him always on the defensive. While she seemed to be doing him no real harm, her unrelenting attack was quickly draining his already depleted reserves of strength, both physical and magical, as well as reducing him to a confusion born of rage and frustration. She was waiting for Vorgulremik to make that fatal mistake, knowing that he eventually would as long as she could maintain control of their battle. And she would be ready when he did.

The end of that game came suddenly. One of Dalvenjah's spells went awry when she failed to wait until she was near enough, and Vorgulremik recovered quickly to dive after her as she shot past. That gave him a moment to prepare his own counterattack, realizing in desperation that he had to put an end to this before he was spent. He spoke his own words, and dense, rolling clouds grew out of the very air in a matter of seconds to fill the night sky. A cloudy sky was a favorite battleground for all breeds of larger dragons. It offered a place to hide for both protection and attack, making up for his deficiencies in speed and maneuverability and setting him on what he considered far more equitable terms with his smaller adversary.

"Flee, Dalvenjah Foxfire!" he roared through the clouds. "Accept my mercy while you may. I know that you have none for me."

But Dalvenjah did not respond. What Vorgulremik had summoned to his own defense was again to her best advantage. While he was most often aware of her every movement even when she was concealed from sight, she was always aware of him. Thus they began a mutual chase in and out of the clouds, striking out at each other with long spears of flame. Each one sought to confuse and rush in at the other as they weaved a complex pattern of feint and dodge between them.

Then Dalvenjah called upon her strongest magic of concealment and knew that she had confused Vorgulremik, who paused to hover in mid-air not a hundred yards below and to one side of where she hid. This was the very chance that she had been waiting for. Angling her wings slightly back, she turned and dived directly àt him. When he still did not seem to be aware of her, she called upon her most potent magical weapon.

Her entire form began to glow brightly, turning swiftly into a spear-point of flame aimed at her target. A steel dragon was invulnerable to almost any attack, protected by so strong a personal magic that no physical weapon could harm one of them greatly. But if Dalvenjah could ram him while converted to her fiery form, then her own flames would blast him utterly. It was the only way she knew to kill him while he still possessed the strength to fight back.

Vorgulremik was aware of her instantly, for there was no hiding such magic. But for just a moment he was unsure of the direction of her attack. And that moment should have been all she needed. By unlucky chance he saw her streaking toward him over his shoulder at the very last instant and was able to bring his massive head around in time to spit a ball of flame at her. Unable to evade, she met the fireball head-on and the two forces exploded in flames. Dalvenjah was hurtled tumbling out of the core of that terrible blast, and in the next instant a blow from the steel dragon's heavy claw knocked her from the sky.

She came away from that double assault dazed and in pain but in better shape than she deserved. She struggled to bring her wings down to control her fall, and screamed as a cracked bone failed under that stress and her left wing was twisted backward at a point where it was not supposed to bend. For the moment she could only allow herself to fall helplessly as she fought against the burning pain to speak the words of command. The damaged length of her wing glowed with a pale blue light, and then she screamed again as the bone was suddenly forced out straight and true and the fragments of bone were locked in place. This was not an instant cure. The break was still present, but it was now immobilized better than any splint could hold it.

The pain immediately began to abate, so that she was soon able to straighten her wings and regain some control over her fall. She completed her descent in a plummeting glide, slipping through the branches of the forest and then breaking her speed with a sharp thrust of levitation before settling heavily to the leaf-covered ground between pockets of lingering snow.

She lay for some time, neck, tail and limbs sprawled and wings lying limply upon the ground as she panted harshly for breath, waiting for the pain to subside. The throbbing in her wing was soon muted to a dull, hot ache, so that she now became aware of lesser injuries. She thought that nearly every rib along her left side must be cracked, although all had fortunately stayed in place, and a great many things hurt that were not otherwise damaged. At least she had escaped rending from those long, sharp talons.

She lay for some minutes in grateful darkness, her eyes firmly closed, as she waited to see if Vorgulremik would return to finish her. At that moment she could not have stood off the attentions of a playful kitten, but she hurt so badly that she hardly cared. Then she heard the sound of rustling leather that she recognized as a dragon backwinging to land only a few feet away, but a dragon small beyond the notice of the likes of Vorgulremik. Curiosity got the better of her and she opened her eyes. Tiny Vajerral was standing before her, wings spread for flight as the dragonet watched her injured mother anxiously with jewel eyes that glittered with concern.

"Are you well?" Vajerral asked softly.

"Well enough. But just what are you doing here?" Dalvenjah asked in return, which she considered to be a far more important question.

Vajerral folded her wings and sat back on her haunches. "I followed you through the Way Between the Worlds so that I could be on hand if I am needed. I think that you need me now."

She seemed rather surprised and just a little indignant that the question should even be asked. She was, after all, the daughter of two of the most powerful magicians among the golden dragons and possessed no small talent of her own. Dalvenjah sighed and nodded her head with weary resignation; it was best not to discourage children, especially where it concerned training for a future profession.

"What now?" Vajerral asked.

Dalvenjah had to close her eyes a moment and consider that very question. The open rift waited invitingly not half a mile away, and a deep instinct told her to get her dragonet out of this place as soon as possible. This was a world completely unknown to her, with any manner of evil monsters that might be lurking about . . . quite aside from the monster she knew was here, somewhere. But duty argued that her place was here, at least until she had recovered enough to face Vorgulremik yet again and destroy him. She certainly could not simply disappear through that gate and leave the natives to deal with that fiend as best they could. Steel dragons were practically invincible except against a magic at least as strong as their own, and her first impression of this world was that such magic might be in very short supply.

But what until then? Dalvenjah reminded herself that the term Mindijarah, golden dragon, seemed appropriate for her kind only from a purely draconic point of view. She was still two hundred and fifty pounds of fighting dragon in dire need of good and plentiful food during her weeks of recovery. She needed a safe place to stay, and certainly shelter and comfort for her child. And she would benefit from access to magical equipment and supplies.

That last requirement decided the question for her. Professional courtesy was known in every world that she had ever visited, whether dragon, elf or even human, and a competent magician would be able to help her in many ways. She would at least have a common cause with a sorcerer of the Light, and she could benefit by knowing more about this unknown world. There was likely to be the problem of language, easily overcome when both parties were telepaths. And if she was going to be stranded in a strange world for some weeks to come, it might as well be with someone she could understand on at least a professional basis.

But where would she find such a person? Dalvenjah cautiously lifted herself up to all fours, and then sat well up on her haunches with her head erect as she turned her senses to scanning the world about her. As she had already guessed, Vorgulremik had fled. Not back through the rift, but somewhere into the wilds of this world. He had his own recovery to make, reserves of energy to be replenished through a long rest and occasional feedings. She was reluctant to consider the nature of that feeding; Morilyekarin, the steel dragons, were ones to feed on whatever they found. Just as he had fed. . . .

Dalvenjah thrust such thoughts fiercely from her mind. There was nothing that she could do about that; certainly not now, nor for some time yet to come. Instead she turned her attention back to the task at hand. There were so few traces of true magic in this world; only a poor diminished remnant of the native faerie folk far to the north. Wizards of any type must be very few and far between. A very primitive, backwards world, forever stunted for want of magic and those who could use it. She could only make the most of what she had.

"Let's get on with business," she said briskly, putting up a calm, secure front for Vajerral's sake. She quickly checked her weapons. "But you keep your ears raised and your eyes open. This is a strange world, after all."

"I'll watch out!" the dragonet declared bravely.

The first matter was to close the Way Between the Worlds. Not because she wanted to trap Vorgulremik here; he had opened this rift and could as easily force another. She was more concerned with whatever other nasty little monsters might be making their way from the world of the dark dragons into this one through that invitingly open way. When she considered it, she had to admit that Vajerral was far better off here than alone in that place where they had been. This world might be short on magic, but it also seemed to be lacking in native monsters.

By the time that the two golden dragons had made their way back to the open rift, walking through the snowy forest to spare Dalvenjah's injured wing, she saw that her worst fears were true. Packs of illeshyan, attracted by the magic of the Way Between the Worlds, were practically swarming through. They were small but fierce creatures, draconic shapes like winged weasels but much larger. Hunting in packs, they were not afraid to bring down any prey, even the largest dragon, that they could overwhelm.

A quick scan with her senses told her that at least two hundred illeshyan, seven distinct packs of various sizes, had come through already to disappear into the woods. There was nothing she could do now but close the Way so that no more could come through. At least the nasty creatures lacked magic, flame or any real intelligence. And unlike the steel dragon, they were vulnerable even to conventional weapons, no real problem for the natives to handle themselves.

Dalvenjah sat back on her tail before the Way Between the Worlds and began to work the magic that would close the rift, mending the tear in the substance that separated the two universes. She considered simply closing the Way, for once closed and secured by her own magic only she could have opened it again. But she saw no need in keeping a ready way into the world of the dark dragons. When the time came for her to leave this place, then she would open her own way and return directly to her own world. Under her manipulation, the edges of the rift slowly grew back together and the tear in the universe was repaired, and any trace that a way had ever been open vanished from sight.

The sorceress had to rest again after that. She realized that her plans for finding a competent wizard to help her would have to wait for the next day, for she was not going to be traveling that night. Her damaged wing was not yet ready for even short flights. Golden dragons, unlike most other breeds, could walk upright fairly well but not for extended travel. They were also very long-legged compared to other breeds and could walk or even run easily enough on all fours. But Dalvenjah knew that, due to her scholarly life as a mage, her leathery hands were still too soft for much travel through such rugged, snowy land as this. Besides that, she was near the end of her strength, cold and sore. And she was now very hungry, even if the stoic little Vajerral would not admit to such discomfort. It was best to find shelter for the night and worry about the next step in the morning.

"Let's find us a warm place where we can spend the night, and see if we might scare up something to eat," she suggested.

"I can hunt!" Vajerral declared eagerly.

Dalvenjah nodded, admitting to herself that they would go hungry if little Vajerral could not catch something. This was not the time of year for berries, and she had her doubt about nuts as well.

The two Mindijaran spent what remained of the night in the only shelter they could find, a crude hut made of branches to form an outer wall for an overhang of rock that they had discovered. Morning came clear and bright, reminding them of their own home in the mountains of another world. Dalvenjah found that she was in very little pain that morning. Her wing was already well on its way to mending and she thought now that she might not have had as much damage to her ribs as she had at first feared. She should be able to travel well enough this day, and they would be able to spend their second night in this world safe and warm in a wizard's den, comfortably full of venison and hot bread with butter and mead.

Vajerral hunted on the wing again that morning and proved herself very adept at this task, returning within minutes with her catch of three of the largest rabbits that either dragon had ever seen. Vajerral also insisted upon skinning and preparing them herself, as she had the night before. Dalvenjah loaned her a knife, then sat back and watched with quiet approval. She could be a doting mother but never overprotective. She thought it very important for children to learn to care for themselves as soon as possible, especially those like Vajerral who possessed such strong magic. Making a fire was never a problem for a dragon, and for much the same reason they were all remarkably good cooks. They both ate well on roasted rabbit, and Vajerral had good reason to feel rather pleased with herself, having provided it all.

"How are you feeling?" Dalvenjah asked the little dragon as they made ready to travel. "Are you cold?"

"No, I'm fine," Vajerral insisted. "Do we go now? I can scout!"

The sorceress frowned, reckoning that she would be traveling slowly because of her injuries, and that Vajerral would be bored with that pace. "Yes, you can scout. But you will not go far."

Tracing the magic she sensed to the wizard she sought was no problem in itself. There were at least two individuals possessing very strong magic in what she believed must be a town some miles to the east. The only problem was that she thought it to be fifty miles at the very least, a fifteen-minute flight when she was at her best but a long day's journey under the present circumstances. She was just a little surprised that no wizards had come to her, investigating the tremendous amount of magic that had been tossed about the previous night.

That would have certainly made things simpler, for Dalvenjah was determined to keep with her original plan of not revealing herself to anyone but the wizard she sought. She would not fight the natives but she was also in no condition to flee, and she had heard too many stories about backwards worlds where the natives could not tell the difference between good and evil dragons. And if there was one thing that she was now very certain of, it was that there were no dragons native to this world.

Resigned to a long journey through the wilderness, the Mindijarah was rather surprised when, only two hours later, she caught her first indication of civilization in the form of a road snaking its way up a steep, wooded hillside. She had been flying slowly just over the treetops, holding her wings straight and propelling herself with lift-magic alone. Vajerral alternated between making brief forays to explore the countryside and flying closely, almost protectively, at her side. They had just cleared a ridge of tall pines and suddenly saw the road immediately below them. Dalvenjah had been so startled that she immediately circled back to land for a closer look.

Her understandable surprise was not just with the mere presence of the road, but with its strange nature. It was certainly no dirt track through the wilderness, and her curiosity was so great that she slipped quietly out of the cover of the woods for a close look.

It was as wide as her own wingspan, divided down the center with a painted stripe, and composed of some hard grey substance, a paving material that was not laid out in blocks as she had known but seemingly pressed or formed into a solid sheet, now cracked and broken near the edges with age and use. It smelled rather bad and seemed to be coated with a film of some oily material, so that she was reluctant to touch it. She could appreciate the design, for it gave better traction for draft animals while preventing wagon wheels from being mired in mud and snow. What she could not easily imagine was the wealth and labor that must have gone into making such a road.

But that turned out to be only the first and least of her surprises that day. She was still peering at the strange road when the sound of something approaching sent her back into hiding. Staring out from the protective shadows of the forest, she could hardly believe her eyes when a curious vehicle shot past. She did know enough about such matters to recognize it as the machine it was, a small, four-wheeled vehicle about as long as herself and no higher than her shoulder. There was certainly no horse or any other beast pulling it—and it was moving faster than the swiftest horse—nor did there seem to be any magic involved.

Just as interesting, and far more informative, was the nature of the two inhabitants of the vehicle, seated in its enclosed center portion. The machine was moving too fast for her to get a good look, but she was sure that they were either mortals or elves. She suspected the former, from what little she saw of them. Nor did she sense any more magic about that pair than she had about their machine, which also suggested simple mortals. She sighed wearily. She had met enough humans in the past but could not count any among her friends, for they certainly were not her companions of choice. She realized that she had also been wise to keep herself hidden.

"We are, I think, in a lot of trouble," Vajerral commented softly.

Dalvenjah sighed again and nodded. She could not deny it.

By late that afternoon, as the late winter sun was setting

quickly in the west, the two golden dragons had seen quite a number of things to cause wonder and concern. Vehicles of various sizes, some large enough to serve as homes, raced along a surprising number of roads, and metal dragons soared through the cold sky. And before them lay a city the size of which she had never imagined could even exist, a city that must be large enough to include the entire nation of golden dragons. They had been skirting out-flung pieces of the city for the past hour, ever since they had first begun to come down from the mountains into the highland plains. Dalvenjah was beginning to wonder just what manner of world the two of them had found themselves in.

She could see that it would not be very easy to get to this wizard undetected. She could now sense clearly that he dwelled somewhere near what could be considered the outskirts of this overgrown city, not a mile from where she and her dragonet watched the coming and going of vast herds of the wheeled machines. Darkness was falling swiftly. That was their only hope, since the entire distance to their goal was across an unbroken expanse of native houses. Well, they could always fly high enough and imitate the circling of soaring birds, an old and favored trick as long as one stayed out of range of the stoutest bow. She regretted that her thick coat was an almost inviting light gold, and Vajerral was hardly any darker. But then, the elves did have a saying that all dragons are black at night.

"Are you ready?" she asked.

"Yes!" Vajerral assured her mother eagerly, spreading her wings. Thoughts of good food and a warm, soft bed were enough to make them both impatient to be on their way. The only thing that Dalvenjah could not figure out was why a city this size did not boast at least ten times as many wizards, even if they were only human.

Many miles away, at the scene of the previous night's battle, a small group of mortal men were puzzling over the few clues that they had been able to find. There were three distinct agencies taking part in the investigation, and each one thought that the other two should not have been there. Once it had become apparent that no one group was going to find any answers, they had at last joined forces . . . only to find that they were still right back where they had started.

"Sheriff, just guessing, is there anything in the local wildlife that could have accounted for this?" Dave Wallick asked, repeating the question that they had been returning to time and again for the past two hours.

"Just guessing?" Sheriff Hansin repeated, making it clear that he would make no "official" judgments on the matter. He had laid aside his resentment of both the FBI and this "special investigator" from the Air Force when it became apparent that no one had any easy answers to this puzzle.

"That seems to me about all we can do," Wallick assured him. "About all that any of us can say officially is that we have no idea of just what has happened here . . . if anything."

"Well, we've all seen the tracks," the sheriff began. Of the three groups, he was the most impressed with just how strange all this really was. "We had two creatures there, obviously the same type but of vastly different size. They walked on all fours for the most part, so we can see that their forepaws were almost identical with our own hands in shape and size, with hind paws that were more canine in appearance, but very long and thin. But I've also seen three separate points where the little one sat down in the snow and left evidence of a hind end that belongs on a kangaroo, at least that tail."

"Could it have been a kangaroo?" Major Newell asked.

Hansin considered that briefly and shook his head very firmly. "I know something about kangaroos from watching television. Animals are my hobby, you might say, and I never forget anything I see. The largest of the kangaroos that I know of are the red kangaroos, which are fairly big but nothing like this. And they have hind paws that can't be mistaken for this, much longer than what we see here when they sit back, but much shorter when they walk on just the forward portion."

"What does it resemble most?" Newell asked, still using his crisp military manner that made his questions ring like orders.

"What it resembles most in this area is a raccoon. The trouble there is that raccoons don't have hands that well developed, or tails like that, and they don't come upwards of two hundred pounds. Which is more or less where I would put the big one.

But neither raccoons nor kangaroos build shelters beneath an overhang, skin rabbits or make fires to cook them. Nor do they simply walk out into the middle of a clearing and suddenly take to the air.''

"The tracks might have been erased," Don Borelli suggested, the first thing that he had contributed in some time.

"Tracks are like pencil marks. You really can't erase completely without scratching the paper," Hansin explained. "Besides, raccoons and kangaroos don't have anything to do with lights in the sky and balls of fire, which is what brought all of us out here in the first place. And don't forget those scores of ratlike tracks streaming out in all directions from that one point."

"Rats?" Wallick asked dubiously. "Even I can see that those things you call rats must be as big as a collie."

"They also have that nasty tendency to be walking along and suddenly take to the air," Hansin added, and turned to Newell. "Do you want to have a turn guessing at what we might have here? My unofficial pronouncement is that we have something here not of this world."

Newell laughed. "If I had to guess, then I would say that an alien boy scout and his little brother were dropped off here last night in their flying saucer, tested their survival skills and were picked up again earlier today. And when the mother ship came in to land, all the rats jumped ship. Listen, I've seen a lot of strange things in the course of my career. For that matter, I've seen things a lot stranger than this. Most of the time there is a very simple explanation for everything. And even when there isn't, we have to see hard physical evidence before we can say that we have something out of this world. All I can say about what we have here is evidence of tracks of an animal of an unknown type. Someone else could have built the shelter and fire and skinned the rabbits."

"That is possible," Hansin admitted. "But if you can identify the animal that left these tracks, then I would very much like to know what it was. I can assure you that it was nothing local."

"I want to know myself," Newell agreed. "But, unless you can see in the dark, we might as well hang it up for tonight and look for our dinner."

They turned and started back toward the cars, easily seen in the growing darkness because of the flashing lights on the sheriff's four-wheel drive. The two FBI agents and Major Newell had driven here in nondescript four-door sedans that were typical government issue, and they were beginning to wonder if they were going to be able to get back out through the mud. At least the ground was fairly well frozen, a condition that was surely increasing by the minute now that the sun had gone down.

"What are you two going to write this one off as?" Newell asked as they walked along.

"Kangaroos from Mars?" Wallick asked, and shrugged to himself. "We don't really have to say anything, I suppose, since we weren't actually sent here to investigate anything."

"Then why are you here?" Hansin asked incredulously, firmly convinced that only direct orders could have brought city cops into the mountains at this time of the year.

"Personal rather than professional curiosity," Wallick explained rather sheepishly. "We were driving back from a business trip last night when we saw all the lights and fireballs, so as soon as we finished our real work today we headed back up here as fast as we could for a look and found the two of you waiting."

"You saw it?" Newell demanded impatiently. "Well, what the hell did it look like?"

"Oh, we tried our best to get in close but the best we could do was about two miles," Borelli said. "That was just what it looked like, fireballs. It was mostly over by the time we got there. There was one last, big explosion that lit up the hillside, and a few seconds later something dark shot past our car just above the treetops. It was fairly big, bigger than most private planes. But it glowed slightly around the edges, and it didn't make a sound."

"So, what did it look like?" Hansin asked eagerly. "A flying saucer?"

"No, it had wings," Wallick said, and looked troubled. "Frankly, it looked for all the world like a dragon. And a great deal larger than whatever made the tracks we saw."

"Sheriff!" Deputy Tucker leaped out from behind a tree directly before them, causing all four to jump in fright and reach for their guns. It was never wise to startle four men with guns, especially in the woods at night during the discussion of such an unearthly subject. As it turned out, the deputy managed by no fault of his own to survive the incident.

"Damn it, Tuck. Why did you do that?" Hansin demanded crossly. "I told you to stay with the truck."

"Sorry, Chief." Tucker panted breathlessly, swallowed loudly and continued. "There's been trouble over at the Muellen place. A witness swears that the farm was attacked by dozens of little dragons, no bigger than a modest-sized dog. Killed and ate just about everything they could find and left nothing but the bones."

"Dragons?" Hansin looked pale even in the dark. "When did this happen? And what do you mean, ate? What did they ate . . . eat?"

"About an hour ago. And they ate everything," the deputy insisted. "Cows and horses, chickens, three dogs and a cat. And the Muellens."

"Oh, great!" the sheriff muttered to himself, then turned to the others. "You might as well come along and see what you can make of it. It seems that we have dragons of three sizes: small, medium and extra-large. I just want to know two things. Where the hell did these things come from, and what am I supposed to do about them?"

· Part Two ·

The Sorceress

ALLAN BREIVIK LOOKED upon that night's cello solo with a great deal of ambivalence. Every musician in the symphony dreamed of a solo during an actual performance, and most would only dream. And yet he was never able to perform solo without the image in his own mind of his sister standing sternly over him, ready to cut him to the quick with a tirade of ridicule for the smallest mistake. He was not one to make mistakes; everyone agreed that he was nothing but a solo-quality performer. But fear of failure and the threat of humiliation were the vultures that stood staring down at him during every performance, distracting him from his playing and preventing him from being even better than he was. Even he recognized this in himself, but he had not figured out how to overcome it.

Nor did he need to pay a psychologist to tell him that it was because he hated his sister. He really did not hate Marie, but there were times when he wished her nothing but ill . . . and there certainly was no one in the world who deserved it more. Marie had raised him since their parents died when he was fourteen, and she had been raising him ever since. What he had never been able to figure out was why she was such a good mother to her own daughter, when she was nothing but strict and unforgiving with him. Perhaps it was because she was so disappointed with him for turning out to be the accomplished musician he had wanted to be, and not the stuffy, secure executive she had planned upon him becoming. That might have seemed, to someone who did not know Marie, to be none of her business, but she had never accepted that turn of events, and she never let him forget it.

"Hurry up!" Danny called from the front room, already halfway out the door. "And whatever you do, don't dawdle through your cadenzas tonight. I have to get you home as soon as possible after the concert so that I can get on with my own affairs."

"Affairs?" Allan asked rather incredulously, and promptly ruined his third attempt on a reluctant bow tie. Where was Marie when he needed her? "Danny, do you honestly mean to tell me that you have a date after the longest concert this season?"

"Exactly, Al me boy!" Danny sounded very pleased with himself. "Being first trumpet includes a professional responsibility to keep your lip in good condition."

"I thought your problem was more a case of being too horny," Allan remarked. "Besides, I don't get to do my own cadenzas in the Dvorak concerto and you know it. If you had told me, I would have driven myself."

"Fair is fair," Danny called back. "When have I not had something cooking after a concert? I need a little help getting settled down again after a performance."

"Speaking of settling down, when are you going to get married?" Allan asked as he attempted the intricacies of the tie yet again.

"And when are you? Or won't Marie allow it?"

"Marie won't allow it, and I don't care enough right now to fight her on the matter," Allan answered. "I'm still grounded from the time she found a girl right here in the house, even if it was only the middle of the afternoon and the dear thing was on her way out the door at the time. And that was over a year ago now."

"That's long enough. So when are you going to get in the mood again?"

"Not right now," he insisted, suspecting another attempt on the part of his older friend to arrange "something" for him. "I'm going to try to get a position at another major orchestra in the next year. Somewhere very far away, and then hope that Marie won't follow me there."

"Want to bet on it?" Danny asked doubtfully. "What orchestras have you auditioned for lately? Berlin? Paris? Or were you planning on going back to the old country?"

"That won't do. Marie speaks perfect Norwegian. I don't." He executed the final twist and fold of the tie and found to his amazement that it had come out perfect. "Ah, there we are. Coming!"

He hurried to the front room, only to discover that Danny was no longer there but, predictably, in the kitchen. Danny Grehan was one of those types that ordinary people found frustrating. No amount of food made him plump, and no amount of drink made him stagger. Just now, in his concert formal wear, he looked the part of the dark and dashing millionaire playboy; at other times he looked more like a dark and daring movie swashbuckler, and he never lacked for a young, pretty and willing girl to keep him company after a concert, or any other night of the week, and a different one each night. Of course he was not about to get married just yet; he knew a good thing when he had it.

Allan could not have been more different. As Danny himself put it, Allan was the eternal teen-ager, twenty-eight going on sixteen. He certainly did not reflect his direct Nordic heritage, being small of build if not short, with nondescript brown hair and eyes that he shared with his sister, although she had long since found the true Scandinavian blond in a bottle. He had dated less than a half a dozen times in his life, and his virginity was certainly in no danger. His sister worked hard to keep him in that state and he usually allowed her the satisfaction of thinking that she was responsible, although he knew perfectly well that the blame was entirely his own. He felt that he was still looking for something he needed before he would feel truly grown up. Perhaps puberty.

"Will you get out of there?" he said sharply. "We have to hurry. It's already dark outside."

"And whose fault is that?" Danny asked as he retrieved

something from the refrigerator before slamming the door. "I thought I should check out the provisions in case we were stranded here for the night."

They paused on their way out just long enough for Allan to collect the rather unhandy burden of his cello case. A moment later they were out the door and on their way to the car, unaware of the two dark, winged shapes that descended at that very moment behind that same house and settled into the concealing shadows of the yard. The two dragons could hear the slamming of metal doors as they folded their wings and looked around.

Dalvenjah was certain that she had come to the right place. Her wizard, the most powerful sorcerer whom she could sense in this entire world, was at that moment riding away in one of the native mechanical carriages. It was just bad timing that her arrival had coincided with his own departure, but she had to consider herself fortunate that he had stayed in one place long enough for her to know where to find him when he did return. She was under the impression that he would be back again that night, and so she decided to wait and make herself known to him in her own good time.

Until then, there was no point in waiting around outside. Professional courtesy was the same everywhere, so she knew that she would be welcome. She walked slowly over to the back door and bent her long neck to peer intently for a moment at the lock. The design was unlike anything that she had ever seen before, small and complex, but hardly beyond her talents. She muttered a word of command and made a sign of movement before the lock. A loud click followed, the knob turned and the door opened of its own accord. Magicians had an understanding about such things; if you could open the lock by magical means, then you were more than welcome.

She paused only a moment to hurry Vajerral inside before slipping in herself and closing the door behind her. She knew that there was no one within the house, but they were in some danger of being seen if they remained outside. She realized immediately that they were in the kitchen, and she looked around for some candle, lamp, fireplace or even a magical glowstone to light and found to her consternation that there were none to be had. Well, perhaps the local magicians used something the likes of which she had never heard.

Anyway, there was certainly food to be had. Her sense of
smell was very sharp and she could detect many wonderful
scents, although the smells of venison, hot bread and mead
seemed to be lacking entirely.

Well, one could not have everything. At least there was food
to be had, and both dragons were led by their noses to the
curious metal box off to one side. Opening this, Dalvenjah
found not only food but the light that she had been wondering
about. Curiously, the light seemed to burn no fuel nor use
magic, and she was at a loss to know how it worked. It was
also cold inside the cabinet, particularly in the smaller compartment. She nodded to herself, recognizing good, solid magic
when she saw it. Vajerral was already helping herself to pickles
and smoked trout, and for the moment that was the most immediate concern. The golden dragons made themselves quite
at home and waited for the wizard to return.

Allan staggered in through the front door some time later,
feeling very much as if it was four in the morning rather than
only half past eleven. Concerts were always hard on the performers; some could barely totter to bed afterward, while others
were so excited and enthralled by the music of their own making
that they would not be able to even sit still until some time the
following day. Allan was variously one or the other, and this
night he was definitely under the influence of the former state.
He should have been excited in knowing that he had played
very well indeed, but he was disgusted with the belief that he
should have played even better. Of course, it was always infinitely worse after a solo performance.

Pieces of tuxedo landed where they may on the way through
the front room. That hardly mattered, since it would have to
be sent out and cleaned before he could wear it again. That
was another of the many curses that plagued most performers,
since music was in fact a vigorous and demanding physical
activity. Symphonies should be conducted in sweats, not formal
wear. His cherished and very expensive cello went immediately
into its own place of safekeeping, something he was very careful about no matter how tired he might be. His career depended
upon the excellent condition of both that instrument and his
hands; everything else was incidental. With that duty attended

to, he tottered into the kitchen with thoughts for the dinner that he was never able to have before a performance.

The fact that he flipped on the light and walked right past Dalvenjah, standing before the back door, without a second glance was a testimony to just how much a solo performance took out of him. He looked right at Vajerral where she sat on a stool at the bar and failed to notice anything unusual as he made his way to the refrigerator. The smoked trout was all but gone, but he failed to recall that he had not eaten it and, even if he had, he would have assumed that Marie and Jenny had raided his icebox in his absence. Just now his only thought was for a peanut butter and jelly sandwich, that manna from heaven and most supreme of culinary delights.

He took out the peanut butter and handed it over to Vajerral, who accepted the large, heavy glass jar and stared at it curiously. Then he handed her the jelly, never once looking behind him but half-aware that someone was there to take it. Allan bent to search the lower shelves for something to drink, and he was in that unfortunate position when reality finally penetrated his awareness like a light in the fog of his sluggish thoughts. He paused in the act of contemplating a can of soda and asked himself if he really had seen a pair of dragons in his kitchen, one of whom had appropriated his peanut butter and jelly. He had to admit that it was a ridiculous notion and no doubt the result of his befuddled state. But who had taken his beloved peanut butter? Curiosity got the best of him, and he had to look.

Allan turned slowly and looked over his shoulder. The little dragon paused in the act of pilfering his peanut butter to stare back. The big dragon was also staring at him with the same patient, polite curiosity. His first reaction was to panic. He really didn't know why, but it seemed like the proper thing to do upon finding dragons in one's kitchen. But he thought about it a moment and decided that he really did not care to. He lacked the necessary energy and the inclination for an honest panic. . . . Maybe in the morning. Panic did not seem likely to accomplish anything constructive, and it certainly would not get these dragons out of his house. Right now he just wanted to know what they were doing here in the first place.

All the same, he thought it wise to put just a little distance between himself and his unexpected guests. Being calm and rational in such a situation as this did not mean being foolhardy. Dragons in the kitchen did not preclude the possibility that he was to be dinner. Unfortunately his kitchen was not the best place to be in a fight, for he was now trapped in a box formed by the cabinets and the bar, the only way out being the narrow opening between the little dragon and the refrigerator, and the securely locked door at his back leading to the garage.

"Ah, hello there," he ventured cautiously. When fight or flight were not strong alternatives, there was always the chance of peaceful negotiation. Assuming that dragons could talk.

"Ashjessah," the larger dragon responded in a surprisingly pleasant and indisputably female voice. He had naturally assumed that dragons would speak in the deeper ranges, like Fafnir, the only dragon he had previously known and who was in fact a Wagnerian bass somewhere offstage.

"Ashjessah," the smaller dragon added cheerfully in a decidedly childlike voice.

Allan frowned. These two might speak, but not in any language he knew. That made things more difficult than he would have preferred, but it did tell him a few things he needed to know. They did indeed speak, which also meant that they were thinking, rational beings and not just fierce beasts. The big dragon wore a harness that held a sword and at least two large knives, which said something about her that was not necessarily reassuring. All the same, he thought that he was not in immediate danger and he was impressed even more by their apparently polite and pleasant manner. That did not answer his most pressing questions, such as why two dragons were in his kitchen, what they wanted here, and when they might be planning to leave.

For Dalvenjah's own part, she was beginning to have some very strong suspicions that this was not the wizard she had been hoping to find. Yes, he was the source of the strong magic that had led her to here; there was no question about whether she had come to the proper place or person. But she had good reason to believe that, for all of his native magic, he was lacking in even the most basic training. This world was so lacking in sorcerers, she was beginning to guess, because none were trained.

She was not caught completely unprepared by that realization. She had begun to suspect it several hours earlier when she had discovered that this house was totally lacking in the most fundamental of magical tools and devices that were a part of even the poorest wizard's household. Even the things that she had first taken to be magical in nature, the cold food cabinet and its bright little light, had turned out to be nothing more than machines. But it was too late to correct her mistake now. She now doubted that she would find a trained sorcerer anywhere in this world, so it was best to make do with what she had. This one did have undeniable magic, he seemed to be calm, intelligent and had certainly adapted to this unusual and trying situation as well as she could have hoped. And he did have a place where they could stay for the next few weeks while her wing was on the mend.

"Dalvenjah," she said, indicating herself. She thought it best to get on with the business at hand, getting him thoroughly involved in helping her with her problems before it occurred to him to show his two visitors the door. She indicated her little one. "Vajerral."

He understood immediately, nodding in a rather exaggerated manner, and pointed to himself. "Allan. Allan Breivik."

"Allan," she repeated, smiling. That was the Mindijari word for a foxlike hunter of her native highlands, esteemed for its cunning and bravery. She did not belong to any school of magic that attached much importance to signs and omens, but she was pleased.

There followed a very long, uncomfortable moment of silence as each waited for the other to do something. Allan was reminded all too well of a particular date that Danny Grehan had inflicted upon him about a year earlier. Danny was the lucky type who sometimes found himself with a surplus of girls and he was perfectly willing to share, but he predictably kept the better one for himself. Which was why Allan now refused to have anything to do with his dating service; he had no wish to be a dumping ground for his rejects. Somehow he found this situation remarkably similar, if not quite as bad. He was, in spite of himself, very interested in discovering just how this was all going to come out. He had gone from trying to assure himself that he had only passed out on the floor and was dreaming all of this to hoping that he had not.

Hardly knowing what else to do, Dalvenjah decided that it was time for more direct action. They obviously shared no language, nor could they learn to speak each other's tongue right there in the kitchen in the middle of the night. When a problem could not be solved by any other means, there was always magic. She stepped forward purposefully, and Allan reacted rather predictably by drawing back in alarm. Dalvenjah paused and indicated very plainly that he had nothing to fear, then advanced more cautiously around the end of the bar until they stood only a short distance apart and stared into his eyes.

In that very instant Allan's own sight faded, to be replaced by the visions from another's eyes. Some were perhaps Dalvenjah's own memories of what she had seen as she rode the winds on her own swift wings. But she was herself in many of the misty images, which might have come from her own imagination. He saw her in some place that clearly was not of this world, a dark and violent land of stark deserts, smoking volcanos and rocky islands in a storm-lashed sea. He saw her fight with Vorgulremik, an airborne duel of fire and magic, until the larger dragon, hurt and exhausted, fled for his life into a new world. He saw Dalvenjah pursue him without hesitation, overtaking the steel dragon within sight of the rift. And he saw what was to have been their battle to the death, and Dalvenjah's failure during her risky death-strike.

The images faded away and Allan again found himself staring into the golden dragon's green-jeweled eyes. Dalvenjah smiled reassuringly and retreated a few short steps. He could see now the swollen portion of her left wing, where he had seen the bone snap like a twig before being set back in position in some manner that he did not completely comprehend. But at least he knew the answers to some of his questions: why she was in his world at all, and why she needed the shelter he and his home could offer. He still had no idea why she had sought him specifically, but he was sure that even this had not been a matter of accident. She had come to him; he was certain of that. And he was just as certain that she meant him no harm.

But dragons, even a pair this small and polite, took some getting used to. They were really very beautiful beings, golden-

scaled with long, sapphire-blue manes that trailed down the
lengths of their sinuous necks, silver horns and immense green
eyes. He had certainly never thought of dragons as golden,
although he had to admit that he preferred golden dragons as
house guests to a dark monstrosity like the larger one in her
visions, bristling with swordlike ridges. Somehow he understood that she was silently seeking his permission to remain
while she healed and regained her strength, but that she would
be gone in a minute if he would not have her.

In the next moment he was startled to hear that polite lady
growling at him, until he realized that it was not her but an
impatient stomach . . . much to Dalvenjah's considerable embarrassment. She had eaten some of what she and Vajerral had
helped themselves to in the refrigerator. But she had at the
time considered it best to not impose too heavily upon the
assumed hospitality of their unknown host, and most of what
they had taken had been subtly directed to the dragonet. They
had both been on very tight rations for the past two weeks as
she had pursued Vorgulremik across three worlds. Aside from
that, it took quite a lot to satisfy even a golden dragon who
had been eating lightly for a very long time, and Allan was
not one to keep much on hand.

"Oh, are you hungry?" he asked anxiously, and looked
around as if expecting to find something to delight a draconic
palate waiting and ready to serve to his remarkable guests. The
answer seemed obvious enough, for Vajerral was still holding
the jars of peanut butter and jelly that he had brought out for
himself some time earlier.

Well, he could certainly imagine nothing better. He hurried
to collect plates from the cabinet, knives from the drawer and
bread from the pantry, and proceeded to make two of the best
peanut butter and jelly sandwiches he could. The jelly was
grape and about as good as he had ever found, and the peanut
butter was the wonderful crunchy type. Who could ask for
more? Allan added sodas cold from the refrigerator, in bottles
rather than the cans that he suspected would have been too
difficult for the slender muzzles of the two dragons.

Dalvenjah sniffed hers cautiously, not at all certain what it
was, but she did think that it smelled very good. Vajerral
certainly had no reservations, even if she was not particularly

hungry. She took a large bite of the sandwich without hesitation and her mother, observing that she did not make a disgusted face, turn colors or fall dead off the stool, took a somewhat smaller bite of her own. And so the two dragons chewed and chewed . . . and chewed, and Allan immediately saw the mistake in his choice. For while it is true that peanut butter is not a particularly substantial food, it has long been the bane of all creatures possessing long, narrow mouths full of many sharp teeth. Dogs knew the hazard but ate the stuff anyway.

"Maybe the peanut butter wasn't such a good idea after all," Allan said, frowning and rather embarrassed.

"Dye, lye dalash mayh," Dalvenjah mumbled in agreement; Vajerral was so encumbered with peanut butter that she looked about to choke.

"Well, let's see what else we can find," Allan said cheerfully as he began a quick search of the refrigerator for other delicacies to serve his guests. "I know that I must have something better than that, so don't eat any more until I've had a chance to look. Let's see . . . cheese, hot dogs, bean dip. I'm taking this all very well, don't you think?"

"Dye," Dalvenjah agreed noncommittally. Then again, she thought to herself, you are not stranded in a very strange world with a broken wing and a four-year-old.

Then she took a long drink from her bottle and immediately began to sneeze violently as her delicate nose was assaulted by an unexpected flood of bubbles. By the stars above, was he trying to kill them both? She was beginning to think very longingly of venison, hot bread with butter and cheese, and mead. And she was now desperate enough to place those images in Allan's mind, with all the subtlety she could contrive in the hope that he would consider it his own idea.

"I'm afraid I don't have most of that," he said without removing his head from the icebox. He knew where those thoughts had originated the moment they popped into his head, since such odd items were not to be found in his refrigerator and never had been. He might have substituted roast beef and cold beer, but he lacked those as well.

What he did have in abundance were hot dogs and buns, which he considered nearly as good as peanut butter. And he could turn those out in draconic volume in a matter of minutes.

He took the sandwich away from Vajerral, who seemed inclined to make a heroic effort to eat it anyway. She had already finished half of her soda and looked ready to fight him for it. She arched her long, supple neck for another drink, then belched loudly. Dalvenjah, who had been rather concerned about where all of those bubbles would go, glanced at her tolerantly.

Allan fed the remarkable pair and packed them off to bed as quickly as he could manage, certain that it would be best to save any more discoveries and surprises for in the morning. Dalvenjah agreed completely and helped him prepare the guest room, although they both looked rather dubiously at the double bed. It was in itself barely adequate for her naturally rangy form; a dragon's idea of a double bed was much wider than it was long. She did not wish to turn Vajerral out of the best bed that either of them had seen in some time. But Allan solved that problem by collecting a large box from the garage and padding it with folded blankets before making a bed on top. That delighted the dragonet, appealing to her instincts for making a den in a warm, secure hole. She leaped inside, buried herself in a blanket, and was asleep in moments.

He retreated gratefully to his own room, certain that Dalvenjah could take care of herself now that he had demonstrated the working of light switches. By that time the combined effects of this very long and eventful evening were beginning to catch up with him. He might have forgotten a very trying solo performance in the excitement of finding dragons in the house, but that leaden fatigue had not forgotten him and moved in quickly to make its presence felt. He found the task of struggling out of his concert tux almost too much.

The door opened silently while he was still undressing, but Dalvenjah remained where she was until Allan noticed her and glanced at her questioningly, wondering if she had some question. She smiled in a reassuring manner to tell him that nothing was wrong, and that she certainly had not come to eat him for dessert, as she took a few hesitant steps into the room. He could tell that she had something very important to say, and he was just as curious to discover what it could be as about how she would go about saying it. He thought that, in spite of her brave outer appearance, she was on the verge of tears. That more than anything made him completely aware that there was a real person, perhaps not too much unlike himself, within this dragon.

"Alyesh thyarnan on iyah derreh min dessah'par on an," she said softly, her hesitation reflecting the fact that her gratitude was as sincere as her unwillingness to impose upon his hospitality.

"No, think nothing of it," Allan insisted, no longer surprised at his ability to understand everything she said. "You are more than welcome here for however long you need. There are no dragons in our world, and there haven't been any for a very long time now. So it's something of an honor."

Dalvenjah smiled broadly. "Lye dalash dahn."

"No, perhaps not," he agreed. "But I am happy to have you."

Dalvenjah did not reply, but walked slowly over to the window of the room and peered out into the frosty night. Icy lines traced patterns around the edges of the glass, and her warm breath fogged the window before she saw anything more than just a star-filled sky. She thought of her own home in the highlands, an ancient fortlike structure that she had found in ruins when she had been looking for a place to set up in business. She had restored it all herself through magic and plain hard work, and she had been very happy there. And had been happier still when she had found someone to share it with her. It was still there, worlds away, awaiting her return. But some things would never be the same.

"Lye aye mayh asheh, asheh sothe'byn," she said softly, almost beneath her breath, weeping silently.

Allan did not answer. He could feel her loneliness; she shared her feelings with him unintentionally along the link she used to allow them both to understand each other. And beneath that loneliness he sensed a larger grief, the bitter suggestion of a far greater tragedy than her own misfortunes. He could not imagine what it could be, and he knew that she was not about to share it with him. At least not yet. That hardly mattered. His concern for her, he found to his considerable surprise, was very real and great. He cautiously stepped forward, as silently as he could, and laid his hand very softly on her neck just above her shoulder.

A quiet moment passed before she seemed to notice. Dalvenjah's ears perked and shifted around catlike toward him before she bent her head around to look at him. She regarded him questioningly for some time, as if surprised by that gesture, seeking its meaning and whether or not she should accept it for that. He did not know her sorrows, or the depth of her pain. He was not even her kind. But magic was a language in which meaning could never be mistaken, and she knew beyond any doubt that his concern was sincere. That alone was all that really mattered between friends. She smiled amid her tears, accepting his gift of understanding and comfort, and there was no need for spoken words between them when their thoughts spoke more directly and plainly of what they really meant.

"Min anneh i dhal lethar," she said gently.

"I hope to be," Allan answered as he used his kerchief to dry the tears from her golden scales. "I will be your friend for as long as you need one. If we work together, we can make everything turn out just fine."

Dalvenjah smiled warmly, and this time her tears reflected her joy and contentment. She had found her wizard after all.

Allan awoke early the next morning, or at least earlier than he would have preferred. The previous evening had been a rather long and trying one, and he could still feel it. He closed his eyes tightly and wished that he was only dreaming that he was awake. That wish might well become reality if he gave it a chance, and he would awaken some time later with only the very dim memory of his foolishness at thinking that he needed to get up so early. Then he remembered that there were dragons in the house and sat up sharply in bed, very much awake.

Was that memory real or only a dream? Just now he was not entirely certain, for if it had indeed happened then he had seen it through a haze of fatigue and unreality that made it seem like only a passing dream in the clear light of morning. He often dreamed silly things, and now he realized that he would be better off if it had been nothing more than that. But if it had been only a dream, then who did he hear rattling about in his kitchen? It certainly could not be Marie, since she would never allow him to remain in bed. He had the very uncomfortable feeling that there were indeed a couple of golden dragons making themselves very free in his refrigerator, eating heaven only knew what for breakfast. Even worse, the banging of pots and pans told him that they were trying to cook it. All the same, he decided to avoid accepting that as true until he could look for himself. It might be Marie after all.

Could he be so lucky?

No fear! He dressed quickly, hurried to the kitchen, and found that all of his dreams had turned out only too true. Vajerral was perched happily on her favorite stool, her head twisted around to peer at him as he entered, while Dalvenjah attended to her cooking. She had obviously made the best of what she was able to find, and was contentedly cooking bacon, frankfurters and bologna in his largest electric skillet, poking at the food with a long-handled fork. Allan hurried over to see if she needed any assistance. He stepped up to her side to peer at the contents of the skillet and noted with some interest that she had somehow found a way to make it work without plugging it in.

"Dhal eldinar," Dalvenjah greeted him pleasantly. At least it seemed that she did not consider it necessary to wear her harness and weapons.

"Good morning," he responded. "Ah . . . we have a very different way of making that thing work."

"Eh lye aht de'lyr shann," the golden dragon replied, unconcerned.

Well, that went very much without saying. Allan pulled the stool beside Vajerral's out from beneath the bar and sat down heavily. He sat for a long moment, his head propped up on his fists, and contemplated what he had to say. As much as they seemed to be communicating perfectly, he wondered just how much the dragons really understood about his world and the way things worked. He was still very much under the impression that, like mythical dragons, they must make their home in a deep cave and sleep on a pile of gold. Dalvenjah would have been amused by that last observation. She made a very good living as one of the best magicians of her world, but if she had that kind of money she would have bought feather mattresses.

"Do you understand what it is I do as a career?" he asked at last.

"Min anneh i shalasijas?" Dalvenjah asked.

"Yes, exactly," he agreed. "Anyway, I play in what we call a symphony, with dozens of other musicians all playing together as one. And we have to practice quite a lot before we are ready to perform. We had a major concert last night, and today we have to begin preparing for our next. We will have only two more concerts, less than two weeks, and then I will have several weeks free that I can spend helping you. What do you think of that?"

"Dhoun ryst," the dragon agreed, obviously pleased by the prospect. "Aval ajahs min ahl di'dhefas?"

"Oh, I should be back some time later this afternoon."

"Eh deshan min ajahs cherran lyr de'min djeri?"

"Yes, we could do that," Allan agreed, but with some reluctance. Having a common language would make things much easier, but he was not at all certain how good he would be as a teacher.

He considered that during breakfast and, before he left, he thought that he might have come up with a partial solution. He paused on his way out the door to introduce the two dragons to the workings of the television and pointed out to Dalvenjah the virtues of the public station. The morning hours, he believed, were devoted to the very programs that could teach the sorceress the very thing she wanted. Dalvenjah was certainly impressed, and she could readily appreciate the rather novel approach to teaching their young that these people had developed. Which was just as well, for they could only learn the hard way. Lacking magic, they could not assimilate volumes of information quickly and easily the way her own kind were able to.

But it did her very little good. For one thing, this way of learning obviously assumed that the subject already knew something of the language and was more interested in learning to read and write it. To confuse matters all the more, there were apparently two languages being taught at once, one much more common than the other, although it took her some time to figure that out. For one thing, she could hardly imagine why any group of people needed to have more than one language, and she was distressed at the thought that she might be required to learn both and, by some complex rule of verbal etiquette, be able to transfer between the two. She soon came to the conclusion that white and black humans spoke the primary language, brown humans had a language of their own, and frogs and monsters were equally conversant in both. It seemed to make sense, at least when she reminded herself that she was dealing with humans and talking frogs.

The two golden dragons watched that program all the way through, then saw a show on paper folding and another on the life of penguins, and followed up with another session with the frog. Dalvenjah rather liked that frog, since he reminded her quite a lot of her first master of magic, nearly twenty years ago, when she had hardly been any older than her own dragonet. She could imagine only too well what dry comment he would have made about her present situation. She did have a well-trained memory and assimilated a volume of new words, but she would have to wait for Allan and the magical contact she had with him to learn what to do with it. Televisions had their limitations; she could not link with it for either direct communication or memory transfer.

Dalvenjah was caught by surprise later that afternoon when two strangers arrived and let themselves into the house with a key. She did not know for certain what to make of that, since Allan had not warned her about it. But she did think that this female must be the older sister Marie who was very much on Allan's mind. She grabbed Vajerral and hurried to hide in the shower with the curtain drawn, and the two dragons became invisible, just to be safe.

"It just doesn't impress me as normal medical procedure," the woman was complaining as they passed by the hall. "Every time I go into Dr. Howard's office, he talks about breast exams. 'Take off your shirt, and let's have a breast exam.' Every time."

"At least he is conscientious," the man explained, obviously at a loss.

"Conscientious, hell!" the woman exclaimed. "Dr. Howard is my dentist!"

They left shortly after, and Dalvenjah hurried to the window for a look. But they were well out to the car by then, and all she saw was a rather tall, slender woman and a slightly shorter, stocky man.

By later that afternoon the dragons had begun to experiment with the television's remote control, and they were contentedly studying the complex and most often violent relationships that existed in this world between n ice and cats when Allan returned. He had wisely remembe:ed to shop for groceries on his way home and pulled into his driveway with his little car loaded with brown bags full of everything that he had thought would appeal to his remarkable guests. He had not been able to find venison and mead, but he did have what he considered to be passable substitutes.

He was returning to the car from opening the garage door when he stopped short, having seen that Mrs. Parsons from next door was scrutinizing the volume of groceries, plainly visible through the rear hatch of his car, enough to have lasted him the better part of three months. "Grandma" Parsons was the chief neighborhood busybody and Keeper of the Cats, but harmless enough once her curiosity was satisfied. But Allan had always been fearful of her watchful eye, suspecting that she was Marie's major source of information.

"Nice concert, by what I hear," she called to him pleasantly, although she handed out even her compliments in a tone of voice that allowed no arguments. "At least by what they say in the paper. The critic liked you."

"I could have done better," Allan admitted shyly. His natural reticence and Marie's careful training left him unable to accept compliments without turning them back into an apology. He positioned himself subtly between the car and that sharp gaze.

"So when will it be on the radio, anyway?"

"Oh, three weeks from next Monday night, I think."

"I'll not miss it," Mrs. Parsons declared, and glanced at the hoard of groceries inside the little car. "Did you know that you have dragons in your house?"

Allan was startled in spite of himself; since the subject had not come up right away, he had considered himself safe. Mrs. Parsons certainly had not approached the subject subtly, since she hardly knew the meaning of the word. And he could not imagine that she considered the subject very important if she had not mentioned it before. "Yes, I am aware of that."

"Friends, or relatives?"

"Oh, just friends. And very nice, polite people, I can promise you that. They flew in last night."

"Yes, I saw them land," Mrs. Parsons said. "Well, I just thought that you should know. They looked like very nice people—for dragons—so I decided not to worry about it. Besides, I couldn't stay up late enough to warn you when you came home last night."

"And the cats don't mind?"

"Oh, they all marched over for a look first thing!" Mrs. Parsons exclaimed, laughing, as she turned to walk away. Then she paused and turned back for a moment. "Oh, I'll not say a word of this to Marie. I know how she is about such things."

"Ah . . . I would appreciate that," Allan agreed, wondering if he really could rely upon that, and why Grandma Parsons was in such a cooperative mood concerning such a difficult subject. She was a great fan of his, but he had always suspected quiet sabotage on her part where Marie was concerned; revenge for an unfortunate remark of his concerning catgut. That in turn led to an even more horrifying thought: He had not warned the dragons to watch out for Marie and make themselves scarce if his sister made one of her frequent unannounced appearances. As if a dragon really could make herself scarce.

He backed the car into the garage and quickly closed the door before opening the kitchen door and calling for the dragons to help him. They were already in the kitchen waiting, which meant that they had not been caught by surprise by his arrival.

"Hello," he said absently as he thrust a bag into Dalvenjah's arms.

"Good morning," she answered pleasantly as she took her burden into the kitchen.

"Ah, close enough," he called back to her. "I think you mean 'good evening' by this time of day."

"Good evening," she agreed, appearing at the door for another load. "Yes. Excuse me."

"Well, you have made some progress!" he said approvingly as he brought her another bag. "I really have no idea how much the three of us will eat, but I did want to get enough to last a while."

"Sure," Dalvenjah answered, her response close enough to be considered appropriate. Of course, she was still having to

rely upon magic to understand what he was saying to her, and
then search through her miserably small stock of words for a
reply.

Working together, they had the rather impressive load of
groceries in the kitchen within a minute and the golden dragons
set about the task of emptying the bags while Allan brought in
his cello and put it away. She had no problem knowing which
things belonged in the refrigerator and which went into the
cabinet. She had an icebox of her own—even if it was kept
cold by a very different means—and she often put away enough
for several weeks so that she would not have to leave her studies
to shop. But there was so much meat and fish that most of it
would have to be frozen, and she decided to leave that for
Allan to do.

"So, you know about groceries," Allan remarked approvingly as he returned, glancing briefly at Vajerral who sat on
her stool looking longingly at this bounty. Surely these two
had helped themselves to lunch.

"What?" Dalvenjah asked, holding up one package of meat
daintily.

"Oh, hamburger," Allan explained, then saw that the dragon
still did not understand. "Ground beef."

Dalvenjah laid the package down quickly, and shook herself.
"Disgusting!"

"What?"

"Grody!" she elucidated.

Allan shrugged. "Anyway, did you have any problems?"

"No, no," Dalvenjah insisted. "Dal laus halladha shen
brin."

"Oh, don't worry about that," he assured her, glancing at
the telephone. "That is a device we use to speak across long
distances. You don't need to worry about answering it, since
you are not here anyway."

"Oh, I see."

"And no one came over?"

"Someone." Dalvenjah explained as carefully as she could,
in his language. "Two. Tall woman. Short man."

"My sister Marie and her boyfriend Rex," Allan told her
as he took an empty bag and began loading it with things for
the freezer. "I wanted to warn you about my sister. She makes

a career of minding everyone's business, especially mine, and she doesn't mind telling you when she doesn't approve of what you are doing."

"Real bitch," Dalvenjah remarked.

"Exactly," he agreed, then turned to stare. "Where did you learn that?"

Dalvenjah only shrugged.

"She saw you?"

"No, no."

"Anyway, she comes over here all the time, even when I'm not here," Allan continued. "I doubt very much that she is going to approve of you two, and if we do have to make introductions then I believe that it should wait until you can speak to her in her own language. I want you to watch out for her, and if she does show up, you have to disappear. If you can."

"Of course," she assured him.

"You can?"

"Oh, for sure," she insisted, and did so. One moment she was standing in the middle of the kitchen, and in the next she faded away and was gone. Vajerral made some comment of either encouragement or approval; Allan was not in contact with her, and the short string of words made absolutely no sense to him. Then Dalvenjah was back, smiling broadly.

"I should have guessed," Allan said to himself, having lost his ability some time near the middle of the previous night to be surprised by anything that happened in his house. "Where did you go, anyway?"

"Right here."

"I see." He shrugged. "I wish you could teach me that."

"Lye iyan."

"You can?" This time he did turn sharply to stare at her in open amazement. "You mean that it's that simple? Anyone can learn to work your magic, just by learning the proper spell or whatever?"

"Dah, lel as dahn mayh akija," she told him in a soft, serious voice. "Min aht asheh innahl dasjerra."

"I have strong magic?" Allan asked incredulously, but with eagerness rather than denial. Then he suddenly understood. "Is that why you came to me?"

"Dye, de'min dasjerra di'len lyr." She told him what he had already suspected. "Min dessah'cherdhan dal'esha de'min dasjerra?"

"Will I?" he asked himself thoughtfully, torn between desire and fear, and looked up her. "Yes. If I have that kind of magic, then I want to learn how to use it. At least, I guess I do. But how?"

"No sweat!" she assured him. "Dal ahst fhal as akija. Min dyerrah'cherdhan dal'heral djeri de'lyr."

"Your language?" Allan asked hesitantly. That sounded like a very tall order; he wondered if Dalvenjah would even be in his world long enough for him to accomplish that rather intimidating task. He was still barely adequate at Norwegian, in spite of the fact that it was Marie's first language. "Yes, I suppose I could give that a try. But why?"

Dalvenjah, however, refused to answer that particular question at that time. She insisted only that it was the important first step in learning to command magic to a specific purpose, and that she could teach him no magic until they could speak in Mindijari, her own language. She did explain to him that the process of learning each other's language would be through the magical link that existed between them, and that learning would be made much easier by a mutual transfer of memory. She considered two or perhaps three weeks to be quite enough for them to master each other's language, and that he would begin learning her magic much sooner than that.

And so their lessons in language began, and progressed as quickly as Dalvenjah had promised. The sorceress found that she was very pleased to have an apprentice, even an informal one. But she was still rather dismayed with herself for taking on such a task. Most accomplished magicians might wait until they had been in the business four or five hundred years before trying their hand at teaching, and she was still a child herself by that standard. The difference was that Allan already had strong magic; he was, for most purposes, a sorcerer ready-made, ready to become a master of his art in only weeks rather than months or even years.

She could also be secure in the knowledge that anything she did with Allan could be counted as nothing more than just practice, a chance for her to see if she was herself ready to undertake the education of a promising student. Once she was gone, all of her work with Allan would not count for anything to anyone in this world or any other. Except, perhaps, to him.

With the concert season coming to a rapid and predictably vigorous close, Allan found that he had to be away from home a great deal more than he would have wished. The presence of ten cellos, the most any standard orchestra ever had, might seem like an exercise in redundancy. And, to a small extent, it was, except that he was principal and his presence was mandatory. Dalvenjah also insisted that he was not to interrupt his schedule to accommodate her and she made certain that he was off for every rehearsal and concert on time. She had a much more agreeable approach to minding the business of others than Marie had ever dreamed could exist. And Allan played better than he had ever played before.

That in itself might seem curious enough, but it was simple to explain. He worried constantly about the two dragons, in spite of their proven ability to make themselves disappear. They had to resort to that simple trick about once every three days, although Marie's visits were shorter and less frequent than Allan could ever recall. Allan thought privately that her own affair with Dr. Barker was finally becoming a major issue. And it should be, after the better part of two years. Rex Barker thought the world of Marie, even if he did have a name that belonged on a German shepherd. And she professed to think proportionally little of him; truer, or at least more honest, love had never existed. Allan had no complaint, especially if it kept Marie out of his house and distracted her from watching his own life quite so closely.

How that related to his mastery of the cello was easily explained. To put matters simply, he was too busy teaching Dalvenjah his language, learning her own and, within a week taking his first simple lessons in magic. All of that, plus worrying about the affairs and general well-being of his dragons, was enough to distract him from worrying about his playing. As a natural result, his playing improved noticeably, becoming less self-conscious and therefore more smooth and natural. Every performing artist should have a house full of dragons. The worries of simple stage fright paled in comparison to the concerns of keeping the dragons fed, entertained and out of sight. But they had to be gone before the start of the summer tour or he would be in real trouble.

At least the Mindijaran ate less than he had first feared, so that the stock of provisions that he had brought in that first day should last for some time. Dalvenjah did all of the cooking and, while she was working with cuts and types of meat and fish unfamiliar to her, she was able to do things with it that were best described as out of this world . . . in every sense. Her secret, Allan suspected, was that she had used her magic to convert his meager store of spices to items more familiar to her. He knew, for example, that onion salt was not blue.

The Mindijaran were certainly happy, and they seemed to be doing well enough. Dalvenjah's damaged wing had long since ceased to give her any pain, and the swelling had gone down by the end of the first week after their coming. Vajerral was enjoying herself thoroughly, completely involved in the delight of discovery of her first new world. But both her mother and Allan were concerned that she should not be spending her life trapped inside a house day after day for so long. Dalvenjah was actually less worried about that than Allan was, since she was used to a climate and a more primitive way of life that made being trapped inside by winter for weeks at a time inevitable.

"We will be going home soon now," she assured him as they sat one night working on their language lessons at the same time that Allan sawed almost absently on his cello. "By then it will be spring here, and warm summer in our home mountains. Vajerral will play in the forests and ride the winds for a long time before the days again grow short and cold."

"How long?" Allan asked almost fearfully, for there was now no question in his mind that he did not want them to go and take away the magic.

"Perhaps five weeks more . . . or less," she said. "Then I will be strong enough to fight Vorgulremik."

"No, we," he corrected her, fearful of the offer that he was making and yet firm in his resolve. "You have fought him alone once and lost. The next time, it will not be alone. I will have enough command of my own magic by that time that I can fight him with you."

"We will see," Dalvenjah answered simply, but in a voice which indicated that she was far from convinced. "When the time comes, it will be entirely according to my loudhen . . . my terms. Then we will see."

Allan knew, of course, that she had no intention of allowing him to have a part in that fight, but he also believed that she would be forced to relent when the time came. He had no desire to fight that vast, armored monster he had seen in her memories. His only motive was concern for her, and for Vajerral. He had already come to understand that Dalvenjah was very much the single parent, that her mate or boyfriend—she had never been married—had been gone for quite some time now. He also understood very well that she possessed such magic that she would never have had a child by accident.

Allan was already considering the next problem, that of finding a place for Vajerral to play as well as somewhere that Dalvenjah could strengthen her own wings. The advantage to living where he did was that the mountains were only a couple of hours away. Solutions to the problems of finding a place for them to go as well as getting them there came from the same source. He regretted having to bring his sister into this, but he needed what Dr. Barker had to offer. And Vajerral needed what Jenny Breivik had to offer, a companion near her own age. There was some difference there; Jenny was a very mature nine-year-old, but the dragonet was an almost frighteningly mature four-year-old. In that respect they were on about the same level.

Dalvenjah, however, would not hear of it. She pointed out that Allan was barely a week away from the end of the concert season, and that he would then be free to go away with them. Their introduction to anyone else in this world, she added, should wait until then. Allan had to agree to the logic in that. He could well imagine the fight that he would have on his hands when Marie found out that there were dragons in his house. He could just as well wait until Dalvenjah had a command of English that would allow her to hold her own. Or even win; Allan was already aware that this mild-tempered lady possessed both a strength of will and self-certain authority that could put Marie to shame.

* * *

It was fair to say that they were all three very happy with each other. The dragons spent their days with Kermit and the monsters and felt very much at home, their routine occasionally interrupted by sessions of standing invisible in the shower while Marie made her brief inspections. At night they studied language and magic with Allan and he practiced bow techniques, while the nightly concert played in the background on the radio. But on Saturdays they gave very strict attention to the Metropolitan Opera, while that night was devoted to old programs like Jack Benny and Fibber McGee.

"Why do your people have so many languages?" Dalvenjah asked one afternoon as they listened to the opera, a remarkably spirited performance of *Siegfried*. She was at first inclined to consider it a tragedy; the dragon died.

"I really don't know," Allan remarked absently. Dalvenjah, immediately assuming her role of teacher, gave him a stern look to indicate that he should think about it. He did; she did not accept "I don't know" as an answer even when the question was unimportant. "It's because we don't have wings."

"How do you come to that?" she asked, intrigued by that rather unusual answer.

"Simple," he explained. "Wings have always made it easy for your people to go wherever you wish, and get there very quickly. But in the old days most of my people had to walk, which meant twenty miles for a hard day's travel. Horse and oxcart were little faster, and most people didn't have those. And so everyone stayed home for thousands of years, and their languages slowly grew apart."

"Interesting," she commented. "Are you sure of that?"

"No," he admitted. "But it sounds good."

They sat for a time in silence, listening as Siegfried sat beneath the linden tree, dreaming of the mother he had never known and listening to the song of the woodbird, blissfully unaware that he was sitting on a dragon's doorstep. Dalvenjah sighed wistfully; something about this was very familiar to her, even nostalgic. Fafnir's den bore little resemblance to her meticulously restored fortress, but both were places where a dragon belongs. But she identified most with Siegfried, so at home and at peace in the forest.

"Why do dragons sleep on a pile of gold?" Allan asked suddenly.

Dalvenjah lifted her head and blinked at him. "Who told you that we do?"

"That's what I've always heard."

"It is true, in part. Just . . . what do you say? Exaggerated." She closed her eyes, and sighed a second time. "Gold is one of the metals, like iron, that are closest to magic. Iron restricts magic, and it can even slay or repel some magic creatures. But don't try that trick on me . . . or Vorgulremik. We are too secure in our powers. Gold, on the other hand, enhances. Or more important, gold can restore powers to a sorcerer who is failing, or at the end of his strength. If I could have called upon gold when I fought Vorgulremik a week ago, perhaps I would not have lost. And then . . ."

"Yes?" Allan encouraged her gently.

She turned her head to regard him again. "This you must understand. I am not like you or any other living creature, not entirely. I am immortal, like the elves. Even the least of my people possess such magic that it is a great part of our very substance, so that we may only die if we are blasted by strong magic or our magic is taken away. And there is magic in gold. It speaks to us in our sleep, and it makes us dream. Such dreams . . . So it is said that dragons sleep in a bed of gold. The dark dragons, like Vorgulremik's kind, they may dream in unbroken sleep for weeks at a time, coming out of their dens only to feed. Only in their gold-dreams can they forget the evil that dominates them and be at peace."

"But what do you dream?" Allan asked before he realized that perhaps he should not. But Dalvenjah did not even glance at him.

"What does anyone dream, but what they want the most?" she asked, mostly of herself. "And yet there is a dark side of the gold-dream, for in them you may dream of other times. Sometimes a past so distant that you can hardly recognize it. Sometimes a future that you would rather not see. I knew, you see. I knew long ago that Derjadhan would die fighting a great dragon. I dream of you . . . but to no point."

She shook her head and suddenly brightened, although with an effort to pull her mind away from such thoughts. "But most often I dream of all the things that make me happy. I dream of magic yet to be learned and mastered. I dream of sharing many long years of happiness with someone I love. I dream of sex more than I should. That is how I got Vajerral.''

"Oh?" Allan glanced at the little dragonet, who was preoccupied with making a castle from building blocks. "I had thought, with all the magic you possess, that such accidents . . .''

"Oh, it was no accident!" Dalvenjah declared, laughing. "I thought at the time that I wanted a child, when anyone else would have waited many years yet to come. That is how I have always been, doing what I want to do when I want it. That is the way to live, it seems to me. I have a lifetime measured against eternity, and yet I doubt that I will ever do all that I want. So I do it right away, and usually I have no cause to regret. And I do not even regret the things that did not come out as I had hoped. My master used to say that is how we grow up, doing all the things that our elders tell us from experience that we do not want to do. I dreamed again and again of how nice it would be to have a child, so I had to find out. The dreams did not mislead me.''

They were distracted from their talk when Siegfried, giving up on his reed pipe, took out his horn and proceeded to make a noise that Dalvenjah thought would have gotten a dragon off its deathbed. She was not offended by the fact that Fafnir was the bad guy; in her own imagination, he looked suspiciously like Vorgulremik. She was also an accomplished dragon-slayer in her own right, and she would not hesitate to fight the evil dragons—as long as she thought she could win. At least dragons were good or evil according to their breed; humans did not have that distinction.

The act was over soon enough. Fafnir was dead, Mime was dead, Siegfried was chasing after a bird who was going to show him how to pick up girls, and it was time for This Week's Opera Quiz. Dalvenjah sighed, wishing that she had a Siegfried to help her handle Vorgulremik so effectively; Allan was quietly measuring himself against that role, and found himself lacking. He also thought that it was time to stop criticizing opera as being unrealistic.

"What of you?" Dalvenjah asked suddenly. "What do you dream?"

Allan looked surprised. "I really don't know. Just the silly things that all mortals dream, I guess."

"Then let me ask again. What do you want?"

He had to think about it for a long moment. "I have most of what I want, I guess. I wanted to be the best cellist I could be. I still have a long way to go, but where is the challenge to being perfect? At least I know that I'm very good, and getting better."

"And if magic could make you the best in all your world?" Dalvenjah asked, then laughed at his reaction of dismay, even disgust. "Ah, at least you are that honest with yourself."

"And I'm not often that honest?" he inquired, too surprised by what she had implied to be properly indignant.

"Few of us are ever completely honest with ourselves," she replied. "You are not so unlike me in your dreams. You dream of the things you want, of the things you need in life to know that you are really alive. But only once have you dared to take what you wanted, when you realized that you must be a musician, and I think that you have not yet dared to take from that all that you might find in it."

Allan did not argue with her on that. He knew that he was an exceptional cellist, but also that he still had much to learn. But he had always thought that he was making very good progress in a very short time. He hardly knew what to make of Dalvenjah's assertion that he was holding himself back through some fault or fear of his own. His first reaction was to tell himself defensively that this winged sorceress knew very little about the realities of being a first-rank performer. Then he reminded himself that she might know little about the cello, but he suspected that her jeweled eyes could see straight into a person's heart and soul and the secrets hidden there.

"Levitation," Dalvenjah ordered suddenly.

Allan knew from long practice what that meant. He quickly looked around for a likely target and saw Vajerral crouched on the floor, hard at work on a fourth variation of her castle design. He said the proper word and sketched a sign of command in her direction—a necessary aid at this stage of his training—and the dragonet immediately left the floor. She glanced around, startled, and instinctively fanned her wings when she found herself in mid-air. That, her own lift-magic and Allan's initial boost was enough to send her straight to the ceiling, squealing in alarm. He immediately removed his spell and allowed Vajerral to return herself to the floor.

"Wrong word," Dalvenjah commented.

Allan needed some time to properly understand what the words and signs of command were and how they made magic operate. In part, his own background was in the way, for he had been brought up to believe that magic did not exist. He did know something of Norse mythology . . . at Marie's insistence. According to his own ancestors a thousand years removed, the command of magic lay in the runes, the symbols first used to identify words before they had been pressed into more everyday uses as record-keeping. The written word gave the magician a certain amount of command over the object or action it represented. This idea was also a part of his problem, since it seemed to him at first that Dalvenjah was telling him very much the same thing about how her own magic worked.

Part of the trouble there was that they had begun their lessons in magic before either had enough command of the other's language to really understand what each was saying. Dalvenjah could not have been more upset, although mostly with herself, when she finally realized just how far he had wandered from what she was trying to teach.

"No, no!" she exclaimed. "You take me too literally. Words have no power in themselves. They are just the tools we use in making magic do what we want from it."

"I don't understand," Allan protested weakly. "What else is there but words?"

"Oh, words are only shadow things!" she insisted. "When you would command a thing, you must first know it. You reach out with your thought, your own inner magic, measure it and sense its true and complete nature. Only after you truly understand what it is can you work magic with it . . . effectively. If your understanding is incomplete, your magic will be incomplete. As you learn the nature of that thing, it will reveal to your mind its shape and form. And, since we think always in words, your mind will—of itself—translate that thought into the sounds of a spoken word. That is the word of command, but it has no meaning in itself. That hardly matters. The rock does not know its name. Neither does magic have a language of its own. Magic does not listen to your words, but your thoughts. The word is for you to know what you are doing.''

"Thoughts?" Allan asked.

"Of course," she said, and frowned as she pondered, her ears laid back, how she might explain. "Listen well. You make the magic, and at the same time you are the magic. That which you call the soul, it is only the part of your being that is magic. You are a creature of lower magic, therefore mortal. I am a creature of higher magic, therefore immortal. Both magics work the same, but the higher magic is much harder to control. Mortal magicians, they can command the lower magic easily enough, but very few can command the higher magic as I do. But you can."

Dalvenjah settled back for a longer lesson than she had first anticipated, folding her long tail beneath her and sitting back on the curious support it provided. "When you make magic, you call upon that inner part of yourself that is magic to work for you. Some people find this easy; they are magicians. Others do not. A large part of the difference is that some find it very easy to determine the inner name of command. Both are needed to make a very good, strong magician, which you are. Sounds simple, but this is where long practice comes in. Your magic is mature. You will learn in months, even weeks, what took me years. But then, I learned so much else growing up besides magic, just like you did."

"Yes, I understand," Allan agreed, and his was the true, almost instinctive understanding of one who not only comprehended what he had been told but knew how to make it work. "But how can I work the higher magic if all I possess as a mortal is lower magic?"

"That is my doing," Dalvenjah said. "You are working my magic, dragon magic, not mortal magic. You are, as you might say here, driving on my license."

"Now I don't understand," he was forced to admit.

"This is not so simple," she said, laying back her ears yet again. "You see, everything has an inner name. Even you and I. A magician cannot work his own magic until he has been given his inner name, and so knows the true essence of himself. The time is not yet that you can take your inner name. Until then, you use mine. You know what it is, even if you do not realize it.''

"Then you are doing the actual magic for me?" he asked, although he knew that this was not so.

"No, the magic is entirely your own. But by identifying yourself with my inner name, you are in your innermost essence becoming me for the short time that you are working magic. And, in becoming me, you naturally have access to all of my powers. But you cannot take my name completely and become me; do not fear that. My inner name is in conflict with your own. I can change your inner name and make you become something else, but there is a definite limit to how much you can be made to change that way. Only the outer form, or part of the inner. Never the whole. You cannot be made to change completely as you must to take my inner name.''

"What is your inner name?" Allan asked.

"Ahlay'sje venna'dashey idhan." She half-sang the magical word-tones.

"That is a very long name," he commented.

"It defines my entire essence," Dalvenjah explained. "Of course, when I mastered my magic and became a true sorceress, my master gave me my inner name properly. No one, no matter how strong their magic, can take my inner name to use against me. Most people can be commanded through their inner name, for they are not protected.''

"And you will give me my inner name?" Allan inquired as evenly as he could to hide the fact that he could not have been more eager to receive his master's status and begin practicing magic that was entirely his own.

Dalvenjah smiled tolerantly. "I am sorry, but I doubt that things will be allowed to go that far. Soon I must fight Vorgulremik, and if I win then I must take Vajerral home. If I do not . . . either way, you are without a teacher. Will you give up your career and come with me?''

She waited, knowing that no answer was coming. It was an unfair question, and she knew it. Allan was caught too unprepared to make such a decision, and she doubted very much that the lure of magic alone could pull him away from what he had worked so long and hard to achieve with his music, let alone leave the only world that he had ever known, to live with dragons. Allan could not even look up, for he quickly came to that very same realization. There was really no question, just disappointment for what might have been.

"I am sorry," she said gently. "Perhaps it was wrong of me to even begin teaching you magic. I had not thought that you would really want to be a true magician, that you were happy enough with what you already are. It was only supposed to be a game."

"No, don't be sorry," he told her. "I got carried away in my expectations. A little magic is better than none at all, and I will always cherish this gift. But . . . the magic will go away when you leave?"

She nodded slowly. "I fear so."

"Then I will have just the memory of your gift," Allan said to himself. "What a lonely world this will be then, when both you and the magic have gone away."

That night Dalvenjah did not sleep well, for she felt evil magic on the move in this unprotected world. Vorgulremik fed and he fed well, growing large and strong. For it was the way of his kind that the Morilyekarin, like most of the evil breeds, lost both size and strength as their reserves were exhausted through many hard trials, but that their size increased with proper feeding. He had come into this world barely sixty feet in length, worn by fight and flight, but after only two weeks of rest and good hunting his form had increased a full fifteen feet. He was now hiding out somewhere in the wild, hoping to escape her wrath. He was waiting for her, well aware that she would come when she was ready. And he meant to win this battle for good, adding her magic to his own. For it was also the way of the steel dragons that they ate not only the flesh but the spirit, ingesting the magic it contained and making it a part of their own. He would slay her and eat her body and soul, and with what he gained from her he would be the strongest of the dark breed.

That night he hunted superior game. He had eaten cattle and horses by the scores of late, and he prospered well enough on such fare. This night he was hungry in his very spirit, and he meant to satisfy his cravings on the flesh and essence of humans. Soul food. Mortal spirits were weak and insubstantial things, but better than animals. He craved better, but the faerie folk of this world were far away, greatly diminished in strength and number. He would have to be satisfied with whatever he could catch; at least it was plentiful.

That night there were other hunters in the wild. Sheriff Hansin, Dave Wallick and Don Borelli of the FBI and Major Newell of the Air Force were quartering that area of the mountains. The trail of destruction was easy enough to follow and to read. The attacks of the two types of dragons were easy enough to tell apart: The little ones ran down their prey and consumed everything but a few scraps of hide and broken bones, while the big one took its prey suddenly, on the wing, and left nothing but blood and occasional tufts of fur. The two dragons of the middle-sized variety seemed to have disappeared altogether.

They were much more interested in the big dragon, the one they thought to be the most dangerous. So far they had been unable to track it to its lair—if it even made a den of any type. But they had every hope that they would be able to catch up with it eventually; then, Major Newell could have fighter planes there in a matter of minutes. The large dragon had attacked a small plane in the dark hours of the previous morning, and the pilot had been able to report only that something was tearing his plane apart. They had been searching for the remains of that plane all day, the major flying with pilots from the Civil Air Patrol while the two FBI agents rode with the sheriff in his four-wheel drive.

"Newell here." The major came on the radio suddenly. Sheriff Hansin brought the truck to a very quick halt, perched rather precariously atop a knife-edge ridge amid ghostly, stunted pines, and Wallick hastily brought up the antenna on his portable receiver.

"We read you," he answered. "Do you have something?"

"Maybe," Newell responded. "I think I just saw his shadow in the moonlight crossing our path behind us."

"Not much in the way of moonlight," Hansin pointed out, speaking loudly to be heard. "But you get the hell out if you think that thing's around. That thing you're flying in is closer to a hang glider than a B-52."

"We are already on our way out," Newell said before he was interrupted. They could hear the impact even over the static, followed by the breaking and rending of metal. Only the fact that the noise continued and the contact remained open suggested that the little plane had not been destroyed immediately.

"Newell, you still there?" Wallick demanded.

"Still here," the major replied with deceptive calm. "The damned thing must be sitting on top of the plane."

"Not quite!" the dim voice of the frantic pilot argued. "We don't have any wings. Whatever it is, it's carrying us!"

"It is a damned sight bigger than we were led to believe," Newell added. "A hundred feet at least, with . . ."

At that moment Vorgulremik broke open the cockpit to get at the inhabitants within, and the radio contact went dead. The three men waiting in the motionless truck could see the scene in their minds only too well as the dragon ripped apart the plane and pulled its screaming inhabitants from its ruined shell, then allowed the twisted wreck to crash to the mountainside below.

"So now what?" Borelli asked after a long, silent moment.

"First thing is that we get ourselves out of here," Hansin said firmly, and he turned the truck around and back down the bare trace of a path. "I doubt there is anything that we can do for them now. We can come back in the morning. I have a very good idea of where we will find anything that's left. And then . . ."

"And then we try a more cautious approach," Wallick said.

On the following Wednesday, the end of their second week in his world, Allan decided that the time had come to introduce the dragons to Marie and Dr. Barker and make some arrangement for getting them into the mountains where they could stretch their wings. Dalvenjah was not actively opposed to this plan. She was the first to admit that she needed to begin exercising her damaged wing very soon now if she was to have it back in perfect shape in time for her fight with Vorgulremik. But she was plainly disgusted with the whole idea of having to bring anyone else in on this. Part of the trouble, although she did not yet realize it, was that she had already developed a very strong dislike for Marie. She was very fond of Allan, even to the point of motherly protectiveness, and she was hardly pleased with anyone who had forced upon him such a burden of false guilt and self-doubt for simply being what he wanted to be.

Allan had already made arrangements to bring Marie, Jenny and Rex Barker home with him after rehearsal. They hardly knew what to make of his request. They were all inclined to believe that his story about dragons in his house was a ridiculous pretext to get them over for some other reason, but they could not imagine what.

Allan had asked Dalvenjah to order pizza by phone a short time before their arrival, so that it could be delivered and served at the proper time, providing an important tactical diversion. Dalvenjah was not unfamiliar with the phone; she would not answer it, for fear of finding Marie on the other end, but she had called Allan at rehearsal on occasion. She picked up the receiver, checked the pizza delivery ad that Allan had left for her, and began pressing buttons. Long arguments with the microwave had taught her a lot about pressing buttons.

"Jarvis Professional Services."

"Oh." Dalvenjah had not expected this. "What manner of professional services?"

"I beg your pardon?"

"I was trying to summon pizza."

"Oh. You have a wrong number."

"I am getting that impression," Dalvenjah remarked, mostly to herself. "So what do I do now?"

"You could always hang up and try again."

"Yes. That makes sense. My regards to you." She put down the phone, then picked it up and stared at the buttons. Technology! And these people had turned their backs on magic to do it the hard way?

"Paramount Pizza Parlor."

Say that three times fast, especially if you're a dragon with sharp teeth. "I need to order three large pizzas."

"What type?"

"Big and round?" In Dalvenjah's experience, there was only one type.

"I mean, what do you want on it?"

What did go on pizzas? Dalvenjah shrugged. "Venison."

That was followed by a very long pause. "Ah, lady, we don't have venison pizzas, and I don't think anyone does."

"What do you people put on pizzas?"

"Sausage and pepperoni are most common."

"Sausage sounds nice," Dalvenjah mused. "What is sausage?"

"Pork, mostly."

"And what is a pork?"

"They grow it inside of pigs."

"Pigs! That is disgusting. Nasty little beasts." Dalvenjah shook herself. "Make that three large pepperoni pizzas."

"You've got it, lady. Your name, please?"

"Dalvenjah Foxfire."

"That's a name?"

It took a little doing, but she finally arranged to have the pizza sent to Allan's name and address. When the person at the pizza parlor called back to confirm her order and had to talk to her again, he decided to take the path of least resistance and send the pizzas.

She had only just finished when she heard car doors shutting outside. They arrived in three separate vehicles, and Dalvenjah watched them through the window for some time as they stood in the yard discussing the matter in words that she could easily guess. They started for the door at last, and she sent Vajerral into hiding behind the large chair where the dragonet had been seated watching some program.

She paused a moment in the process of switching off the set, observing as one character on the screen came up behind the other, placed his hands over her eyes from behind and said "Guess who?" An old game in this world, but new to her. She turned off the television and quickly retreated into the kitchen, becoming invisible in the process.

Allan unlocked the front door a moment later and pushed it open wide, looking around quickly. He had fully expected to find the dragons waiting just inside, and he was at a loss to understand why they had made themselves scarce. He took another long step inside the front room, peering questioningly into the doorways leading into the kitchen and back hall. Jenny ran in behind him and stood in the center of the front room turning in a slow circle, fully expecting dragons to step out of the closet. Marie and Dr. Barker were close behind, glancing about the room with tolerant curiosity.

"Well, where are your little visitors?" Marie demanded in a voice that stated in no uncertain terms that she was no longer amused with this little game and that she was beginning to have very serious doubts about him. Marie was very good at getting her point of view across in a very few words. Dalvenjah, standing not ten feet away, snorted quietly and could have breathed fire.

"They must have gone into hiding," Allan said defensively. "I've told them to keep themselves hidden so often that they must have decided to disappear until they find out if everything is all right."

"And how can two dragons disappear?" Marie asked sarcastically.

"They're very good at it, believe me," he assured her as he laid his cello on the sofa. He was beginning to wish that he could resort to the magic that would allow him to disappear. He knew that Dalvenjah was in the house; he could sense her presence clearly enough, but his talents were not yet developed to the point that he could trace her even from this close. He glanced only briefly into the kitchen, already suspecting that the dragons were in one of their usual hiding places in the back of the house. "Dal, are you in there?"

She did not answer, and even went so far as to hold her breath. She was not yet finished having a good look at these newcomers.

Jenny she liked well enough at first glance, since the little girl reminded her so much of Vajerral that they might have been the same person in different forms. She was both old and small for her age, but such a skinny rack of bones and knobby joints that she appeared taller than she was. There had as yet been no official pronouncement about whether or not she was a true genius, but there was no question that she was a precocious brat. Not that she was given to actual misbehavior, but she had a store of energy to match her indomitable curiosity. At least moving her ahead two years in school had done some good in keeping her occupied. Dalvenjah, who was a genius of the second order as well as a first-rate sorceress, could identify well with her. But most important, at least as far as she was concerned, was the fact that the girl radiated nearly as much raw magic as her adept uncle.

Her mother, on the other hand, hardly had enough magic to bother with. Recessive genes, no doubt. If she was less than a genius, then it was not by much. Allan had called her the best independent financial consultant in town, which sounded impressive enough but really did not mean a damned thing to the sorceress. She was, curiously enough, taller than her younger brother, which had always been an important psychological advantage. She also reflected her Norwegian heritage more clearly, although she had cheated by getting her blond from a bottle. Even so, if her hair was braided and she was put into armor, she would have looked the part of the perfect Brunhilde, although her temper and constant interfering made her a more perfect Frika. Like her brother, she still looked younger than her thirty-four years, and there was no doubt that she had the looks to make the wolves pant.

One of those wolves stood just behind her, the one with the name, as Allan was fond of saying, that belonged on a German shepherd, still looking around the room as if he expected dragons to jump out at him any moment. Rex Barker certainly did not look the part of the brilliant young surgeon. He was stocky and barrel-chested, looking more like a short weightlifter than a sawbones. Nor could he be described as remarkably handsome, for he had a round face that was warm and friendly, almost comical, as if he was always laughing at some jest. He certainly did not seem like a match for Marie; but he and Jenny were a match, and they had both been working on Marie for over a year. Just now he looked like he would have been delighted to see a dragon, but he could see that this was a matter between Marie and Allan and wisely stayed out.

"Dalvenjah! You can come out. This is Marie and Dr. Barker," he called out, and waited a moment for a reply. At last he shrugged. "She seems to be reluctant to come out. I'll go look for her in the back."

"I suspect a plot in this," Marie said softly, although she did not wait until her brother was safely down the hall to make her opinion known. "If you ask me, he has another girl in this house and is trying to break the news to us. He must be thinking that, after leading us to expect dragons, an ordinary girl will be an improvement.''

"We won't let him get away with that, will we?'' Rex said suggestively, which was about as close as even he dared come to admonishing her for her behavior.

"Just as long as it's not a little spitfire like that last one.''

Dalvenjah twitched invisible ears.

Marie stepped back toward the recliner where Vajerral was hiding and brought a heel down about three inches from the end of Vajerral's tail, which was snaking out from beneath the chair. The startled dragonet squeaked in alarm and jerked away her tail, nearly tripping the rather startled Marie in the process.

"Allan, when did you get a cat?'' she demanded, but he did not answer.

But Jenny was not so easily misled. She was sure that she had seen something odd about that tail, and she was prepared to trace it to its source to solve that mystery. After all, there was supposed to be a little dragon in this house. She peered cautiously around the back of the large chair before climbing in between it and the wall. At the same time Vajerral streaked around the front of the chair and came in behind Jenny just as she emerged out the other side. The girl stood for a moment looking rather mystified; she had not found a dragon, but she had not seen a cat either. She circled around the front of the chair to try again.

"Come on, Allan,'' Marie said impatiently. She could hear her brother in the back of the house, searching the bathrooms. Whoever he was supposed to have in the house, he could not seem to find her . . . it. "Where is this monster of yours?''

"Monster?'' Dalvenjah huffed indignantly, and decided that it was time to take matters into her own hands and put an end to this nonsense. She stepped forward into the front room, becoming visible at the same time. She calmly walked up behind Marie and placed her hands over her eyes. "Guess who?''

"Oh, what the hell is this?'' Marie demanded, blissfully unaware of the very wide-eyed stares that were directed at her and "the monster'' from good Dr. Barker and her own daughter. Then she paused and cautiously felt the large, tapered hands, covered with smooth scales, that lay over her eyes.

Marie was hardly slow of wit; Jenny certainly had not inherited her IQ from her father. She stopped short in her measuring of those aquiline hands by touch, and in the next instant she exploded out of the dragon's light grasp and leaped into Dr. Barker's arms. Of course, he was not at all prepared to catch her, and she was a tall girl in the first place. The result of that most ill-considered move was that she bowled him over and the pair crashed to the floor in a sprawl of arms and legs.

Vajerral, her natural curiosity drawing her to the sound of that mishap, grabbed the back of the recliner and pulled herself up to the limit of her long neck, and found herself almost eye to eye with Jenny. The girl screamed, an automatic reflex rather than any considered plan, and the dragonet replied in kind. Unfortunately she was undecided about screaming and breathing flames, and the result was a rather feeble mixture of both. She ducked back behind the chair, which shook in time with her choking coughs.

"What?" Allan entered the room at a run, but stopped short at the doorway. After searching the house for Dalvenjah, she seemed to be all that he could see. "So there you are!"

"Your sister?" the sorceress asked complacently, indicated the tangled mass of bodies between them.

It was at that fortuitous moment that the pizza arrived.

Things were, needless to say, off to a less than glorious start. Allan had to bring everyone into the kitchen and seat those who could sit down at the table. Then he carefully explained from the beginning how he had come to have not one but two dragons living in his house, where they had come from and what they were doing. He had, of course, related the entire story once before. But that time no one had actually believed that he really did have dragons in his house and they had not paid the same attention they would have if they had thought that it might actually be true. Dr. Barker seemed to be taking it all well enough, since he was a very hard person to upset anyway, and Jenny was actually delighted. Marie, predictably, sat at the table with her head in her hands, and she appeared undecided about whether she should faint dead away or fly into a fine rage. Dalvenjah sat on her tail a short distance away, looking rather sullen; Vajerral and Jenny were perched on stools at the bar.

"So that's it," Allan concluded. "Dalvenjah came here to help us, so it's only fair that we do something for her."

"That sounds fair to me," Rex agreed.

Marie did not reply at once. After a moment she glanced almost hesitantly over her shoulder at the dragon. Dalvenjah responded pleasantly with what she intended to be a warm, encouraging smile. Unfortunately, a dragon's long snout was not built for friendly smiles, and it came out as little more than a broad, toothy grin. Shaking her head hopelessly, Marie buried her head in her hands and moaned, "Oh, shit!"

"Oh, come on, Mom! They're neat!" Jenny admonished.

Marie looked over at her impatiently, and sighed. "Don't sit so close to that . . . that thing."

Allan looked about ready to explode, his rage greater than what he would have ever managed for his own sake. Unlike his sister, he thought of Vajerral as no more a monster than Jenny was. But Dalvenjah had a much calmer, simpler method of handling this. She bent her head forward and quietly said, "If you say anything like that again, I'll set fire to your pants."

Marie looked over her shoulder at the dragon, rather startled, but wisely decided to avoid arguing the point. As Allan had predicted, there was no real question about who possessed the most forceful personality. One of Dalvenjah's advantages was that she saved her fire for when it did the most good; when she growled, everyone knew that she meant it. Marie reconsidered and turned her attention back to Allan, who represented a much safer target for her wrath.

"Well, what happens now?" she demanded.

"That seems obvious enough," Rex answered. "Allan has the right idea. He can use my van to take these two dragons up to my cabin in the mountains. And his memory does serve him well: There probably will be no one near enough to see as long as they're discreet about their flying. It's a good time of the year right now, too late for skiing but too cold for anything else. You should have nearly the whole mountain to yourselves."

"And tomorrow night is my last concert for nearly two months," Allan added eagerly. "That's more than enough time to get Dalvenjah back in shape and through our fight with Vorgulremik.''

"My fight," Dalvenjah corrected him gently. "You will not have a master's control of magic by that time, however strong your powers may be."

"His powers?" Marie demanded incredulously. This was the part that Allan had been too bashful to explain himself.

"Strong magic," the sorceress insisted, and turned to her student. "The next time you need to convince someone that you have dragons, why don't you just show them your magic? Why do you not allow your sister to see how we disappear?"

Grinning like a conscience-stricken Cheshire cat, Allan spoke the proper word of command in his mind and faded quickly from sight. Dalvenjah followed him into thin air a moment later, and Vajerral rounded out the demonstration by vanishing as well. Jenny exclaimed in delight and even Dr. Barker appeared to be quite impressed, but Marie only buried her face in her hands and swore to herself. She wondered where she had gone wrong as a surrogate parent; it was bad enough when he wanted to be a cellist, but now he had made himself into a sorceress's apprentice. All she could think of was Mickey Mouse and all of those brooms and buckets of water. All three returned after a few moments.

"Where did you go?" Jenny asked excitedly.

"Nowhere," Allan insisted. "We were here the entire time."

"Back to the subject of this fight," Rex interrupted. "I still find it hard to believe that your wing can be ready for flying that soon, let alone fighting. I can hardly believe that such a long, delicate bone could even mend properly in the first place, and it doesn't seem like you ever have tried to keep it splinted."

"Magic," Dalvenjah explained. "Magic holds it firm. Magic makes it go back together well. That is no problem."

"I would still like for you to allow Dr. Barker to take a look," Allan suggested.

The fact was that, as worried as he was about her wing, he was even more worried about what his world could be doing to her. Few things here, food, illnesses and climate, even the very dust and pollen in the air, were exactly like she had known in her own world. But even more than that, he was worried that she might have new injuries needing to be tended after her next fight with the evil dragon. His thought was that, if Dr. Barker knew what signs were associated with her condition now, while she was in reasonably good health, then he might know more about what shape she might be in when she really needed help. Rex brought out his trusty black bag and began by checking her eyes, ears and the sharpness of the points of her silver horns. Then he brought out a wooden tongue depressor and a small light.

"Open wide and say 'Ah,' " he said absently.

Dalvenjah complied, opening her mouth as wide as her canine jaws would allow. She was in the process of saying "Ah" and Rex was bending forward for a closer look when he suddenly realized what he was doing and leaped back.

"Whoa, there!" he exclaimed. "Ah, are you the type of dragon who breathes fire?"

"Of course," she said tolerantly, frowning admonishingly. "But it's not the type of thing that one does by accident. I will not burn your nose any more than you have to worry about one of your own kind biting you."

"I've been bit," Rex remarked. But, holding the tongue depressor before him as if it was St. George's lance, he moved in for a quick peek down her long throat. The problem was that it was long; even her vocal cords were nearly a foot down the hole, which was the reason for the odd hollow quality to her voice. "Ah, ha! I believe I see a light at the other end."

"I had a light dinner," she explained. And so they were the very best of friends from the start; Rex Barker took an immediate liking to anyone who could appreciate a bad joke.

He continued his examination externally, since there was little he could do about investigating her internal structure. He would have given a lot to have been able to get decent X-rays of her undoubtedly curious wing and shoulder structure, the two joints being only inches apart and each with its own pectoral muscles. Even Marie had to admit that the dragons were beautiful creatures, a strange, alien beauty that had to be seen to be properly understood. Most people thought of dragons as massive beings with thick, stocky bodies and short, stumpy legs. But Dalvenjah was very slender of body and long of limb, which gave her an almost elfin beauty and grace; even her sinewy neck was not much thicker at the top than a human's.

After a time the good doctor's investigation moved into regions that one did not normally associate with dragons, and Dalvenjah began to have a hard time maintaining her professional impartiality.

"Honestly, Rex!" Marie exclaimed when he all but crouched down between her legs.

"Oh, not to worry," he assured her absently. "I'll do you next."

She could not have been more scandalized. "Rex! Not in front of the child!"

"I didn't mean to in the first place," he remarked dryly. Marie seemed about ready to explode a second time, but he took no notice. "Listen, I've learned over the past year that Jenny has a very good theoretical understanding of just what is going on, and she'd probably have a more personal knowledge if her apparent physical age did not lag as far behind her real age as her mental age exceeds it."

"What?"

"I know what's going on when we spend the weekend up in the mountains," Jenny said for herself. "I figured that out the first time we went, when Rex stuck me in the room off the kitchen with a new color television."

Marie once again looked likely to faint.

"And the other child present apparently does not speak English," Rex added.

"Can too!" Vajerral declared.

Rex glanced over his shoulder at her, and shrugged. "How much is this evil dragon like you?"

"Not much," Dalvenjah answered. "The golden dragons like myself live in the cold, high places, and we are comfortable there even without magic. The great dragons can survive in such places as this or my own home, but they need their magic to protect them and they are always slow. Vorgulremik is not happy here, and he must feed."

Rex glanced up at her, as did the others, alerted by something in the way she had said that. "Feed? You mean he eats people?"

"Oh, yes. People have strong spirits. He must consume their souls, to have the magic of their essence to add to his own."

"But not virgins?" Rex asked. He noticed her lack of comprehension. "A girl who has never . . . you know. It's part of our myths about dragons that they only eat virgins."

"No, not . . . virgins?" Dalvenjah said. "Anyone."

"Oh, that's a shame," he remarked sadly as he returned to his seat at the table. "Considering the lack of virgins in this world, we could have just waited for the old boy to starve. But, for now, I can indeed solve two of your problems. Allan, your last concert is tomorrow night, right?"

"Right, boss," he agreed.

"Well, the next morning I'll bring my van over—less the second row of seats—and you can take your friends up to my cabin. Marie, Jenny and I will be along Friday, the following night, although we can only stay until Sunday night. As much as it must pain her, Jenny does indeed have school to attend. Just as it pains me to know that I have patients to see and surgery to do and golf to play."

Jenny did indeed look very sour at the thought of having to go to school and only see the dragons on weekends. But then, she thought it a worthy trade if being in the mountains meant that she could see them fly and breathe fire and do all the other neat things that were against zoning ordinances there in town.

"Come on!" Jenny said to Vajerral as she hopped down from the stool, having decided to take advantage of the time she did have. "I got a really neat book at the school library today. All about the famous chateaus of France. Would you like to see?"

"Dye, asheh aludeh," the dragonet agreed enthusiastically as she leaped down from her stool.

The two raced out the door into the front room, where Jenny had abandoned her books on the sofa. Marie sat for a long moment with her mouth hanging open, clearly on the verge of protesting that she did not want her daughter to be alone and unsupervised—or unprotected—in the presence of monsters. She stopped short when she saw that Dalvenjah was glaring at her rather fiercely, and for the first time in her life she was daunted by a will far stronger than her own. She was not about to give up without a fight, but Allan and Rex both added the strength of their glares to Dalvenjah's when they saw that she was sure to win. And Marie did indeed relent quickly enough, humbled in the face of superior resolve. We have met the enemy, and she is ours. But she did not intend to surrender that gracefully.

"What are shat-oh's?" Dalvenjah asked, abruptly changing the subject, or at least putting it back on track.

"Castles," Rex explained simply.

"Oh, Vajerral should like that," she said, pleased. "It will remind her of home. Of course, our castle is really more of a fortress, very big and dark and all rock. But I have tried to make it a home."

"You live in a castle?" Marie asked, surprised, quite in spite of herself.

"Oh, yes," the dragon assured her. "Very expensive to keep, since it was abandoned when I got it. But I can afford it. Upwardly mobile, as you say. I do have professional appearances to maintain."

Marie only shook her head slowly.

"Are you sure that the three of you will be all right up there for the next few weeks?" Rex asked, returning to the subject of why they were there in the first place. "You can't count on the area being totally abandoned, even at this time of the year. You should not have any trouble in the area around the cabin itself, but I am worried that someone might take a shot at our friends if they go flying too far. Or, at the least, dragons are probably very hard to explain away."

"I will watch out," Dalvenjah assured him. "It is too hard to fly and be invisible at the same time, but there is easier magic that makes it very hard for a person to look right at me. And I will not allow Vajerral to fly very far by herself."

"Yes, but will she do what you tell her?" Marie asked. She was naturally skeptical about the restraint children could maintain, since Jenny had none. At least it was completely overshadowed by curiosity.

"Vajerral is very responsible," Dalvenjah insisted. "I taught her very early how important that must be, if she is to be a Veridan, a sorceress and a fighting dragon."

"If you'll excuse my saying so, you don't impress me as

being very big and strong even by the standards of your own kind," Rex remarked.

"No, I am not so big," she agreed. "But I am still very strong, and the ways of fighting of the Veridan, the warrior-sorcerers, have little to do with strength. My battle with Vorgulremik will be one of magic."

"That sword of yours..." Rex suggested, indicating the blade she carried in her harness.

"Not much good against steel dragons," she said, drawing the sword and holding it before her with both hands. The blade was nearly five feet long. "The first Veridan were mortals, not so much unlike yourselves. They needed the weapons that the Mindijaran do not. They use the sword not just as a blade, but as a focus of magic."

As they watched, the length of that shiny blade began to glow with a misty blue light that flowed and dripped. "My people have some contact with them, even a colony in their world. But I have never had much business with mortal folk. Before now."

"This one is my favorite," they could hear Jenny telling Vajerral in the next room as they peered through the picture book of castles. "I like the way they adapted that high roof to fit smoothly into the lines of those rows of small turrets."

"Lye dalash derreh aeya lendan fer ghennah," the dragonet said.

"Yes, I've often thought so myself," Jenny agreed.

Marie was thoroughly mystified. "How do they understand each other?"

"Magic," Dalvenjah explained simply.

"It all sounds clear enough to me," Rex added. "You really don't understand a word of it?"

"No, none."

"You do not have great magic, like Allan and Jenny possess," Dalvenjah told her. "You have more than Dr. Barker, but he is not afraid of his."

"I have magic?" Rex asked, surprised.

"Not much," she admitted. "Just enough that you can share the link that Vajerral has made so that she can speak with Jenny. But then, nearly every member of your race has that much magic. Vajerral is supplying the real magic, so that you cannot do it without her. Only Allan and Jenny possess the magic to do that for themselves, but one has to be taught how.''

"Well, I'm still amazed," Rex commented, mostly to himself.

• Part Three •

The Mountains in Spring

ALLAN KNEW WHY he had decided upon the cello over the violin only a second after the string broke. The violin string had become a symbol for very high tension and stress, and the violinist had to live with the awareness that half of a broken string could snap toward his face with force enough to do serious damage, even put out an eye. It was startling enough to see one of the things shoot off the front of a cello, but at least the danger was not quite as great. The trouble was that strings most often broke during tuning, when the cellist might be leaning over the instrument with an ear almost on the bridge, listening to the tone while turning the pegs that tightened the four strings.

Allan swore to himself for a moment, but very quietly, and not until he had taken the replacement strings out of his pocket and began taking the broken string off the cello. One of his teachers had once warned him, during his advanced studies, to always keep a complete set of spare strings with him when he was out on stage. It saved quite some time in fitting a replacement and eliminated the possibility that there would be none to be found. Of course, strings did not break all that often.

This was the first one this season, and he might not break another for months.

The orchestra continued tuning after the brief pause resulting from the incident, which had also had the effect of quieting, if only slightly and briefly, the noisy pre-concert crowd. Such careful tuning was an old and honored tradition among orchestras and almost a part of the entertainment as far as the patrons were concerned. They would probably be disappointed if it was lacking, and some insisted that it helped to get talkative patrons to their seats. But there was always the question of whether so much protracted and noisy effort was really necessary. An entire orchestra could re-tune quietly in a matter of seconds between movements of a work, or even tune to a new key when required. Some instruments, like the big, loud tympani, were in an almost constant state of tuning even during the work itself. The players themselves certainly were not going to tell.

There was also the possibility that extroverted musicians simply liked to sit out in the middle of the stage and make noise. It was a cheap substitute for a solo, if nothing else. And the shy types, like Allan himself, were often very quick tuners as well.

Danny Grehan, acting as if this was no more than another rehearsal before an empty hall, walked over and stood staring over Allan's shoulder while he deftly attached the new string. He waited, unconcerned, with his horn tucked under his arm as if it was a walking stick, then quietly applauded when Allan was finished.

"Allegro non fumbo. Very good," he remarked. "So, last concert of the season. What are you going to be doing for the next few weeks? Off to some musicians' workshop, no doubt."

"No, not at all," Allan said, with a note of self-satisfaction that caught Danny's attention and interest. "My friends and I are going to spend the next four weeks in a cabin in the mountains."

"Oh, ho! Friends indeed!" Danny declared, and half the orchestra turned to stare. "You Norwegians never get your English right, using the plural when you mean singular. So who is this friend?"

"No one you know," Allan said absently. "And I intend to keep it that way, thank you."

"What? You don't trust me?" Danny sounded incredulous and aggrieved.

"Not for a minute."

"Ah, you are learning. But what does Marie have to say about this? Or doesn't she know?"

"She knows," Allan answered. "She does not completely approve, as you might guess, but so far she has not had her way. I hope to keep it that way, if I can."

"If you can?" Danny asked. "Listen to me, boy. You're off to a damned good start, so don't blow it. That's the other problem with Scandinavians; they think they have to do what they're told. Do you think the Vikings sacked the western world because they wanted to? No, they would have preferred to have stayed at home and read those incredibly long, dull epic poems. No, they all had big sisters telling them what they should do with their lives. Jews have mothers, and Scandinavians have sisters."

"Eh?" Efriam Lifshitz glanced up from tuning his violin.

"Too bad you don't have any Irish in you," Danny continued. "The Irish, now they don't let anyone tell them what to do. And that's in spite of the fact that they don't hesitate to tell each other or anyone else what they should be doing."

"Case in point," Allan remarked softly.

"Let me show you something." Danny looked around, and found Dean Larkin seated among the oboes. "Dean, me boy!"

"Sure, and what can I do for you?" Dean responded appropriately. Like most of the rest of the orchestra, he had been listening in on the conversation. He was the group's native Irishman . . . unlike Danny, who was only a reasonable facsimile. He saw his part coming, and he knew what was expected.

"So do tell us," Danny began eloquently. "Why did the Irishman cross the road?"

"Sure, and I don't see how that's any of your damned business," Dean said in an exaggerated brogue without looking up from his instrument.

"You see!" Danny declared triumphantly, turning back to Allan. "That's the proper Irish spirit you need to deal with a Norwegian sister."

"Sure, and I'll bear that in mind, so I will," Allan agreed.

"You do that!" Danny said, very self-satisfied. "So do tell. Where are you and your friend—singular—going to be? I might just drop by and say hello."

"Sure, and I don't see how that's any of your damned business," Allan quipped, and plucked experimentally at his new string.

Danny straightened, looking rather astonished, then nodded approvingly. "The boy learns fast, so he does."

With that he turned and marched away toward his proper region of the orchestra, ignoring occasional smiles and sly glances. The maestro had told him more than once that the reason the brass section was located near the back of the orchestra had nothing to do with the instrument, unlike the percussion and double basses.

Allan thought that he should have been pleased with himself, but the fact was that he was feeling vaguely dissatisfied. He was indeed going away for four weeks with a very pretty girl, but she was also a dragon and their relationship was purely platonic, even one of student and teacher. But Danny, playboy of the western world, thought that he was taking up residence with a lady friend, much as he might himself be doing, for an extended romantic and sexual interlude. And he found, to his surprise and personal embarrassment, that he would very much like to be doing just that. He was even more surprised to realize that he would like to be able to tell Marie that he was doing just that . . . and get away with it.

Freud would have had a wonderful time with such errant thoughts.

After he had a moment to become used to the idea, Allan asked himself why he should not be allowed to do as he pleased. Marie went away for just such weekend flings herself. There was no secret that Dr. Barker had acquired that very remote cabin for just that purpose, and they had the audacity to take Jenny with them. Why, then, was that a horror of horrors where he was concerned, that he was lectured if Marie thought he even took notice of anything female? Even Dalvenjah did exactly as she pleased.

But Allan knew the answer to that. He was afraid. When he had decided upon music as a career, it had been with the personal understanding that it was because music was all-important in his life. And he meant that literally. He had never known sex, hardly dated, hardly even kissed a girl. He had explained to himself again and again that strong talent, especially when it clearly bordered on genius as his own did, made too many demands upon the one who would try to use it. Real talent left no room for a personal life; it was not fair to someone else to come to expect his attention, only to find that she was forever second to a cello. And it was not fair to himself.

And so he kept his virginity locked away in his cello case, and he had always felt pleased that he was doing the right thing. But he wondered then, for the first time, if he really was just afraid. Did he live with the fear that any attempt to satisfy his personal desires would mean losing his exceptional talent? Or was he simply afraid that he was not adequate as a person to enjoy the privileges that all the rest of the world took for granted? And was he really being fair to himself? He wondered if it was possible that he could not make the right choice whatever he decided.

And that, he thought, might be the real reason why he was content to never face those questions. There were too many possibilities, and too many chances of deciding wrong. He might be dissatisfied, lonely and lacking, but he thought it better to hold onto what he was sure of rather than take a chance of losing it.

Allan was almost afraid to go home that night, for fear that Dalvenjah was able to read his thoughts. It was an ambivalent fear, for he found, also to his considerable surprise, that he wanted very much to tell her how he felt. He thought that she would know the exact solution to his every trouble. She did seem to be able to manage an apparently awesome talent and still enjoy all the romantic and sexual affairs she wanted. But she was a very strong and secure personality; she knew the secret for taking what she wanted and enjoying it without guilt or regret. He knew that he was not that secure, that he could not even admit to himself that he possessed the same capacity for love and desire as anyone else.

Dalvenjah was indeed waiting for him, although Vajerral had long since gone to bed. The sorceress professed that she would never understand why his people insisted upon making music through the middle of the night, but she was always very patient in waiting for him to come home, a soda and a peanut butter sandwich waiting for him. He wished that she could have heard each concert as he played it, but the radio broadcast was delayed more than three weeks; she had not yet heard his solo from the night they had first met.

She was aware that something was bothering him from the start, and he knew it. But he was grateful that she did not resort to Marie's tactic of demanding an explanation right away; instead, she waited quietly until he was ready. He ate his dinner in silence, and by the time he finished she knew that he was waiting for her to ask.

"Allan, is something wrong?" she inquired cautiously.

"You don't know?"

She looked surprised. "What am I, a mind-reader?"

Allan raised an inquiring brow. "I'm not sure."

"Well, sometimes," she admitted. "But I do not go around digging into people's thoughts any more than I want them in mine. But I do not think that I need to read your mind. I think that you are feeling lonely tonight. I can understand that."

"You can?"

"Yes, certainly," she insisted. "I am lonely much of the time. That is why I am glad that you can be with me most of the time now that your . . . your season is over. We will practice magic and talk about all the things we need to do, and I will not be so lonely. Perhaps not you as well."

"Perhaps not," he agreed, although he sounded completely unconvinced.

"Oh, so it is that kind of lonely," Dalvenjah observed. "Well, I can't do anything about that. I am a Mindijarah, a dragon, and immortal."

"And I'm a cellist," Allan agreed dismally. "We don't have all that much in common. But you could be human, if you wanted?"

"I could be . . . what you call an elf, the immortal equivalent of what you are," she answered somewhat guardedly. "If I wanted."

"But you wouldn't care to be?"

"Not hardly! Would you want to be a dragon?"

Allan shrugged. "No, I suppose not. It would not be very

beneficial to my career, and I think that a dragon would find the cello deucedly hard to play.''

"Easier than the violin," Dalvenjah remarked, and sat back on her tail in silence for a long moment. "Perhaps it is that I am too much of a bother in your life. Taking too much time, perhaps.''

"No, not at all!" he assured her. "You're still the best friend I've ever had, and I want to learn all the magic that you have to teach me.''

"Even if the magic will all go away when I go?'' she asked gently.

"Yes, even so," he said without hesitation.

"Then that is your decision," she said. "For four more weeks or so, you will have magic. Then you must return to the real world, at least as you have always known it, and to your own life. But I hope that you will learn that your life is your own, for you to take from it all the riches you can find in it. There is no reason why you should be lonely, nor lacking in anything else that life has to offer.''

Dr. Barker brought his van over at practically the break of day, parking it in the driveway and leaving again with Marie without saying a word. Allan was pleased, since he had been prepared for two hours or more of advice and admonishments from his sister before she would allow him to leave for the country for four weeks in the company of dragons. He wondered if Rex had something to do with that.

The van was bright blue with decorative stripes and a great deal of chrome trim, fully carpeted on the inside with big, soft seats, gentle lights, a better radio system than Allan had in his house, and even a color television. There was a large side door for Dalvenjah. The back windows were deeply tinted and had blinds on the inside to prevent anyone from stealing a casual glance inside. And Rex had removed the second set of seats just inside the door, leaving only the long bench seat in the very back and plenty of room for the dragons. But the machine also looked twice as big as anything that Allan had ever driven in his life, since he had always owned the smallest of the small and found it adequate for his needs.

The first problem was getting the two dragons into the van

without making a public spectacle of the affair. That was easy enough for Allan to figure out; he removed his own car from the garage, drove the van inside and closed the door. It was easier said than done, since he found parking the large van inside his small garage similar to trying to dock a battleship the first time behind the wheel, but he managed it without disturbing the original shape of the van's fenders. He placed his bags in the back—the dragons had none—and parked the van in the street before he returned his own car to the garage and locked the door.

He accomplished all that and turned back to the van, intent upon being on his way, only to find to his horror that the side door was open and Grandma Parsons had climbed inside. He hurried to discover what was going on, but Mrs. Parsons saw him coming, slammed the door and took off at a spry trot across the yard.

"So long, Allan!" she called. "Have a nice trip."

"Right," he answered absently as he opened the driver's door and climbed inside. Vajerral was perched in the passenger's seat where she could look out easily enough, with firm instructions that she was to hide herself when any cars came to a stop beside their own. Dalvenjah was seated on her tail behind them, her jeweled eyes glittering in the dim light.

"What did she want?" he demanded as he shut his door.

"Just talk," Dalvenjah answered. "And a gift."

"Do you think we can trust her to keep her mouth shut?" Allan asked as he started the motor. He paused a moment as he cautiously pulled away from the curb, then continued. "She's kept quiet so far."

"She will not tell," Dalvenjah said with considerable conviction.

"You're sure of that?"

"I told you last night that I can hear the thoughts of others," she explained. "There are times when it becomes necessary. Perhaps I should not say this, but I trust your sister less."

"No doubt."

Dalvenjah brought her head forward between the seats. "You have not told me that Vorgulremik is destroying so many of your people."

"You got the lowdown out of Grandma Parsons?" Allan asked. "And how did she know?"

"She knows what everyone else seems to know, that a lot of your people are disappearing by what they call 'mysterious means.' She has the advantage of knowing about me," Dalvenjah said. "From that much, it is not very hard to understand."

He shrugged as if to show how unimportant he considered the matter. "What could you have done about it? You won't be ready to fight him again for another four weeks at least, and you've only been here two."

"You should have told me," she insisted.

"I will not have you going after that dragon until you're ready," Allan told her firmly. "I want you to promise me that you won't."

"There is nothing gained in failure," Dalvenjah agreed. "I will know when I am ready, and I will not fight before."

"Remember that," he declared, then sniffed. "What do I smell?"

"Cookies," Dalvenjah said.

"Chocolate chip!" Vajerral added with considerable pleasure.

Dr. Barker had described the journey to his mountain cabin as an easy two-hour trip, but in that he had failed to consider three important points. First, he usually drove his very expensive, high-powered sports car that made little work of the steep mountain grades and relentless snaking turns. Second, he drove like a madman at the best of times, especially so during his trips to the cabin when all he could think of was getting his hands on Marie, while on the way back he had to get home and rest in time for surgery the following morning. The police along that stretch of highway had long since learned to ignore him, knowing that they were no match for car or driver. Nor did he always tell the truth, and in this case he had deliberately underestimated his own driving time by an hour.

Vajerral could have cared less. She sat upright in the front passenger's seat and enjoyed every moment of the trip, or at least the novelty of riding in the machine. Dalvenjah was somewhat less enthusiastic. She was not all that impressed with machines in the first place, and she was forced to spend the entire journey sitting back on her tail and holding on as well as she could through the endless progression of sharp turns. For his own part, Allan found it a hair-raising adventure. The van itself was not all that hard to drive except for its tendency to pull slightly but consistently to the right, so that he had to be always on his guard.

Allan realized one very important point about halfway there, and stopped at a combination service station and small grocery store along the road to collect supplies to last them at least a couple of days. He left the van parked well away from the store to make it more difficult for anyone to steal a casual glance inside, at the very edge of the gravel parking lot in the shadows of the surrounding forest. He concluded his shopping as quickly as possible, threw the sacks of groceries in the rear compartment and climbed behind the driver's seat for a hasty retreat.

"Hold off!" Dalvenjah said urgently before he had a chance to turn the key. "Vajerral has disappeared."

"What?" he paused in confusion, and suddenly realized that the passenger seat was empty. "How did she get out?"

"Opened the door," the dragon explained. "She needed to visit the bushes, so I told her to get out your door so that she would not be seen from the store. But she has not come back. I think that she is distracted."

"I'll distract the underside of her tail," Allan declared, and looked around. "Throw me that blanket. I'll catch her as quick as I can and bring her back in that."

Vajerral had indeed been distracted, although not for all that long. The forest was not new and strange to her; in fact, it reminded her more of home than anything that she had seen in the past two weeks. That was why she wandered farther than she should have. After a couple of minutes she realized that she was already in trouble, and that the amount of trouble she would be in would be the same whether she flew straight back or continued to explore for a few minutes longer. She reasoned with irrefutable if impeachable logic that she might as well get all the good she could from the trouble she was in.

The late morning air was still chill, and snow lingered in wide patches beneath the forest and hung in the branches of the trees, which were bright evergreen and so did not have the destitute look of winter. The dragonet threaded a path between the stretches of snow, preferring dry ground even if the snow was no real discomfort to her hands and paws. She walked along slowly, lifting her head on its long neck to stare into the trees or peer into dark holes, feeling happy and very much at home.

But she had not gone very far when she happened across a citizen of this forest who did not look like anything she knew from back home. Even so, she thought she knew what it was at first glance. It had to be a cat, not unlike one of the delegation kept by Grandma Parsons, which marched over to visit every morning and often told her very interesting stories about their daily rounds and successful hunts. They certainly came in many colors, and so she did not find it at all odd if this one was black with a white stripe down its back. She sat down in its path and waited, certain that any cat who lived and hunted in the forest would have some very delightful stories to tell.

Brother Skunk, on the other hand, was not much given to idle conversation, nor did he trust strangers. And there was surely nothing stranger in his woods than this dragon. Vajerral did not yet know about skunks, but he had never seen a dragon . . . even if the local mountains were fairly crawling with dragons of assorted sizes, at least compared with most parts of the world. He was also rather nearsighted, and very intent upon his business. And so it was that he was not even aware of Vajerral until he almost bumped into her.

He drew back, startled, with his hackles raised and his tail on end. But he did not attack at once, seeing that the dragonet only sat and stared at him with polite interest, not at all threatening. They stood for a long moment, staring at each other. Then Vajerral cordially inquired about how hunting was this time of year, and that surprised the skunk greatly. No one had ever spoken with him before; no one ever made the effort to talk to skunks. But instead of being properly appreciative, he was instantly suspicious and wondered if he was about to be a victim of foul play. Whatever this creature was, it looked to him like an unnerving cross between a fox and a snake. He immediately turned tail to run, a move which had the advantage of bringing his personal long-range artillery to bear.

It was fortunate for Vajerral that dragons are quicker than skunks. That sudden move was startling in itself, even if she did not know what it meant, but she did sense a hostile intent. Her own reaction was rather similar in its way, even more dangerous if less disgusting. The two opponents faced—or did not face—each other for a bare moment, but Vajerral shot first. There was a loud electrical snap, a blinding flash of light and a fair amount of billowing blue smoke. The unfortunate skunk emerged an instant later from that small explosion, four feet high in a trajectory that described a lazy arch across the clearing, chittering in alarm and anger while he trailed smoke from his magnificent tail. He landed on all fours and kept on, running and cursing like he had never run and cursed before.

Allan was unlucky enough to arrive at that precise moment, following his own quarry by magic and then alerted by that explosion. He had just stepped out from behind a tree when he saw the skunk racing toward him, a rather ragged and dejected-looking tail exuding wisps of smoke instead of more potent clouds. It hit him in both legs at a full run, again foiled by bad eyesight, with the result that they both crashed into the bushes. The skunk recovered first, and Allan looked up to the sight of the beast hissing at him not two feet away before reversing himself to display his smoking tail. The skunk knew humans and considered them fair game, but he had also had enough surprises for one day and elected to continue his hasty retreat.

Allan was so intent upon finding Vajerral and getting her under cover that he decided that he would have to be startled later. He jumped up, collected his blanket and hurried on to the clearing. The dragonet was nowhere to be seen, but evidence of the explosion lingered in the form of a haze of blue smoke and a path of scorched ground.

"Vajerral!" he called softly.

"Allan!" She squeaked in delight from almost directly overhead and leaped down from the branch where she was perched, without waiting until he was prepared to catch her. He tried, but his hands were burdened with the blanket and she plummeted into the middle of that before striking him in the center of the chest and bowling them both over.

"Got you!" Allan wheezed, the breath momentarily knocked

out of him, although he still managed to wrap the ends of the blanket about the dragonet and tuck her under his arm. "Stay quiet for a moment, until we get back to the van. What did you think you were doing?"

"I thought I saw a pussycat," the dragonet replied, muffled in the folds of the blanket.

Vajerral, remembering how much trouble she was in and why she should not be seen in public, kept silent and motionless while Allan hurried her back through the woods to the parking lot and opened the side door to pass her quickly into Dalvenjah's waiting arms. He slammed the door and turned to hurry around to the driver's side. Only then did he see the police car parked before the front of the store, facing his direction and with a pair of constables seated inside and wearing startled expressions. His first thought was that they must have seen Dalvenjah through the open door of the van; he did not know that Vajerral's long, golden-scaled tail had been hanging out of the folds of the blanket and clearly visible.

Allan did not pause to argue the point, since he knew that he could not win such an argument. The only thing that he could think to do was to make as hasty a retreat as possible. And hope that the good officers, who had surely seen something very odd, were still not too sure just what they had seen but would decide that it had not been odd enough to warrant a closer investigation. He climbed into the van, started the motor and left at what he considered a hurried but unremarkable pace.

"I think they saw us," he warned Dalvenjah once they were back on the highway.

"Who?" she asked in return.

"The police back at the store," he told her. " I wouldn't worry that much about anyone else catching just a glimpse of you, but they might decide to take a closer look. Especially when you consider all the recent murders and disappearances in this area, and all the talk about strange creatures."

"That's bad," Dalvenjah remarked, and returned Vajerral to her usual perch by pushing her over the top of the passenger seat, then turned to peer out the rear window. "Bad news."

"I see it!" Allan snapped.

"Floor this sucker!" Vajerral declared, bouncing in her seat with excitement. "Más pronto!"

Allan frowned at the dragonet, suspecting that she had been watching a little too much television.

The patrol car had not yet turned on its lights, so Allan could not be sure if this was an actual chase. That was the problem he faced: If there was to be a chase, then he needed as much of a head start as possible. But he did not want to provoke pursuit when there might have been none by running too soon. He had no illusions about his ability to escape; as quick as the van was, fast for just about any automobile except for the likes of Rex's sports car, he would still lose the race here in the mountains to steep grades and tight turns that would force him to brake harder than the smaller police car or risk losing control.

The problem was not long in resolving itself. The road began to climb steeply immediately after leaving the store, snaking in and out amid hills and ridges. After about three miles, the patrol car turned on its lights and began to close. Allan hit the accelerator without hesitation and the van's powerful engine roared in response, so that it turned out a far more even contest than he had dared to hope. But it was hopeless all the same, for the police closed the distance between them slowly but steadily. Then the road began to rise even more steeply than ever before, and he knew that they had lost.

"Can you take wing out the side door on the move?" he called over his shoulder, not daring to look while he was fighting the van for control. "I could stop and let you out, but they're going to see. Unless you can keep yourselves invisible."

"That is no good," Dalvenjah declared. "I would not willingly leave you to such trouble."

"I won't be in that much trouble if they don't get a good look at you two," he answered. "So far I only have to worry about a ticket for speeding. But if they catch you, it will be much worse for all of us."

"So there's a law against being a dragon?" she asked haughtily.

"Of course not!" he snapped impatiently. "People here don't believe in dragons. So they might be surprised and scared and very likely to shoot first. Or worse."

"I understand," she assured him calmly. "But there is a better solution."

"What?" Allan demanded, then had to pay full attention to the road when he saw a particularly sharp turn coming up, a steep cliff bordered along its top edge by the road. He was just beginning the turn when the wheel was suddenly ripped from his hands by some unseen force, intent upon leading the van through a small opening in the guardrails and into open space. At the same time it leaped forward, accelerating up the steep rise much faster than its engine could have moved the massive machine.

"Dalvenjah!" he cried desperately. "What do you think you're doing?"

"Trust me," she said in her typically calm voice.

He had no choice, it seemed. The van shot through the opening at what might have been a good take-off speed for a jet plane; the speedometer went all the way up to one hundred and twenty, and they had left that well behind. The van hurtled well out from the edge of the cliff and began to descend in a long, graceful arch, sure to crash into the woods that choked the bottom of the narrow valley far below.

But Dalvenjah's magic, supported by the considerable talent that Allan had to lend, was more than enough for the task. The van glowed faintly even in the bright morning sun, trailing thin blue mist. Dragons in flight were always enveloped in that same blue light, marking the magic of levitation that made flying so effortless for them. The van slowly recovered from its fatal dive and even began to gain altitude. The patrol car slid to a screeching halt at the opening in the guardrail, and two officers watched in silence as two tons of van flew away through the morning sky. A moment later the car reversed itself and headed back the way it had come, faster than ever.

But the flight was a short one, for the van was indeed heavy. Dalvenjah guided it across the valley to the side of the next ridge and over the same road, cutting off more than half a mile of a wide loop. The police could have still overtaken the fugitives, except that they were now headed in the wrong direction. Dalvenjah brought the van down gently in the middle of the road and sat back on her tail, looking very smug and self-satisfied. Allan needed a few seconds to recover from his surprise, but he did not look especially pleased even then.

"Was that the best you could do?" he demanded softly.

"What the hell did you want, parting the Red Sea?" Dalvenjah asked in return, rather miffed.

"No, something subtle," he insisted. "They saw this van flying through the air, and you can bet that they found that very strange."

"No doubt," the dragon agreed. "But who will they tell?"

Allan considered that briefly and shrugged, and they continued on their way.

Dr. Barker's cabin, as it turned out, was slightly larger than Allan's entire house. It was a massive A-frame situated on a forest-crowned hill above a small mountain lake, very rugged and outdoorsy in appearance but also very large and comfortable. There were no less than three bedrooms, two filling the peak of the steep roof with the larger of them having a big redwood deck outside wide windows, and a third downstairs behind the generous kitchen, which was complete with an indoor freezer for supplies. The den or front room in the forward portion of the house was large enough for three vans. And there really was no one around for miles, the neighbors either absent or nonexistent. Allan was just a little curious about how Rex had found such a secluded location; the question of why hardly needed to be asked.

The place was in an advanced stage of neglect, at least compared to Marie's usual fastidiousness in regards to housekeeping. Obviously she did not often have time for such mundane affairs here. Dalvenjah was rather disgusted and set to work at once, giving the place a cleaning like it had never known before—and all in less than ten minutes. She employed magic for the task; she had a spell for every conceivable chore and a couple that had to be seen to be believed. That, of course, was how a full-time sorceress and fighting dragon managed to keep a small castle with a minimum of time and effort. And without the need of employing a dwarf or wyvern housekeeper; Dalvenjah would tolerate no strangers in her home.

The cleaning was finished by the time Allan had the van unloaded, and he was still bringing in a rather hefty supply of wood for the fireplace when the two dragons appeared on the back porch. Vajerral made some excited comment in her small, high-pitched voice. From the woodpile he was too far away to hear just what she had said, and they were no longer in magic contact, which he did not ordinarily need to understand their language. Then the dragonet spread her wings and leaped from the back of the porch straight into the air, sailing downhill toward the lake before circling out over the water. Dalvenjah remained on the porch, obviously not prepared to join her daughter in flight, but watching with a look of keen pleasure and contentment.

"You will not fly?" Allan asked as he joined her on the porch a few moments later.

"Not ready," she answered simply.

"You look very happy," he observed. "Lye aye sharn dal'fren lel."

"Lye aye sharn," Dalvenjah agreed. "Asheh sharn. Vajerral likes it here. I am glad that we could come."

"She does seem to be enjoying herself," Allan remarked, watching as the small dragon dived at the wavelets nearest the shore. After two weeks of being trapped inside, she was putting her wings to the test. He sighed. "I wish that I could fly."

"I could teach you."

Allan turned to look at her in surprise. "I don't have any wings."

"Don't need wings," Dalvenjah insisted. "Wings make things simpler for dragons to fly for a long time, but we depend more on magic. For us it is instinctive, a part of what we are. We know the magic from the day we first start to fly. But you can work the magic consciously just as well. And you already know the magic."

"Well, yes," He did indeed know five different words of command for levitation; he had just never thought of applying any to himself. It sounded very simple, now that he considered it.

"You will learn?" she asked.

"Yes, of course," he answered eagerly. Was there any question? This made learning magic really worth the effort.

"Then fly," she said.

"What?"

Dalvenjah stepped off the porch only a short distance and turned to look up at the second-story deck. "Fly up there. That is short, and so a very good place to begin. If it goes wrong, then I can help you.''

Allan looked up at the deck. He had to go at least eleven or twelve feet straight up to clear the rail and come down inside, a comparatively short flight compared to what he wanted to do but a good way to begin, and wiser than trying to come down the same distance. He considered his choice of words of command and selected the one that seemed most appropriate, reciting it to himself. An instant later he felt himself being lifted effortlessly from the ground. He overshot his goal in his excitement before he remembered that he could guide himself by will, and landed on the rather precarious perch of the cabin's very steep roof.

"Not bad, considering that you did not end up where you meant to go," Dalvenjah remarked sardonically. She did not doubt his ability to fly, but she was a little anxious about his ability to balance on the peak of the A-frame in his present state.

"Not bad?" Allan asked in disbelief. "That was great! I could have flown a mile and chased Vajerral around the lake."

"Then do so," she told him. "That would be good practice."

And so it was that Allan was flying some two weeks before Dalvenjah would be ready to try herself. She could have flown the same way he did, without the use of wings. But she did not trust herself to not employ her wings, the instinct being so strong that she might forget, and that could have been damaging. Not taking the chance was the best way to insure that nothing did happen.

Allan at least considered it to have been a very productive day, and the two dragons certainly had no complaints. Vajerral had endured her two weeks of captivity remarkably well, never making a complaint. Even Dalvenjah had found being trapped inside for two weeks to be somewhat difficult, for dragons led far more active lives than most mortal folks and needed to stretch their wings almost every day. Dalvenjah also found it harder than ever to keep herself grounded, now that the opportunity to fly had been restored. And Allan, after the elation of his own learning to fly had dimmed somewhat, could sense a return of that shadow of loneliness and dejection that was always ready to darken her life.

Later that night, after dinner as they sat around the fire in the large den listening to the concert on the radio while the wind outside grew biting cold, he brought her the gift that he had kept in hiding. Since music was very often a topic of discussion between them, he knew that she was a rather accomplished amateur musician on an instrument that, from her description, sounded to be not unlike a six-string classical guitar. He had managed to find an inexpensive one and had transferred it to the back of the van along with his cello without her knowing.

"I don't know if you will be able to play it," Allan said rather apologetically as she took it from its case. "It seems that you have a ten-note system of music compared to our seven, so the frets should be practically worthless to you. But you might be able to play it by feel, with a little practice."

"Ayeh, Derjadhan..." Dalvenjah said softly in her own language, a word that Allan did not understand. Her jeweled eyes misted with tears. "It is beautiful."

She sat well back on her tail and braced the guitar against her chest, having just a little trouble with its odd shape. With her long neck bent nearly double so that she could see, she began plucking notes experimentally from the unfamiliar instrument, then modulated a few quick chords that flowed smoothly into a piece of alien music. Despite what Allan had said, she had very little trouble with the guitar and needed no practice. She was, after all, a sorceress, and was expected to be able to do anything with or without the use of magic. Vajerral abandoned her roasted nuts and lifted her head to listen, ears perked.

"It... it is beautiful," She repeated softly, and looked up at him. "Why would you do this? You have given me so much already."

"And you gave me something just as beautiful today," Allan said shyly.

"But that is not forever. It will go away too soon for you."

"I will always remember."

She considered that briefly and nodded slowly. "That is the important thing, is it not?"

Dalvenjah bent her head low and began to play again, while Allan hurried to collect his cello. And they made music of other worlds long into the night.

Dr. Barker, Marie and Jenny made the trip up to the mountains very early the next morning. Marie might have just as well done without another visit with the dragons, but both Rex and Jenny could hardly wait and she was not about to let them associate with "monsters" without her supervision. They arrived not long after dawn, tightly packed in the good doctor's sports car. That was something of a trick, since it had only two seats. Jenny, as always, was packed into the rear deck beneath the glass dome with the rest of the baggage. It was fortunate that she was skinny, almost astonishingly double-jointed, and not subject to claustrophobia.

They were driving up the long dirt road from the highway and had just come around the last corner before the cabin when they were treated to a rare sight. Vajerral was riding the morning breeze on her broad wings, which was something to see in itself. Then, as they watched, Allan came sailing through the air like some comic-book hero. He landed a little too swiftly on the seat of his pants in the dust before the front porch, where Dalvenjah was watching his activities critically and trying not to laugh. Rex and Jenny both made appropriate noises of appreciation; Marie nearly fainted.

"Hail the Masked Cellist!" Rex called as he climbed out of the car. He flipped the switch that released the rear dome and Jenny popped out like a jack-in-the-box. He shook his fists over his head. "Way to go, kid! Now that's something Rostropovich can't do."

"I'm not so good myself yet," Allan remarked sourly, brushing the seat of his pants. It was still very early in the morning and too cold to properly enjoy flying.

"Comes from having no wings," Dalvenjah said. "Hello, Rex. Hello, Jenny. Vajerral should be back around in a moment."

"Here she comes!" Jenny exclaimed, and ran to intercept her draconic friend as Vajerral hurtled around the corner of the house and circled for a landing.

"Hello, Marie," Dalvenjah said pleasantly as the woman climbed slowly out of the car.

"Charmed, I'm sure," Marie answered tightly, and turned to her younger brother. "Allan, would you like to tell us what you were up to?"

Allan looked mildly surprised. "That depends upon what you mean. Actually, I've been up to as much as a hundred miles per hour and well over five thousand feet."

"You do that again soon and you'll get spanked!" Dalvenjah added. Marie could only fume in silence, seeing that the forces of evil were allied against her. She had given up even trying to have her way around the dragon.

"Oh, I'd better let my puppy out of the back," Rex said suddenly, and hurried to the rear of the car. He began unpacking. "I thought that you might appreciate having a good watchdog, up here by yourselves."

"You've got to be kidding," Dalvenjah remarked with obvious sarcasm. With a sorceress and fighting dragon at hand, they hardly needed a dog.

"I meant that you might like having a dog's keen ears and nose to help make sure that strangers are not sneaking around."

"You've got to be kidding," she repeated. Enough said.

Rex finally got the travel cage open and what looked like the biggest, most miserably skinny-looking German shepherd hopped out of the back of the car—much to the amazement of Allan and Dalvenjah, who could not begin to figure out how three people, a wolf and their baggage could all fit in such a small car without the use of magic. The dog shook himself vigorously, as if shaking out the folds and creases, then trotted happily around the back of the car to join the others.

He came to a very quick stop when he spied the dragon suddenly, staring for a very long moment while he seemed to try to figure out what to make of this strange creature. Friend or foe? He decided upon the latter, no matter that the dragon was several times larger than himself. Bristling and growling loudly, he stepped forward and made himself ready for battle in a menacing, stiff-legged stance. Dalvenjah only stood her ground calmly, lowering her head for a closer look at her smaller adversary. Then she arched her neck, thrust her head forward, and roared. It was an interesting roar, higher in pitch than that of a lion and more than half a sharp bark, and backed up by a four-foot tongue of flame that nearly singed the shepherd's whiskers. The dog stood for a moment, blinking in bemusement with his ears laid back as he reconsidered this matter.

His tail tucked between his legs, he hurried over to stand behind his master.

"You brought this to protect me?" Dalvenjah asked.

"He's still a pretty good old dog," Rex said defensively. "His name is Rex Barker Jr."

"Well, that figures," the sorceress said under her breath. The name fit the dog better anyway.

They unloaded the car quickly and took everything into the house, since there was not very much in the first place, and with the added admonition that Dr. Barker was to take his "son" back home with him when they left Sunday night. Which seemed to suit Rex Jr. just as well anyway, for he had learned a healthy respect for the dragon that bordered on terror. And so he had that much in common with Marie, aside from the fact that she could be a real bitch. Neither of them cared very much for dragons, but there was nothing that they could do about it.

The most immediate problem was one of space, for the cabin was not really all that large. Arrangements had to be made, and not all of those arrangements were entirely comfortable. Rex and Marie took their usual room, confirming Allan's rather certain guess that they did not come here to play Parcheesi. Curiously, she was very hesitant about allowing her younger brother to observe such irrefutable proof of what was really going on, much more so than with her own young daughter. Perhaps she thought that Jenny was still young enough to be completely fooled.

Jenny was placed in her usual room off the kitchen, with Vajerral stuffed into a blanket-filled box for the night. Marie liked that even less, but she kept quiet. Finally, Allan was moved into Dalvenjah's room, although he brought in a narrow cot of his own, since the dragon needed the largest part of the room's double bed to be comfortable. Marie was upset with that plan enough to overcome her fear of dragons and protest, although she found herself largely ignored.

Rex Jr. stayed in the kitchen at night, and outside all the rest of the time, and was quite pleased by that arrangement. It was entirely his own idea.

"Next time we'll come down Friday night," Rex said as they worked in the kitchen after lunch. Allan washed and Dalvenjah dried, a feat she accomplished in a perfectly mundane manner as much as Rex would have liked to have seen her say a magic word or blow the dishes dry with her "hot, steamy breath." And he did not care if he said so. Marie then put away the dishes, handling them as if they were bombs and wondering if she could ever bear to use them again. Rex, in the manner of all great physicians and surgeons, appeared to do nothing more than supervise.

"Wonderful," Marie said under her breath, although she refrained from expanding upon that. By this time, there was hardly any need.

"I would have thought that you would want to be here as much as possible, to keep an eye on things," Allan said rather pointedly. No one, least of all Marie, failed to recognize the new note of confidence and determination that he was using in the face of his sister's overprotectiveness—or that it was growing steadily. "You don't know what we might be up to."

"Like what?" she asked fearfully but still wrapped as a challenge, pausing a moment in the act of placing a plate back in the cabinet.

"Summoning demons," Dalvenjah said before he could find an answer. They all looked at her questioningly, although Allan and Dr. Barker were both quick to figure out that she was joking and laughed. Marie did not find it at all funny.

Dalvenjah suddenly perked her ears and swung her head around to face the smaller room that Jenny and Vajerral shared. The others, alerted by her apparent concentration, stopped what they were doing and turned their less acute hearing to the task of investigating whatever could have caught her attention so completely.

"Are you ready to try again?" They could hear Jenny saying in a soft, almost conspiratorial voice.

"Dye, lye dalash mayh," the dragonet answered in equally soft tones.

"Then take a deep breath and let her rip!" Jenny declared.

That was followed by the sound of Vajerral drawing in a very loud breath and then a pause, a moment of deep, profound silence. Marie finally figured out just what was going on. She threw the plate that Dalvenjah had just handed her over her shoulder and ran toward the open door of the bedroom. "No, don't you . . ."

But it was too late. They could hear Vajerral blow with all her might, which amounted to quite a lot. A moment later the sound took on a new, curious note, not unlike a cutting torch with its flame not yet adjusted to optimum. Marie stopped before the open door, stared in amazement for a moment, then leaned wearily against the door frame so that she could beat her head against the wood. "No! No! No! Jenny Breivik, you get your nasty ass out here right now!"

"Ah, Mom!" Jenny protested as she marched out the door. Vajerral followed her out a moment later but made her way to her own mother, responding to a silent command.

"Now don't you try that tone of voice on me!" Marie declared, determined to have her say if she had to fight the biggest dragon ever to do so. "What do you think you're doing, encouraging that little monster to spit fire? You're more than twice her age, and old enough to know better."

"I am old enough to know better," Jenny declared, not at all daunted. "I considered the matter in a mature, logical manner. Dragons are supposed to breathe fire. Even little ones."

"There will be no more problems," Dalvenjah interrupted gently. "I have talked to Vajerral about it at some length."

"And what did you tell her?" Marie demanded, turning to glare at the two dragons. There hardly seemed to have been time for them to have talked at length about anything, and Marie could not recall hearing them say a word.

"This is a wooden house, not at all like the stone one we live in," she explained simply. "I told her to do it outside from now on."

"Oh, great," Marie muttered dismally. She stood for a long moment, rubbing her chin as she stared at the floor, as if trying to find her place in the child psychology manual she kept in her mind's eye. D for dragons—nothing. "Jenny, why don't you and your . . . ah, do something safe?"

"I'll read Vajerral a story!" Jenny declared, and the two ran through the kitchen to the front room.

"Read?" Marie asked herself in a slightly frantic voice. "How can she read a story to a dragon who doesn't speak English? Oh, don't answer that. I know they do it. I've seen it done. It just isn't logical."

"Don't worry, Marie," Rex told her cheerfully. "Three more years and she will be a teen-ager. Then all you have to worry about are drugs, skyrocketing auto insurance and the pill."

"I can do without that kind of optimism," she answered tartly, and bent to collect the pieces of the plate she had tossed.

Dalvenjah stood for a moment, staring at her, obviously deep in thought. Or so it seemed, for in fact she was debating with herself about whether she should offer some advice that would be scorned anyway, or just keep her big mouth shut. Logically, she knew that she would be better off with the former choice. She also found that she could not help herself.

"You worry too much," she said simply.

"What?" Marie paused, and straightened to stare at her questioningly.

"You worry too much," the dragon repeated. "Life is doing. Life is seeing and hearing, and touching. If you could look upon the strange and unexpected as an adventure and a challenge to your abilities, then you might even enjoy such things. Instead of worrying."

"You're a fine one to talk!" Marie declared indignantly.

"Am I not?" Dalvenjah challenged. "I am the one in a strange world, with a four-year-old in a place where she does not belong. And I have the fight of my life ahead of me before I can go home again. If I let things worry me as much as you do, then I would fall over dead with fright."

"Well, that is true," Marie admitted, although she said it so fiercely that it still sounded like a denial. Then her mood softened somewhat. "All right then, monster. I can put up with you for four more weeks—since it is only on weekends—and then I'll be rid of you. But I don't have to like it, not one bit!"

"I should never have expected that much."

Jenny returned at that moment from the front room, followed closely by the little dragon. "Rex, what's a mule-skinner?"

"Golly, I don't know, possum," He said, scratching his head in a rather exaggerated manner. "I never knew that there was a market for mule skins in the first place."

"Stop that, Rex," Marie said sharply, as if Jenny was too young to know when her leg was being pulled. "A mule-skinner is a person who drives a wagon that is pulled by mules."

"Like in laundry soap?" Jenny asked.

"That's right. Although usually less than twenty."

"That's what I thought, but I wanted to be sure," The girl said as she turned to leave. "Vajerral seems to have some trouble with her translation of that, and I've already had to tell her about dinosaurs. And that's all on the first page!"

"I can't imagine any story that would have two such diverse elements on the very first page," Rex mused to himself.

"Oh, heaven only knows what she may be reading, with all the weird things they have out these days. Probably that Sendak or one of those other strange writers. . . ." She paused in her tirade and looked up, stunned. "God, what am I saying? My baby daughter is reading stories to a little monster, and I'm only worried about the content of the story!"

"The term 'monster' is a purely relative one at best," Dalvenjah remarked politely. "But if you want to see a real monster, you just call my baby daughter that one more time."

Marie drew back in alarm, suddenly aware that she was asking for trouble. She seemed to have some trouble keeping her mouth shut once she started, and so she found herself saying things that she should not say in front of Dalvenjah. But even she knew that Dalvenjah's threats were nothing more than that; the dragon was undeniably a more civil person than herself, and certainly not given to sudden violence . . . at least not under this degree of provocation. Marie's dislike of the two dragons was due to a simple, illogical fear, just as she would immediately fear being in the same room with a lion or a bear. Even she recognized that.

Of course, Dalvenjah was not a lion or a bear but a dragon. She spoke in a fairly reasonable manner considering a two-week familiarity with the language. There was no question that she was a person in her own right, and not an animal. That was exactly the problem. If it had been just a lion or a bear in the house, Marie could have simply screamed and run for her life. That was her instinctive reaction in treating with Dalven-jah, but she also realized that the dragons were people and she should regard them as such.

That was the source of the tension that existed between them.

"Hey, Junior!" Dr. Barker interrupted suddenly, breaking the stress of the moment. "Do you know how the boulder got away with pretending to be a cliff?"

"Golly, I don't know, Doc," Allan responded appropriately, looking over from his work at the sink. "How did the boulder get away with pretending to be a cliff?"

"He put up a very good bluff."

"Yeh? Well, you're so dumb, you think a dive-bomber is a person who blows up cheap bars."

"Oh, enough!" Marie declared as she helped her brother finish at the sink. "Allan, why do you encourage him?"

"He can't help it," Rex answered for him. "He's so dumb, he thinks that a bottle of scotch is where they keep the ashes of his Uncle Angus."

"Oh, yeah?" Allan demanded in mock fury. "Well, you're so dumb that you think viola da gamba was an Italian explorer."

Dalvenjah obviously found that last joke funny enough, for she buried her long muzzle in the damp towel she had been using to dry the dishes, in a largely unsuccessful attempt to hide a broad smile. Marie turned to stare at her in considerable amazement.

"You mean to say that you understood that?" she demanded.

"Of course," the dragon replied. "I know every word that Allan knows, and I recognize them when I hear them. I just don't sometimes find them fast enough when I use them."

"Every word that Allan knows?" Rex mused. "Well, a lot of people get by on a third-grade vocabulary."

"Don't be facetious," Dalvenjah said smugly, plainly pleased with herself for coming up with that one. Marie turned to stare, and the others laughed. She shrugged helplessly. "Surely you have heard the one about the horse and the sparrows?"

"Do tell," Rex said, taking the bait.

"Well, it seems that there was once an artist who was hired to paint a very famous racehorse who had since retired from the track. He was still a handsome horse but he seemed to have some type of sleeping sickness, for if he stood in one place for very long, he would go to sleep. This actually made things very easy for the artist, until the second day when sparrows began building nests in the horse's mane. The artist did not appreciate this, for he did not need the sparrows and they tended to awaken the horse.

"Finally he asked the trainer what he could do to get rid of the sparrows, and the trainer told him to rub dry yeast in the horse's mane. The artist had his doubts about this, but he tried and it worked.

"'I still can't believe that it worked,' he told the trainer later. 'Is there something about yeast that those pests do not like?'"

"'Well, it's like this,' the trainer said. 'Yeast is yeast, and pest is pest, and never the mane shall tweet'"

Dalvenjah grinned broadly at her dramatic conclusion, but her smile faded when she saw that the others were only staring at her. She laid back her ears and would have blushed, except that she lacked the capacity. "Did I not get it right?"

"Oh, your joke was good enough," Allan quickly assured her. "It just came as something of a surprise to hear anything that . . . that . . ."

"Silly?" Marie offered.

"Witty," he corrected her pointedly, "coming from a . . ."

"A dragon?" Marie suggested.

"A visitor from another land, who is not well versed in the subtleties of our complex language."

"Meaning that maybe you aren't as dumb as you look," his sister added by way of conclusion.

"Marie!" Allan said sharply.

"I know what you mean," Dalvenjah said, trying to sound cheerful, although her ears were still laid back.

"Where are my rings?" Marie demanded suddenly. The dishes were done and she had finished tidying up, but she could not find her rings anywhere. "I know I laid them down here somewhere."

"No great loss," Rex commented sourly, indicating his desire that she never find them.

"Don't be that way," she told him sharply. "James Donner

may have been a worthless bum, but the rings are worth something. They are solid gold."

"Not solid," Dalvenjah remarked. "The rings are under that bowl."

"What?" Marie lifted the bowl and found the two missing rings beneath. She snatched them up and inspected them closely, as if looking for the marks of a dragon's teeth. "How do you know?"

"I can sense the magic in gold."

"I mean about their not being solid gold?" she asked impatiently as she put on the rings.

"Everyone should know that," Dalvenjah explained. "Solid gold is too soft to make jewelry. Usually it is combined with other things to give it some strength. But your rings are real enough, for the magic is strong."

"There is magic in gold?" Rex asked.

Dalvenjah nodded. "Gold strengthens magic. Had I gold when I had fought Vorgulremik, I might not have lost."

"Speaking of magic, I had better go see what the children are doing," Marie announced, turning to leave.

"Vajerral knows what she is doing," Dalvenjah assured her, with a note of defensiveness in her voice that was just barely discernible.

"Perhaps, but she has been dealing with magic ever since she was hatched," Marie replied on her way out the door.

"Hatched?" Dalvenjah demanded in a soft, icy voice. Her ears were laid back, this time in a gesture that was unmistakably one of agitation.

"Hold on, Dal," Allan was quick to reassure her. "She doesn't know any better. Most people here do think that dragons lay eggs."

"Hatched!" she declared gruffly. "What does she think we are anyway, chickens?"

"It's too cold to cook outside!" Marie complained, not for the first time but for about the tenth.

"Nonsense!" Rex declared as he carefully stacked the small, black bricks of charcoal into a perfect pyramid. "Best time of year for cooking outside, while the sun is going down and the shadows are lengthening, and there is just a little nip to the air.''

That was all true except for the part about the little nip. In fact, it was already well below freezing. But the dragons did not notice, and neither did he, nor anyone else but Marie. And so she suffered in silence, except for occasional bouts of suffering out loud.

"Ready?" Allan asked.

"Ready," Rex declared as he carefully balanced the final brick. Then he straightened his stiff back slowly and looked around. "Now, what did we do with the starter fluid?"

"We didn't seem to remember to bring any," Allan remarked, being very careful to emphasize the pronoun.

"Great."

"No problem at all," Allan declared, and looked around. "Vajerral!"

"Dye?" The little dragon trotted over quickly to see what he wanted, with Jenny following close behind. Allan bent quickly to snatch her up, tucking her under one arm.

"Do you think that you can make a little fire?" he asked as he aimed her in the direction of the grill.

"Dye, lye dalash mayh," she assured him without hesitation.

"You'll have to hold it for several seconds."

"Lye iyan par derreh. No sweat."

"Fire when ready!"

Vajerral took a deep breath, arched her long neck until it was as stiff as a rod, and blew flames. She was still very new at this; the narrow tongue of fire was barely a foot long, and it was accompanied by a sound like that of a poorly adjusted blowtorch. But it was a good, hot flame all the same. She was able to hold it nearly thirty seconds, and by that time the charcoal was glowing warm and red, almost ready for cooking.

"Well done!" Allan complimented the dragonet as he lifted her away from the grill. "You're getting very good at that."

Vajerral only nodded, unable to reply because she was panting so heavily.

"We've been practicing," Jenny said. Then, noticing the beginning of a warning glare from her mother, she explained quickly. "We practiced among the rocks down at the edge of the lake."

"That is very good," Dalvenjah put in quickly before Marie had a chance to protest, thereby having her own word on the subject. She was seated, rather precariously, like a cat along one bench of the table, her long arms and legs tucked up beneath her. Rex Jr. sat shivering behind the woodpile, not because of the cold but out of frustrated longing. He enjoyed cooking out better than anyone, but he could not compete with dragons. He peered out from time to time, drooling with desire.

"Say, if you have dragon magic, why can't you breathe fire like they do?" Rex asked suddenly.

"He is not . . . equipped to breathe fire," Dalvenjah said before Allan, who looked rather startled by that question, could answer. Marie opened her mouth and shut it, recognizing the futility, but the sorceress ignored her. "That does not mean that he cannot work the same fire magic. All good magicians can throw fire."

"Throw fire?" Allan asked, confused.

"Yes, throw," she insisted. "You need some way to aim your fire. Dragons do that with their breath, but magicians of other races do so with a simple gesture of throwing or pointing. Try it. Do you know the word?"

"I think so," Allan said uncertainly.

He stepped over until he was facing down the length of the clearing behind the house and stood for a moment in silent contemplation as he thought this thing through. The mechanics seemed simple enough, so he brought his arm around in an exaggerated circle and threw his imaginary fireball forward. The make-believe fireball had only just left his hand when it became real, a blazing comet with a fiery tail that hurtled across the clearing to strike the woodpile with an explosion of flames. Howling in terror but otherwise unharmed, Rex Jr. leaped out of his hiding place and ran toward the lake, perhaps instinctively looking for the nearest water. Dalvenjah said a soft word and the flames died swiftly away.

"Very good," she commented. In fact, it was rather more than even she had expected.

"Good?" Rex demanded incredulously. "With a pitch like that, this boy belongs in the majors!"

Allan thought that he had reason to feel very pleased with himself. He could now do everything a dragon could do: fly, make fire, and work other magics. He did not yet do any one of those things very well, and it seemed unlikely that he ever would. Dalvenjah would be returning to her own world in only a few short weeks and would take the magic with her. But he certainly meant to enjoy himself until then. This promised to be a better vacation than any he had ever had or could imagine, better even than taking a cruise up the fjords of Norway. But he also knew that it would be even harder for him to accept, when the time came, that his vacation was over and he had to go back to work.

He had only just settled into bed that night, with the blankets pulled up over his head, when Dalvenjah returned from the bathroom. He could hardly imagine how she managed to use native facilities, considering the placement of her large tail, but he did not consider it polite to inquire. She climbed in beneath the covers of the larger bed and, by an interesting series of contortions, managed to fold herself into a circle that still occupied most of the bed. She had to pull the pillow down a short distance so that her horns would not catch in the wooden headboard.

"You sleep in the nude?" Allan asked.

"Don't be funny," she muttered, then lifted her head slightly to look at him. "Can I ask you a question?"

"Do I have any choice?"

"No. What is the meaning of the rings that Marie wears?"

"What?" Allan brought his head out from under the covers to stare at her. "Those are her wedding and engagement rings."

"I thought that Marie and Rex were not married."

"No, of course not. Those are the rings she got from James Donner, who she was married to . . . Jenny's real father."

"Was married?"

Allan sighed and resigned himself to a long night of this. "Jimmy Donner married Marie twelve years ago, when she had just finished her undergraduate studies. They were very happy together . . . for a while. But then Jimmy changed in some way. It was like he didn't care about anything in life anymore. He wasn't unhappy or depressed. No, he was off in some blissful little world of his own. And he started drinking a lot, so that he could spend even more time in his blissful little world. He started getting into trouble for that, doing things that no one should when he has been drinking too much. Then, one night, he was driving his car much too fast and took an unscheduled turn off the side of a very high bridge. That was the end of him.''

"Oh, I see." Dalvenjah lay in silent thought for a moment. "And she misses him very much."

"Marie?" Allan demanded incredulously. "She never misses a chance to tell the world what a shiftless, drunken lout he was."

"So she says," the dragon said, totally unconvinced. "But I could tell from the first time I met her that she hurts for someone very much. She does not want us to know how much she misses him, and so she lies."

Allan considered that carefully for a moment and shrugged. "You know, you probably are right. Is that what you wanted to know?"

She shook her head. "No, I really wondered why Rex hates those rings as strongly as he does. I could not imagine hating rings. But now I know. He hates the rings because Marie will not part with them or her memories of the one she knew before. He does not know how to compete with that, and so he is dissatisfied with the object rather than the situation he cannot change."

"I see," Allan said thoughtfully, then looked up at her sharply. "But is there anything that can be done?"

"Done? Don't be ridiculous. It is nobody's business but the turkeys'," Dalvenjah remarked as she pulled the blankets over her head. "And if you are finished asking your silly questions, then turn out the light."

Not so many miles away, a single car bounced along a narrow dirt road that was nearly too rough for such a vehicle. In warmer weather, with the road wet after a rain, it would have never forced a path. Fortunately it was near the middle of a cold, clear night, and the ground was already nearly frozen.

Agents Dave Wallick and Don Borelli spent this night as they had every one for the past week, searching the country-side for monsters. Their superior had been forced to admit to the need for assigning them permanently to this rather unusual case. At least after they had proven the need to him by dumping the mangled body of one of the small monsters on his desk.

And they alone, working closely with Sheriff Hansin, had been successful in tracking and destroying some of the little dragons that had been plaguing the mountains for the last two weeks. At least the nasty beasts traveled and raided in troops, and they hunted according to a pattern more like that of a marauding horde than a pack of carnivores. They were predictable, and once the small group of hunters had learned their patterns, they had been able to outguess a pack and be waiting with shotguns when the things arrived.

Which was no mean trick in itself. The miniature dragons were fierce, fearless and exceedingly stupid. They attacked anything living in a single swarm and drove at their prey with mindless intensity, heedless of their own losses, never stopping until they died. Fighting a pack of the little beasts amounted to a very long minute of frantic shooting. The three of them, together with Sheriff Hansin, had successfully endured two such battles.

There was no question that Hansin could not have held off an attack by himself. And yet he may have attempted just that. They had taken off together the moment the news of the sighting of the dragon pack had come in. But the two agents had been delayed, left far behind on the rough mountain roads in their heavy car while the sheriff had gone on ahead in his four-wheel drive. He had known the night's target, a secluded farm in the narrow valley below, and he had rushed in to warn the people who lived there before it was too late. And he had not come back out again; at least there had been no response to their calls over the radio in the past fifteen minutes.

They suddenly saw the lights of the farm ahead, and Wallick pulled the car to an abrupt stop. He turned to his partner. "Well, Don. Do we go on in?"

"I don't see why not," Borelli answered without hesitation. "We know from past experience that the little devils don't take long."

"Right," Wallick agreed grimly.

They knew even before they arrived that it was too late. The sheriff's truck was stopped before the small farmhouse, its lights on and doors open, the motor running and exhaust steaming in the cold night air in the glare of the bright outdoor lights. The door of the house stood open as well. Discarded shotguns and a pistol lay in the hard dirt yard amid scattered bones and scraps of blue-green hide. The illeshyan turned upon their own dead and wounded, and even hunted one another when there was no other game to be found.

"I don't see any," Wallick said as he stopped the car a short distance from the sheriff's truck. He did not want to drive over bones that were all that remained for burial. He collected his shotgun and opened the door, then paused. "Do you want me to go take a look?"

"Oh, lay off, Dave," Borelli said impatiently. "You can take your look, but you need for me to cover you."

"Right," Wallick agreed.

There was little else to be learned in taking a closer look. Five people had taken a last stand just in front of the truck, firing out into the night as the brilliant outdoor lights illuminated the attacking dragons. The sheriff's two shotguns and a third were empty, although someone had been in the process of reloading all the weapons while Hansin had tried to hold off the monsters with his pistol. It had been valiant, but hopeless. The spines of eleven of the alien beasts, with their dorsal plates like long hunting knives, were intermixed with the scattered bones.

"That big, half-picked rib cage does remind me of Hansin's barrel chest," Borelli remarked softly, and cleared his throat. "What I don't understand is why they left the bones and so many scraps of hide. They don't usually leave anything."

"They ate all they could," Wallick explained. "It must have been a very large pack, but eleven losses of their own on top of humans here and animals in the barn over there meant that they had more than enough meat."

"I see," Borelli said, and turned to watch the flashing lights coming over the top of the ridge behind them. "Well, here comes the deputy. He can help us hold the fort until the coroner can get here. So now what?"

"We do the best we can," Wallick told him firmly. "We'll get the rest of this pack tomorrow night. That will leave three more that we're sure of. But then we have to find the big one."

"That should be easy enough. But what do we do with the thing when we find it?"

He shrugged. "We find someone who can help us. An expert."

Borelli laughed bitterly. "Who's that, St. George?"

• Part Four •

The Magic

THE OUTER SIGHT. The inner sight. The endless cycle of life. Dalvenjah was a sorceress, and being such she was aware of the more subtle things that were woven into the fabric of time. There was never any one future to be seen, but instead an endless fanning-out of possibilities. And yet there were times when too many paths that led into what will be came to rest on the same doorstep, and she had to admit to the inescapability of what awaited her in days to come. Only once before had she dreamed the golden dreams and had seen them shape themselves into a nightmare of hurt and sorrow, and then seen it come to pass before her waking eyes. Now she dreamed again.

But not all dreams were dark and ugly. She did not yet know how to judge this one.

Dalvenjah was not an impulsive person. That might often seem to be the best word to describe many of her past actions to one who did not know her well, or even to some who thought they did. She weighed all of her choices to a nicety of detail, and nothing, no possibility or alternative or consequence, ever escaped her careful notice. But she was also tremendously intelligent; her thoughts flew so much more quickly than even

those of others who had good cause to be proud of their quick
wits, so that she hardly seemed to consider her choices at all.
She was almost at a loss when confronted with a question that
required no answer for some time to come. It gave her too
much time to brood, to run through in her mind again and again
the balance of alternatives and consequences, aware only too
well that she would not know how to respond until the time
for that answer came due.

It was too much time to measure the limits of her own
resolve, her own courage, and the hidden depths of her own
heart and will. For when the mind failed to recognize the
answer, then she must trust her heart. And trust as well to the
inevitability of her dreams.

The weeks she spent resting and recovering her strength in
the mountains were among the best she had ever known, as
there can sometimes be a poignant beauty in melancholy. Past
hurts were soothed in a balm of present pleasantries, so that
the healing was more satisfying for the closeness of the pain.
She was at peace and content, except for occasional troublings
from her dreams. And the awareness that she should be going
home.

Dalvenjah had never had a friend quite like Allan. They were
alike in many ways, sharing many interests. He was the perfect
student, understanding readily everything she had to teach him.
He always knew her moods, if not her motives, and just what
to do to soothe her pains or turn her happy moods into something grand. And she knew him so well in turn, better than he
even knew himself. She thought it unjust that a person like
himself had to remain trapped within the limitations of a mortal
form, and she was troubled all the more by the knowledge that
it did not have to be.

It was one thing, she learned, to have the answer to one's
problems, and quite another to be certain that it was the right
answer.

The weather became somewhat warmer with the beginning
of their second week at the cabin. At least the nights were less
bitter, although the melting snow retreated only so far as the
edge of the forest before drawing a final battle line beneath the
trees, perhaps waiting in hopes of reinforcements.

Allan and Dalvenjah walked together through the edge of

the forest below the cabin one evening just as the last light of day was fading from the sky. Allan was just a little cold but tried not to show it. But night was a dragon's time, and darkness kept few secrets from a dragon's sensitive eyes. Vajerral was somewhere along the boulders of the lake's rugged shore, winging back and forth through the shadows.

"I like this place," Dalvenjah announced suddenly, her pleasure very evident. "It reminds me of my own home, with woods all around. Far away from everyone else, so that the only sounds you hear are those that belong."

"I like this place, too," Allan agreed. "I like being alone."

"You do not," she corrected him gently but firmly.

He looked up at her in considerable surprise. "I don't?"

She shook her head decisively, pausing in her slow stride. "Consider again what you feel. You say that you like being alone, but you will likely find that you mean 'we.' You and I have had a good time together here, but soon it will be done. Would you really stay here long, entirely by yourself? This is a wonderful place, but there would be no one to share it with you. So often you do not know how good times are until you have other times to compare, and you cannot measure happiness until it is done. Mortal or immortal, we judge the value of our lives by what we have done with them. But we are no judges of the worth of our own lives, or we get lazy and sit alone and do nothing . . . as you would like. No, we need others to see the reflection of our own lives in their eyes."

"You are in a philosophical vein tonight," Allan remarked as they continued on.

"I know what I know," she answered. "I learned the hard way. I have been alone too often. I would not ever be alone again. Two lives together add to far more than two lives measured alone. And what of you?"

"Me?"

Dalvenjah paused, seeming to find a place she liked especially well. Heedless of snakes and other crawly things, which her magic told her were not there to begin with, she lay down on her side in a bank of dry leaves that cracked with splinters of ice beneath her weight. She indicated that he was welcome, and Allan sat down in the leaves before and leaned back against her warm body, sheltered somewhat from the frigid breeze that she seemed to never feel. Here they sat beneath the trees and could look out across the small clearing and down the partially wooded slope to the lake. Everything was awash in golden moonlight. And yet, even as they watched, the fitful moon was hidden behind the hazy clouds and they were lost in darkness.

"What of you?" Dalvenjah repeated gently. "Why do you pretend that you are happy with the way your life has been, when you are so unhappy?"

"Do I have any choice?" Allan asked almost fiercely, as if challenging her to say that it could be otherwise.

"Yes, you have a choice," she told him. "You wish often that your life could be otherwise. Have you never dared to even try to do what you wish?"

"No, never," he said sullenly.

"No, Allan. I hear your thoughts tonight, not your words," Dalvenjah said, which was the same as telling him that she was too good a telepath for him to successfully lie to her.

"Well, once," he admitted reluctantly. "Not that long ago, in fact. But Marie would have none of it."

"No, Allan," she reproached him softly. "Tell yourself the truth."

Allan frowned as he forced his reluctant memory back in time. "It was about a year and a half ago, when I was attending special classes at Tanglewood the summer before last. There was a girl from our own orchestra, a violinist, who went with me. She was very pretty . . . at least I thought so. And a wonderful person. And I never realized just how good a friend she was to me until it was too late."

He sat in silence for a long moment, poking into the layers of old leaves with a stick. Dalvenjah waited patiently, never making a sound. After a long moment he sighed sadly . . . or perhaps fondly. "I'll never forget the time she had words with Marie. You see, we used to have a small group of musicians, members of the orchestra, who used to come over to my house two or three times a week to practice chamber pieces. Well, she was all the time bringing over things to eat while we practiced, and so I gave her a key so that she could let herself in when I wasn't there and get everything ready. We would often come straight from rehearsal, and I would have to make some stops along the way, so that she would be there before me.

"Anyway, she eventually felt herself at home enough to use the shower in my bedroom when she changed, and it happened that Marie had just met up with Rex at that time and she wasn't checking on me all that often. So she didn't know what was going on. One day she let herself in, and she thought she heard me back in the shower. It was that other girl, of course, and Marie walked in just as she was stepping naked out of the shower. Well, you know my sister. They had half an hour of very heated words before I arrived and walked into the middle of it."

Allan paused a moment, smiling in fondness of that memory. But then his smile faded when he remembered the rest. He shrugged. "Anyway, I got mad and told Marie that anyone I invited into my house could do as they pleased. But this girl took that personally, and she began to think that perhaps we should be more than just friends. I knew she did at the time, and maybe I should have gone along with that. But I was afraid. I never dared consider such a thing, and it frightened me half to death.

"Well, she eventually lost her patience and got mad at me for not finishing what I had started. So she decided to move away, and auditioned for other orchestras . . . and was accepted somewhere else. I don't even remember where. And all that time she told me every detail of what she was doing, and she waited for me to ask her to stay. And I should have. Damn, I really should have. We would have been so happy. But I never could. I was too afraid. And then she was gone."

He broke the stick and threw it away, then sat for some time in the heavy silence, staring at the ground before him and forgetting that Dalvenjah was even there. He had brought the old memories up to taste again and found them bitter, more bitter than ever. Regret grew strong in the dark places of a person's past.

"What was her name?" Dalvenjah asked gently after some time.

"What?" Allan glanced at her briefly over his shoulder, as if to remind himself that she was there. He shrugged. "Meade.

Meade Lenardon. I never did hear from her again. I guess it was really my own fault.''

"I understand," Dalvenjah said simply.

"You do?" He turned to look at her, not in doubt or accusation but in simple disbelief. "I don't suppose that you would have ever allowed yourself to get into such a state. You are always so sure of what you want."

Dalvenjah did not answer at once, but turned her head and looked away into the night. After a long moment she took a deep breath and sighed heavily. "Derjadhan."

Allan looked at her questioningly. "Vehr as derreh?"

"Lyr dashahn," she answered absently. "The one with whom I was to share my life. Vajerral's father. But I dreamed of him, the gold-dream, and I saw terror and sorrow. And then he was gone."

"How?" Allan asked, almost accusingly. He thought immediately of Marie and James Donner, and how it must have been someone's fault. And he felt immediate loathing for anyone who could have caused Dalvenjah such pain.

"Not his fault," she assured him. "He was like me, a sorcerer and a fighting dragon. A Veridan warrior. And when he was needed, he went. Just as I have, and always will. And he fought Vorgulremik, and lost. Just as I fought Vorgulremik and lost, only he lost far more."

"He died?" Allan asked needlessly.

She nodded. "It was in my dreams. But why? De'an kherasj osh'dejash di'as mayh lahn, eh lye aye mahy sothe'byn."

Allan could see the tears forming in her eyes, and feel her breathing fast and uncertain behind his back. Distressed by her sorrow, he reached up without even thinking and laid a hand gently on her cheek. "Yes, your days were short, but better than none at all. I never dared to take what you had, if only for so short a time, and I guess that I lost even more."

Dalvenjah blinked away her tears and shook her head firmly. "I should not bother you with my troubles."

"I am your friend. At least I like to think so. Your troubles are my troubles," he told her. "So now we're even."

"I guess so," she agreed, forcing a smile that did not completely hide her sorrow.

Allan hardly knew what to do, but he did not like to see her so distressed. He sighed and looked out across the clearing toward the lake. The night was so still and peaceful, but it was a peace that concealed a hidden tenseness. Winter was passing, even here in the high mountains, but Dalvenjah would be gone before she would have a chance to see the coming spring.

"I wish that you could see this place in spring," he said.

"Spring?" Dalvenjah asked suddenly, as if she agreed with that as an excuse to change the subject. "Why should we wait for anything as trivial as that when we can make our own?"

"With magic?" he asked cautiously, as if he hardly dared to believe that the dragon was capable of such sorcery.

"Oh, of course," she insisted.

She rose so suddenly that Allan had to leap up or risk being tossed aside. She stood for a moment, looking into the nocturnal shadows and up at the grey clouds hiding a bright, full moon. There was a tenseness in the world, as if it awaited her word. Then she spoke the words of magic softly, under her breath, without even a gesture of command. It was as if the working of such awesome magic was a simple thing to her.

And the world listened to her, and responded to her command. The silence that came over the land could not have been more complete. Then she spoke a final word, and the magic flowed out from her like a circular wave caused by a stone cast into still water. Allan could see it glowing like a silvery curtain moving ever outward through the air around her. Then it passed, and the world was silent for a moment longer as it gathered its strength for the sudden pushing forth of new life.

A breeze stirred through the trees, a warm, gentle, springtime breeze. It really was not all that warm, but it certainly seemed so after the previous chill. And it might have almost been the hot breath of summer, to judge from the response it generated. The banks of snow retreated with visible speed into the dark corners of the forest, and there was a brief rain as the lingering icicles melted from the branches of the trees.

Then the magic returned, drawing back to its source, and in its passage the world seemed to reverberate with a deep, heavy note. A second wave of magic washed away from Dalvenjah, its source, and in its passage the brown, brittle grass stood up straight and turned green and alive, and dead, naked branches pushed out new growth that unfolded before their very eyes into leaves of green. The grey clouds parted and raced away, and golden moonlight filled the night to show off these new wonders. Dalvenjah looked around, seemingly satisfied with what she had caused to happen. Then she turned to Allan.

"There should be flowers in springtime," she said simply. "Quickly now, while the magic still moves. Can you make flowers?"

Allan nodded, although he was not at all certain that he could. He considered his plan of action quickly before speaking his own words of command, and he ended with the inner name for flowers. It was a broad, unspecific name and not really what he had meant, but it brought a response. The world around them suddenly bloomed, and plants that had never before borne flowers were abruptly ablaze with colors. Tall, dark pines brought out blue roses, and elms brought out red daisies to complement their new green. Even the moss on the rocks and the grass below them bore flowers.

"Very good," Dalvenjah commented, as if she saw nothing wrong with what he had done.

"Ah . . . if you say so," he answered somewhat sheepishly. "But how far does this extend?"

"Not too far, I am afraid," she admitted. "Listen."

Allan listened. The warm breeze continued to stir through the new leaves and shake the golden tulips that hung with the mistletoe. There was a strange sense of perfection to this magical night, too intimate to be truly sacred but beyond that which was merely worldly. A pair of foxes, an older couple out on their nightly hunt, paused at the edge of the forest not forty feet away to test the air with their long noses and listen.

"Spring again," the old fox remarked. Allan could understand his thoughts through the same magical link that had once allowed him to speak with dragons. "My, my! Where has the winter gone? It will soon be that time again. Time for sweet grass and young hares."

"And kits," the vixen added with a note of both wistfulness and weary resignation.

"Ah, but that's the best part, my dear!" her husband insisted, nudging her tenderly. "Making love in the moonlight with a pretty girl. How many kits have we had, my dear?"

"Don't you know?" the vixen asked.

"Know? I don't really even care!" the fox declared. "A person should no more count the passing of the years or the coming of kits any more than a couple should try to measure their love. All we care about is that we've had plenty of all three. But I'm not about to let go of this life until I've gotten all I can from it. What do you say, my love? There is magic in the air tonight."

"You old rascal! Soon," she said as they disappeared back into the woods. "Very soon."

Dalvenjah smiled gently. "They know."

Allan blinked, as if released from a spell. "Know what?"

"They know what matters most," she said. "Everything comes at its proper moment, but then you take hold of what you want and never let go."

Dalvenjah swooped down in a tight arc before pulling up and rising sharply, straight up as she allowed gravity to check her speed. She held her broad wings open, but their long, slow sweeps were more for balance than actual lift. She remained poised in mid-air, suspended motionless by the lift-magic that surrounded her like a pale blue mist. It was so wonderful to be free to fly the way that dragons were meant to fly, after weeks of rest and recovery followed by days of careful gliding and a slow building of strength. To wear the harness that bore her sword and knives. Once again she was back in her element, and that brought with it a final restoration of her old confidence, her certainty in herself and in her magic.

Holding her place in mid-air, she looked down to watch as Allan moved toward her in a more gradual arc. Having no wings at all, his flight was in fact a hover even when he was moving, his arms spread like wings solely for balance. The blue mist of the lift-magic enfolded him like a transparent cloak. He actually flew very well, mostly because he was using dragon magic rather than the mortal magic commanded by other human magicians. It was a magic that made flying come very naturally, for it was a magic that was an innate part of a dragon's being rather than an external factor. Which was a very good thing for Allan, at this altitude. They were up among the clouds, leaving the forested hills that surrounded the lake a mile below.

But even the best lift-magic could not completely take the

place of wings. She knew that Allan must be tiring after several minutes of continuous flight, especially considering the playful game of chase that they had been engaged in almost from the start. He came to a stop in the same way that she had, letting gravity reduce his speed until he was even with her. She reached out and took his hand, extending her lift-magic to Allan to allow him a few moments rest.

"All right?" she asked.

"Fine," he assured her, although he sounded slightly winded.

"Fly with me, now," she told him. "Ready?"

"Ready," he agreed.

Still holding on to Allan with one hand, she dipped over suddenly and began to gather speed in a steady descent. He did not permit her to do all the work but allowed her magic only to supplement his own. He moved out and down to get himself clear of her wings until they were flying side by side at arm's length, faster and faster. Allan flew barely half as fast as a dragon could, mostly because he could not endure the cold since he lacked their thick, protective scales. Of course, he was hardly aware of such trivial matters under the present circumstances, but Dalvenjah remembered and she was taking him back down even now. But she also meant to make his trip home worthwhile for him.

Riding the wind with the sun at their backs, they descended a shaft of the late afternoon sun slowly back to earth. Dalvenjah led, dodging them in and out of small, scattered clouds before completing the final portion of their descent in a tight spiral, using her wings to hold them in a sharper turn than Allan was able to manage alone, circling down in the manner of a great bird of prey. Vajerral flew with them part of the way, but she abruptly turned and darted away at a furious pace as they were nearing the treetops.

"Company," Dalvenjah warned, dropping their speed even more.

"Who?" Allan asked fearfully, remembering too well the danger of being seen by people who should not see the dragons. Especially hunters with guns.

"Friends," the sorceress reported. "And your sister."

Well, you could not get more specific than that! Allan was

privately amused by which category Dalvenjah considered Marie to belong to, and he was certain that the feeling was mutual. Moments later they were coming down for a landing outside the cabin, at the same time that the others were getting out of the car. Dalvenjah released his hand and allowed him to fly down on his own, which had the effect of looking more impressive and of upsetting Marie all the more. Dalvenjah was often looking for new ways of accomplishing the latter, but she was rather disappointed this time. Marie was becoming somewhat reconciled to the fact that her little brother was a sorceress's apprentice. Instead everyone had eyes only for her, for this was the first time that they had ever seen her in flight. A dragon on the wing was an awe-inspiring sight, even if it was only a little dragon. Even Marie was enchanted.

"Lady, you are beautiful!" Rex called out to her as she backwinged before settling gently on all fours. The fact that Allan made an equally graceful landing on only two legs did not go unnoticed, just overshadowed. They had seen him fly before.

"Then you'll be going home soon?" Marie asked hopefully.

"Soon," Dalvenjah said. "But I first have some unfinished business."

"But not too soon," Allan warned.

"Well, it had better not be too long," Rex said. "I have my sources, you know. And my sources say that there have been forty unexplained deaths in all, including a sheriff in the next county, and the recent closing of large areas of the local mountains by the National Guard hasn't helped. There are a lot of rumors going around, including the suggestion that there are little green monsters from another world. Which means that they have at least half an idea of just what they are fighting."

"Your people are able to deal with the illeshyan," Dalvenjah said with certainty. "They have to, since I cannot do everything. The illeshyan are nearly all destroyed now anyway."

"Which leaves the big one," Rex pointed out as he went to the back of the car and began unloading.

"Now, he is perhaps more than your people can handle," she told him. "The immortals are very difficult to kill short of outright destruction, and the great dragons more than any other.

Even your biggest guns which would slay me in an instant will be of little consequence to Vorgulremik.''

"But you can kill him?" Marie asked dubiously.

"I know the proper magic."

Any additional arguments were forestalled as Dr. Barker released the lid on the travel cage and Rex Jr. hopped out and made an immediate dash for the relative safety of the trees. The dog had not paid a return visit the previous week, but his fondness for dragons had not grown in the absence. He paused at the first large tree to glance back around his own bony hindquarters at the entire group with an extremely sour look. Then he raised a leg at the base of the tree in a gesture whose meaning was unmistakable, especially since he never took his eyes off Dalvenjah the entire time.

"Why did you bring him back?" Allan demanded. "You know that he doesn't get along with Dalvenjah."

Rex shrugged. "That doesn't stop me from bringing Marie. But, to answer your question, I could not find a keeper for him. I couldn't find a keeper for Marie either, so here we are."

"Funny, Rex," Marie commented acidly as she retrieved her suitcase and started for the cabin.

Allan took no notice as he walked over to where Rex Jr. stood with his head down so far that his shoulder blades poked out through his fur. He bent down a few feet from the dog. "You don't have to be afraid of Dalvenjah, you know. She wouldn't harm anyone."

"I don't?" Rex Jr. asked in disbelief, taking his magical ability to communicate completely for granted. Almost all dogs understand the human tongue, but cannot speak it in turn because nature gave them big, wet dog tongues to sweat with and slobber on everything. The exception being small, yappy dogs who are too stupid to understand much and too lazy to care. It was just that most dogs hardly knew what to make of half of what they heard.

"No, you don't," Allan assured him. "You just got off to the wrong start with her. And it was entirely your own fault, barking and growling at her like that."

"But she threw fire at me," the shepherd said in aggrieved tones.

"Oh, I did that, and it was entirely an accident."

"Oh." Rex Jr. had to stop and think about that for a moment. "Well, I still don't much like her. She sleeps in a bed and gets a plate at the table, just like she thought she was people."

"She is people."

"Oh." He chewed on that for a moment. "And the little one, too?"

"Of course."

"Damn! Now I don't have any choice in the matter, do I?"

Allan laughed. "Just mind your manners and you should get along fine."

He rose and turned to join the others, but stopped short when he saw that Rex and Marie had paused on their way into the house and were staring at him. He shrugged helplessly. "I just don't want any misunderstandings."

"Oh, sure!" Marie said skeptically. "Allan Breivik, were you talking to a dog?"

"With a dog would be a little more accurate," he said. "I talk with quite a few of the neighbors. Except for Bill Badger, but his kind wouldn't give you the time of day."

"Thank you, Dr. Dolittle!" Rex exclaimed, and made a face of pure disgust. "Ye gods bear witness! Now I'll have to become a vegetarian for sure!"

Contrary to that oath, he had the fire burning in the grill within ten minutes. This time Dalvenjah had to do the honors, since Vajerral was nowhere to be found. She had disappeared with Jenny immediately after their arrival without a word of where they were going. Dalvenjah and Allan both knew that the dragonet was teaching Jenny to work simple magic. There was certainly no harm in that, they thought. Jenny would be working on Vajerral's magic, which meant that they both had serious limits to the amount of trouble they could generate. But Marie had already guessed as much herself. She kept that very much to herself, never showing a hint of displeasure. But that hardly meant that she approved. Quite to the contrary; she was rehearsing a glorious fit.

"That's entirely too much salt!" Marie complained, to no effect. Rex continued to let salt fall like snow on several draconic-sized cuts of beef that Dalvenjah could not recognize. Unlike Marie, she kept her mouth shut on the subject. To complain about the food on this world was to go hungry; there was so much she was unsure of.

"No, not hardly!" Rex assured her. "Salt is good for you."

"Now, you're a doctor; you know better," Marie admonished.

"Nonsense!" he insisted cheerfully. "Why, the ancients knew the worth of salt. It is, after all, the world's oldest preservative. You should be able to appreciate that."

"I'm not a herring," she insisted. "And I'm not in need of preservatives just yet."

"Why, salt was used for currency in some ancient civilizations," Rex continued blissfully. "Roman soldiers were often paid in salt, while some ancients salted the fields of their conquered enemies."

"And that's the gospel according to Salt Peter," Allan quipped.

"What . . . ?" Dr. Barker turned to stare at him. "Oh, what do you know? You're so dumb, you think . . ."

"Dahl!" Dalvenjah exclaimed suddenly, and leaped straight up from the ground and into flight, her broad wings snapping out as she took to the air.

"My sentiments exactly!" Marie exclaimed approvingly.

"No, something is wrong," Allan insisted urgently, and indicated for them to remain quiet while he appeared to listen. They could all hear Rex Jr. in the distance, perhaps a quarter of a mile or more away along the shore of the lake, barking hysterically. And they could tell by the fierce, frantic note of his barks that he must be fighting for his very life. Dalvenjah was streaking at her best speed in that very direction.

"Get the guns from the cabin!" Allan ordered sharply.

"What?" Rex asked, confused.

"Get the guns!" Allan snapped as he too leaped into the air and followed after the dragon's hurtling form, barely to be seen against the darkening sky. He could not hope to match her speed, but he would not arrive more than a few seconds behind her. Rex and Marie both stood rooted for a long moment in their confusion, listening to that distant barking. But that stopped suddenly, replaced a moment later by a mortal scream. Swearing, Rex turned and ran toward the cabin door.

They collected and loaded the two hunting rifles that Rex

always kept in the cabin, then ran the entire distance in little more than five minutes. But it was all over by then. Bodies were scattered over a large area of the forest, but only the small, green bodies of illeshyan. And the almost shredded remains of one valiant dog. Jenny and Vajerral still stood back to back in the middle of a small clearing, gasping with their recent exertions, while Dalvenjah and Allan went about the grim business of making certain that the small monsters were dead. The smell of burnt flesh hung heavy in the cold evening air, for many of the dead still smoldered lazily.

The story was easy enough to determine, for there was not all that much to it. Vajerral, Jenny and Rex Jr. had walked along the shore of the lake until they came to a place they considered secure enough to practice a little magic. The illeshyan pack had attacked suddenly, but the little beasts had not taken them by complete surprise. Vajerral had refused to leave Jenny and the two had made their stand in the clearing, Vajerral stunning the monsters as they came from the darkness of the woods while Jenny calmly dispatched the momentarily senseless things by braining them with a long stick that possessed a heavy knot at one end. Rex Jr. had come running to give battle, but he had been no match for the heavier, stronger adversaries. But the children had done well enough on their own, dealing away half the pack before Dalvenjah and Allan had arrived to handle the rest with their superior flames. Although they never knew it, the two youngsters had fared far better than Sheriff Hansin had done even with his powerful guns.

The two were not at all distressed. If anything, they looked like they were ready to take on another pack of illeshyan. Vajerral quite literally had her hackles up, the blue scales of her mane lifted from between her ears to the base of her neck. And she still stood at attack stance, her long arms and legs braced wide and her neck stiff and held well down. Dragons were most vulnerable at the neck, and they knew it instinctively. Jenny looked more than anything like a half-grown valkyrie, her own stance tense and battle-ready as she held the club in her hand and one of her mother's fierce expressions on her face. Under other circumstances, they would have made a comic sight.

"Jenny!" Marie exclaimed with an odd mixture of exasperation, impatience, astonishment and awe.

"The four of you get back to the cabin now," Dalvenjah ordered in a tone that permitted no argument. "I sense no more illeshyan, but Allan and I will patrol all the same."

"But, Allan . . ." Marie started to protest.

"Is far safer than you," the dragon insisted. "He can fly, and the flame he can command is a better weapon against these creatures than your guns."

"But . . ." Marie began to protest a second time.

"And no lectures until we get back!" she added.

Marie shut up and went back to the cabin without further protest, partly because she liked nothing better than the idea that they should be getting out of this dark, cold forest where little monsters were running around eating innocent little children and stupid dogs, and partly because she was speechless in the first place. Jenny did not much care for leaving Rex Jr.'s torn remains there in the woods with the bodies of his fallen enemies, but even she did not suggest that they do anything about it just then. Both she and Vajerral were still shaking with a barely contained battle fury; only Rex was visibly upset about the fate of his scrawny dog, sniffing and wiping at his nose.

Dalvenjah and Allan crossed each other's trail many times over as they searched the area about the cabin for ten miles around, but they found no trace of any other illeshyan. They returned together, finding the others seated in silence around the fire in the main room, the four widest sets of eyes in existence. Dalvenjah glanced at the four of them only once before heading straight to the nearest bathroom to wash her hands. She would have liked to have washed her entire self, but it took too long to blow-dry a dragon. Then she went to the kitchen and returned with two cold beers and a box of chocolate cupcakes. She sat down on her tail in the middle of the floor, facing Marie squarely.

"Okay, shoot!" she said impatiently.

Marie only blinked. "What?"

"Tell me that it is all my fault." She paused a moment to stare at the top of the first bottle of beer, and its lid flew off. She took a long drink and belched, wiggling her ears. "I will tell you now what you may have guessed. The illeshyan were attracted to this place by the magic that Allan and I have been exercising. And, in the event that you were wondering, I knew that they might come. I was hoping that they would. Then Allan and I could have dealt with them easily. As you can see, things did not work out quite as I had expected. The best laid plans of mice and dragons . . .

"Anyway, it comes out as my fault that this happened. If I had not been here, then they would not have followed me. I had not thought that they could have gotten anywhere so near without my being aware. Cultural pred- . . . prejudice, you might say. I have magic. Vajerral has magic. Even Allan has magic. What danger were we in? Immortal folk find illeshyan to be far more a bother than a danger. My concern was for your own people, all those who have died because Vorgulremik opened a way into your world and allowed such evil things to accompany him."

"All right, I can agree with that," Marie said. "It was all your fault. If you knew that those creatures would be heading in your direction . . ."

"I knew," Dalvenjah agreed. "What choice did I have? I had to have everyone in this world who was making real magic in one place, away from everyone else. What would you have done?"

"There had to be a better alternative," Marie insisted sharply. "I can almost see how you wouldn't give a damn about putting the rest of us in danger, but your own daughter . . ."

"Vajerral did not have to be in danger," Jenny interjected suddenly.

"What?" her mother demanded, turning to glare in astonishment at the impudence of children.

Jenny swallowed nervously, but quickly found her courage. "I said that she never was in any danger. Vajerral could have flown away at any time. I tried to get her to. But she would not leave me."

"Oh," Marie looked completely dumbfounded. "Well, I suppose that is true, of course."

"It was the bravest thing I ever saw," Jenny continued, encouraged by her success.

"You were very brave yourself," Dalvenjah told her.

"Bullshit!" she declared. "I didn't have any choice. Vay did. Not that we were in any danger of losing, of course."

"Oh, of course not!" the dragon agreed with exaggerated sincerity.

"Then again, if you let Vay teach me to fly, we never will have that problem again," Jenny added hopefully.

Marie turned toward her sharply, her mouth already open in reprimand before she thought better of it and surrendered the argument. Somehow it was beginning to make sense. She closed her mouth and stared at the ground, frowning at the hopelessness of it all. Dalvenjah opened the second beer and handed it to her, smiling. "I brought this one for you."

"Good idea!" Marie agreed, and took a deep drink.

"Does it help to know that it is never all that easy, no matter who or what you are?" the dragon asked.

"I'm beginning to realize that your problems must be multiplied tenfold," she observed. "Considering how your mere presence has multiplied my problems fivefold."

"Friends?" Dalvenjah asked hopefully.

Marie had to think about it for a moment. "Well, that's going just a little far. Truce?"

"Truce."

"Ah, just one more thing," Marie added cautiously. "This big dragon. The one that you came here to fight. Will he come looking around here as well?"

"No, no," Dalvenjah insisted. "He is waiting for me, and when the time comes I will go to him."

"That's good," she said, and turned suddenly to Allan and Rex, fixing them with an icy stare. "Well, what about you two staring baboons? I suppose that you have something witty to add."

Rex considered that briefly and shook his head. "Not for all the world."

"Lys des'ahlar avah?" Vajerral asked suddenly.

"Eat?" Rex asked, and leaped up in alarm. "Oh, my God, the steaks!"

Marie frowned. She had understood what Vajerral said for the first time since she had met the two dragons, but she kept that carefully to herself. By no means was she about to admit that she was getting used to magic to the point of having any part of it.

They ate that night seated around the fire, roasting frankfurters in the open flames. The steaks were still edible, at least to someone who had a very expansive idea of well done. But the pieces looked too much like portions of illeshyan that had been caught in dragon-flame for comfort. A festive mood developed quickly, more open and relaxed than any they had ever known before, even if it did have a slightly hysterical edge to it at first. Rex had been the most affected of anyone by the fight, perhaps because of the loss of his dog. Jenny and Vajerral were, predictably, the least affected and by far the first to recover. As far as that went, Vajerral had never been anything more than hopping mad in the first place, and it took the better part of an hour for her ruffled mane to settle completely. Marie took things in amazingly good grace after her initial confrontation with Dalvenjah. The two of them seemed to agree that it was best forgotten, and immediately put the entire matter out of mind.

"We seem to be out of beer," Rex said, returning from the kitchen with a large handful of cans and bottles of soda to go with their hot dogs. "Can you drink Canada Dry?"

"Gee, I don't know," Dalvenjah said, mimicking Allan's dopey delivery perfectly. "Why don't you and me give it a try some time?"

Rex just afforded her an impatient look. "Some jokes are so old, they've percolated into the deepest den of the dragon world."

"What's the matter?" Allan asked, laughing. "Can't stand the competition?"

"Why do you call these hot dogs?" Dalvenjah asked as she applied mustard to her bun very cautiously. She liked the taste of mustard very well, but the slightest sniff of the stuff made both of the dragons sneeze.

"What do you think is in them?" Rex asked, then thought of his own dog and turned momentarily pale. No one else appeared to notice.

"Hold still!" Jenny told Vajerral. They were seated at opposite ends of the sofa, while Jenny executed the dragonet's portrait in pastels. Like everything else she decided to do, she did it very well.

"Stuff it!" Vajerral retorted. The setting was complicated by the fact that Vajerral was still trying to finish her dinner. Allan leaned back to steal a look at the drawing, which was still in its beginning stages.

"I hope that someone has thought to take a few pictures of our friends," Rex said.

"You just did," Marie told him. "I put in your camera. And six rolls of film."

"I wonder what you look like," Allan mused to himself.

Dalvenjah turned to look at him, twitching her ears in mild consternation. "Me?"

"I mean, as a person. Or, rather, my kind of person."

"I know what I would like to look like," she said.

An image immediately appeared in their mind's eye, that of a young girl. She was tall and very slender of build, light of frame but well muscled. Her hair was long and the same brown as Allan's, her features beautiful without being delicate. Dalvenjah was not the delicate type. Her skin was an even tan all over, easy to tell since she was also quite naked. Everyone was rather surprised by that, but Marie and Rex were more amused than anything else. Jenny hardly cared, and Vajerral did not even seem to know the difference. Only Allan blushed, because of some personal guilt only he knew.

"I forgot something, didn't I?" Dalvenjah said rather contritely.

"I think so," Rex said. "Do you want to try again?"

"Well, let me see."

Dalvenjah had to think about that for a long moment. It led the others to wonder if she thought of all humans in terms of their naked selves, as if she automatically deleted clothes in all her images as a random variable. She finally came to some conclusion and sent out her new image. It was not the same person at all, but clothed, as they would have expected. The clothes and hair style were very flamboyant but rather dated, and the young, beautiful woman was suspiciously familiar. In fact, it was . . .

"Ellenor Powell?" Rex was the first to figure it out.

"It is!" Marie agreed, equally surprised. Allan did not seem to remember just what Ellenor Powell looked like, so he was still unsure.

"But why Ellenor Powell?" Rex asked, mystified. "I could understand someone like . . ."

"That's who you wish she was," Marie said, with a note of warning in her voice. She had no doubt who he would have liked to find in his cabin. Naked—in the spirit of that first vision.

"Very pretty," Dalvenjah explained. "And she could dance like no one I have even seen. I like dancing. Dragons really are not built for it. Not dance like that."

"Marie, didn't you used to dance?" Allan asked.

"Yes, I was pretty good, too," she said, her Norwegian accent becoming just noticeably stronger. It had a tendency to do that when she went back in time through her memories. "I'm not especially musical, unlike you and Jenny. But that was one thing I have that you don't."

"What, tits?" Rex asked drily.

"No, grace and coordination," she insisted, and glared at him briefly, as if she was reluctant to admonish him for what she seemed to take as a compliment. "Does it always come down to sex with you?"

"No, but that's my favorite position," he said. "Speaking of music, why don't we make a little of our own? I brought my beast."

Rex's "beast" turned out to be a full-sized concert accordion a la Lawrence Welk, which he played with surprising finesse and proficiency. The dragons were fascinated by the thing, so unlike any musical instrument they had ever known. Even the piano, which Jenny played like a true child prodigy when she was not drawing, composing, or calculating cube roots, was not too unlike a keyboard instrument of their own world. Dalvenjah got out the guitar that Allan had given her, and which she now played surprisingly well in either her own or the local musical notation. And the two dragons were also exceptional singers, Dalvenjah possessing a remarkably broad range across five full octaves, her normal high contralto somewhere near the middle. Vajerral was limited to a high soprano until her voice "filled out," as her mother phrased it. Only Marie had

nothing to contribute to the evening's music-making, except
as a captive audience.

Following Jenny's suggestion, they began by rehearsing an
off-world song that Dalvenjah introduced. Both Jenny and Allan had the necessary command of musical theory and technique
to be able to master the odd harmonics almost immediately;
especially Allan, who was well versed in the neoclassical. And
Rex knew enough to be able to add some background chords
on his accordion. After only half an hour they were able to
play the song through more or less flawlessly, Dalvenjah playing the guitar as if it was a harp with Jenny supporting on the
piano, accompanied by cello and accordion. Dalvenjah naturally took the lead vocal role, in her own language, although
Vajerral joined in on vocal accompaniment in a surprisingly
full, rich voice, supporting just a line or two now and then,
most often at unexpected points rather than the more predictable
portions.

It was a haunting, stirring song that spoke of nothing but
very common things, and yet with a subtle sentimentality that
might have been more at home in a ballad. Dalvenjah shared
the meaning with them magically, not just the words but also
the deep feelings that this song inspired in Mindijari. It spoke
of home, the home she knew well and longed for in her dreams.
And it spoke even more softly of love, of the type of deep,
satisfying love that she longed for as well, that she had known
and lost. The final deep, echoing note that Jenny added almost
as an afterthought on the piano came almost as a shock, like
a faraway cry of hurt and longing cutting through all that
beauty.

Then Allan and Dalvenjah played together a few more mundane selections, often things not originally meant for cello and
guitar but which they somehow made to work well together.
Allan was a great improviser, or perhaps a thief, of things he
"liberated" from the violin repertoire. He maintained, almost
as a professional motto, that many of the more delicate pieces
written for violin, music of love and gentle fondness, really
belonged on the cello. Perhaps because he always thought of
love and sentimentality with the same subtle note of longing
and regret that the cello could bring out so much better than

the lighter strings. It certainly fit in well with the themes that
Dalvenjah had established from the start.

They finished the night by turning the floor over to Dr. Rex
and his magic accordion, playing the rousing Norwegian polkas
that Marie preferred, and which she seemed to regard as sen-
timental in spite of the fact that they were quite vigorous enough
to bring the squirrels out of hibernation early. She and Allan
danced a couple of polkas. Then, just to find out if dragons
really could dance, Allan and Dalvenjah took a turn. It turned
out that dragons did indeed dance a lively polka, although she
had to be careful about swinging her long, thin tail in the
crowded room. At least the ceiling in that room was high
enough to accommodate her long neck, even when she stood
fully upright.

After that Rex and Marie said that they had to go outside
for a moment to cool down, and the former looked like he
honestly needed to. They went out the front door, and Jenny
and Vajerral disappeared quietly out the back a moment later.
Allan and Dalvenjah returned to their own experimentation on
their two instruments but Jenny returned only a few moments
later and quietly indicated for the sorceress to follow her back
outside. Her expression was very serious, although by no means
alarming, but she refused to explain.

What she wanted Dalvenjah to see needed no explanation.
They slipped as quietly as they could around the corner of the
house until they were able to peer out of the shadows at Rex
and Marie standing together in the front. It was by that time
very late into the night, perhaps an hour before midnight. The
moon was still very bright, although its full radiance was now
more silver than the golden that it had been only days before.
It still reflected brightly in the light dusting of frost that covered
the dry grass and leaves and glazed the windows of Rex's car.

"Seeing that dragon polka is something that I'll never forget," Rex said in what seemed to be a very obvious attempt
to break a lull in their conversation that had persisted while the
spies had been moving into position. Marie only shrugged.
Dalvenjah perked her ears, having determined that this was
indeed more serious than it seemed.

"This night reminds me of that early cruise we took up the
Norwegian coast, just about this same time last spring, and

that same cold, clear night in Bergen," he continued after a moment. "And those same woody hills like we have here, only ten times as steep. Your Bergen dialect was so good that people kept asking if you were bringing your American husband home to meet his new relations."

"Wrong on both counts," Marie said, just a little remotely. So that was the game! Rex was getting very serious on the subject of rings and doing all the time what they now saved for weekends, and she was on the defensive. Poor Rex! He was a victim of the magic of Dalvenjah's song, while Marie had not been so deeply stirred by that sense of urgency. Dalvenjah was beginning to appreciate that dragon magic was a very dangerous thing for mortals.

"We did see your grandparents," Rex persisted, almost hopefully. "And your relatives. You didn't mind playing at being married to them, at least as far as I could tell. So few of them spoke any English, and my Norwegian wasn't so good back then."

"I didn't want to disappoint min bestemor," Marie answered, admitting nothing.

"No doubt," he agreed guardedly. "Your Uncle Bernt figured things out very quickly, but I don't think you ever knew that. He was a funny old guy. Riktig morsom."

"Ja, svaert," she agreed absently. "You've been practicing."

"Ja, jeg snakker Norsk svaert bra na," Rex continued, in rather stilted Nynorsk. "Hvordan star det til? Bare bra, takk. Jeg er fremmed her."

Marie smiled. "Can you say anything that you haven't memorized off your language tapes?"

"Ja, selvfolgelig," he insisted, without hesitation. "Jeg elsker du, min kjaereste."

"Hestelort!" Marie declared skeptically.

Rex shrugged, frowning. "This night reminds me of that cold, clear night in Bergen, outside that little restaurant on the hill overlooking the city and the harbor. There was frost on everything, and I thought how beautiful the evergreens looked with a twinkle of frost on the tip of each needle. And I remember that one tree right outside the room we shared at your grandparents' house. I wanted one outside our window here, so the first thing I did when we came back was plant that little one here.''

They walked slowly over to the small, withered sapling that stood near the far corner of the house, just outside their window. Dalvenjah and her fellow conspirators had to lean out just a little farther to follow them. Rex stood beside the tiny tree with his hands stuffed down the pockets of his pants, looking very crestfallen. He did not know that Marie was weakening in her resolve, although surrender remained a long way off.

"You just laughed when I planted it," he continued, almost despondently. "You said that I would never be able to transplant a pine and make it live. You laughed all the more when I said that it was a token of my love. You said that you might just consider marrying me when you saw the thing live and put out new growth."

"The offer still stands," she told him. "But I think I'm safe."

"It's not dead yet," he pointed out.

"That remains to be seen. I cannot yet see any sign that it has survived the winter."

Rex frowned again, bitterly. "How long do we have to wait? How much of our time do we have to throw away on something that has been dead and gone now for twice as long as I've known you?"

"That has nothing to do with it," Marie said coldly, her warning unmistakable. "Matters are pretty well decided already, I will grant you that. But not for certain. The time is not yet right."

"When will the time be right?"

"I will know."

They turned and walked away, around the corner of the house, speaking now of simpler things. Dalvenjah could have followed their conversation with her sharp ears, but she did not try. She had heard what she had been brought to hear, and she understood the problem. She knew what the question was, but how could she answer? Jenny trusted her too much. They stepped together out of the shadows, walking over to the sapling that Rex had planted. It did indeed look quite lifeless, like a dead stick that would not even stand upright except for the stake that it was tied to. But it was not dead yet; Dalvenjah could still sense faint life within it. Allan and Vajerral remained slightly behind when they paused to look down at the tree.

Jenny turned to face her squarely. "Can't you do something?"

Dalvenjah only shook her head sadly. "I am a sorceress. I deal in real magic, not illusion. I could make them think that they are in love, but it would not be quite the same as if they found it for themselves. You would not have me lead them into something false."

"What's the difference?" Jenny demanded. "As long as they love each other, what does it matter where it came from? Wouldn't it be just as real to them?"

"Perhaps," the dragon conceded. "I could give them the illusion that you would have me make, and they would live happily ever after. But I would know the difference. I am a sorceress, and I have a responsibility to use my magic properly. I must be true to myself, if not just them. I will not meddle to that degree."

Jenny turned away, so utterly dejected that she looked about to cry. That sight touched the softest part of Dalvenjah's generous heart, so that she knew that she had to do something. She laid a gentle hand on the girl's shoulder, and smiled reassuringly.

"They really do not need my help," she said. "They already have all the love they need. But . . . perhaps there is something I might do to hurry matters along."

She took a small step forward until she was staring straight down at the withered little tree, and she said a word of command. The sapling shook itself as if awakening from a long sleep, and immediately seemed to stand up straight and proud. Then, even as they watched, it began to extrude new green needles from branches that no longer appeared quite so dry and fragile. Dalvenjah smiled, very satisfied with the effect. Vajerral made a comment of approval of her own, and Allan stepped forward to lay a hand on the base of her neck.

"Will that be enough?" Jenny asked anxiously.

"Should be," Dalvenjah promised her. "We must be very subtle; that is the key. Too big a push would only break the bridge that we work to mend."

"I hope so," Allan said. "My sister never seems all that willing."

"She pretends that it is only play, of no great or lasting consequence," the sorceress said. "She is afraid to love again. Afraid that it will only go wrong, as it did before. Perhaps the way to help her overcome her fear is to hold her to her promise."

"Will that work?"

"With magic, all things are possible."

• Part Five •

The Exiles

FUNERAL SERVICES WERE held promptly at ten the following morning, in a secluded forest glade far from the bodies of the fallen—which had themselves been shoveled into a pit and burned with dragon-fire. Rex insisted upon it, even though the process of interring the remains meant first collecting the parts. And no one argued, not even in thought. Dalvenjah spoke a few appropriate words, since there was some consensus that a sorceress was second best to a holy person. At least when the competition consisted of a cellist, a surgeon and a financial consultant. And the others had already recognized that she had a way with words; effectiveness and accuracy, if not proficiency. Rex shed a few tears for his beloved cur and namesake and Jenny put in her two cents, and they formally erected the monument that the two of them had hastily carved in a piece of plywood.

In Fond Remembrance of
Rex Albert Barker Jr.
Man's Best Friend—But None Too

Fond of Dragons
'He ate what was set before him.'

The rest of the weekend did not pass without further incident, even in comparison with what had already happened. Everyone had already guessed that Jenny was having Vajerral teach her magic. They tried to maintain the strictest secrecy, which was a task comparable to expecting such subtlety from a bull elephant. But no one, not even Marie, had been especially worried because there seemed to be little real magic that the dragonet had to teach. All except for Dalvenjah, who knew better but who also adhered to the philosophy that everyone stood to prosper by learning a little magic.

What the others overlooked was the fact that Vajerral did indeed know one bit of magic very well, which all dragons came by instinctively, and which was very easy to teach to anyone with even a small amount of talent. And Jenny had about as much potential as any mortal deserved, second only to Allan and not by very much. The trouble began when Marie happened to glance out the window the next morning and saw Jenny and Vajerral flying down to the lake.

What happened next was predictable, except that it was rather hard to discipline an errant child who could hop from tree to tree like a sparrow. Jenny was a very good judge of just how much trouble she was in with her mother, especially since she was in trouble quite a lot of the time. Many mothers create hardships by trying to force perfectly normal children to pretend to be gifted. Jenny's problem was that she was exceptionally gifted but her mother preferred that she act perfectly normal. Her questing, imaginative mind was a restless bull in the china shop of her mother's restrictions. The inevitable result was that neither of them was very happy.

"Jennifer Breivik, you come down out of that tree this instant!" Marie declared after chasing the errant children down to the edge of the lake before any of the others could intervene.

"No way!" Jenny said in return. In this way she was still somewhat a child; she was quite prepared to spend the rest of her life in a tree rather than face her mother's present level of wrath. Of course, there were any number of alleged adults who faced their own music by turning tail in much the same way. But in Jenny's case, it was perhaps best for everyone that she did keep herself out of reach.

"You're going to get the whipping of your life!" Marie declared, contrary to her policy that spankings were for toddlers.

"Don't you think I know that?" Jenny asked with considerable surprise, which also served to state her own position in this matter. Mother had a point of discipline and moral and social ethics to discuss, if in a somewhat violent manner; daughter was out to save her ass—quite literally.

Marie looked up and judged whether or not she could climb the tree; she knew that she could, but not fast enough to prevent an escape. Jenny did have a tactical advantage: victory through air power. Indeed, she did not even seem particularly concerned. Or at least not frightened; she meant to make her point, and more than that, to win. In that she was anything but a child, or considerably less so than her own mother. Dalvenjah sat a safe distance away and simply watched, even less concerned, and Allan took his cue from her. Rex was plainly amused by the whole spectacle. Only Vajerral took the matter completely seriously. She sat even higher in the same tree, shaking with such fright that she seemed in danger of falling off her branch.

"You come out of that pine tree before I chop it down!" Marie declared.

"I think that's a poplar," Rex said, deciding that it was time to intervene. "I always thought that Jenny must be very poplar."

"Oh, cut it out!" Marie snapped.

"Can't," he said, and shrugged. "Didn't bring an ax. Which is a good thing, or I would have used it on a knot-head like you."

"What?" Marie turned on him abruptly, so distracted that she forgot all about Jenny for the moment.

"You heard me," he declared. "Just shut up long enough to think about this for a moment. Flying has been one of mankind's oldest and dearest dreams, one that we have conquered only lately and then only by machine. Jenny has a rare

opportunity to do what no one else in the history of our race—
with the exception of her Uncle Al—has ever done. Don't
spoil it.''

"Are you kidding?" Marie demanded incredulously. "This
is dangerous!"

"So is riding a bicycle in the street. And that's probably a
lot more dangerous than this is. But millions of kids do it every
day, including her. But you don't object to that."

"Of course not. That's different."

"Just how is that different?"

"Why, I have insurance to cover that!" Marie declared.
"Just how could I tell the insurance agent something like she
ran into a tree when she was out flying with a dragon?"

Rex rolled his eyes impatiently and sighed. Time for a new
approach; trying to reason with her had failed, so maybe he
should just tell her. "Listen. I have just as much a stake in
this as you do, and I say she can practice all the magic she
wants while she can."

"And who says you do?" Marie demanded.

"I do," he said defiantly.

"I second the motion!" Jenny called down from the tree.

"Motion has been made and seconded," Rex announced.
"All in favor say aye. Aye!"

"Aye!"

"The ayes have it. Motion is carried by a two-to-one margin.
I say she can practice her magic."

"I still say no!" Marie declared.

"I say yes!" Jenny added.

"Lyr kas!" Vajerral put in her own vote, having sensed that
things were beginning to go their way.

"The motion is carried," Rex announced with an air of
unarguable finality, and turned to look up into the tree. "You
can practice all the magic you want, as long as you are careful
about it. No fire."

"Ah, Rex!"

"This is a compromise," he pointed out to her.

Jenny considered that a moment, and saw the logic in it.
"All right. I have that down pretty good anyway."

After all that, Marie was so bemused and bewildered that
she allowed herself to be led away without another word of

protest. She looked as if she would still like to protest, but she had either forgotten quite what she had meant to say or how to counterattack in the face of such overwhelming illogic, when children were allowed to vote on whether they were in any real trouble. And while no one else had mentioned it, she was only too aware that Jenny would have been in no real danger the previous evening if she had only learned to fly a day earlier. She also found, once she had taken the time to consider the matter, that she was actually rather proud of having a daughter who could work such serious magic. That was quite enough to cause her to question her very sanity.

Dalvenjah found a unique method for teaching Allan to practice the finer points of levitation: She made him play darts. This was no small trick, since she insisted that they play according to her rules. The only real difference in the way she played the game was that she did not permit throwing the darts. Instead the dart was laid flat in the hand and directed toward its target by magic. After a couple of rounds, Dalvenjah was obliged to even the odds somewhat by the unprecedented concession of actually throwing her darts. Allan considered it giving him a sporting chance, like a five-second head start. She had never played darts in her life, needless to say, but she was predictably good at it either way.

Allan was letting the board intimidate him. He was so afraid of missing the board altogether that he was aiming too far in toward the center. The result was that he was finding it almost impossible to hit a double, on the outer rim of the target area, that he needed to begin the game. Half the time, Dalvenjah had won the game before he even got his double and began counting down his points. According to British dart-player's tradition, a person who was "brushed," defeated without getting that necessary double, owed the winner two beers. After only three nights of practice, Allan owed Dalvenjah over two hundred beers.

"Darts!" Dalvenjah declared with satisfaction. For good reason. Double and triple eighteen combined for a gratifying total of ninety points, and the final twenty-four points was concluded with the necessary double twelve.

"Good darts," Allan conceded grudgingly. "So, that comes to two hundred and forty-eight beers. You prefer bottles?"

"Long necks."

He afforded her a very sour expression as he stepped up to the line to start again. Laying the first dart in his hand, he drew an imaginary line between its sharp point and the place on the dartboard he wanted to hit. Then he launched the dart with a gentle thrust of magic, careful to avoid upsetting his aim with the very force used to propel the dart. For once it flew straight and true, his personal cruise missile, right to its intended target, the double twenty. Allan stared in disbelief for a long moment, then beat his chest and did a Tarzan yell. But his next two darts wandered right, into the single one.

"Forty-two the hard way," Dalvenjah commented. "You just can't stand prosperity, can you?"

"I'm doing better," he protested as she took his place at the line. "I just managed to avoid two hundred and fifty beers. You seem to think that double twenties come easy."

Dalvenjah said nothing. She threw her first dart, and in pure perversity got that same double twenty. She followed that with the single twenty, and then the elusive triple twenty.

"Shanghai!" she declared, strutting like a peacock. "Ohh, I'm bad!"

Vajerral looked up from where she was building a fortress out of blocks and chirped some word of approval. The little dragon never seemed to tire of building castles; she seemed to have a real inclination toward architecture. Which was a shame; her mother obviously intended her to take up other lines of work.

Allan stepped up to the line to launch his next salvo. Satisfied with getting the double twenty in the previous game, he returned to the lower regions of the board. This area suited him best, since he was not required to thrust the dart to much greater altitude than the hand it was launched from. He surprised himself greatly by getting his double on the first try, second game in a row. A total of fifty-nine points from the round was very gratifying.

Pleased with himself, Allan stepped aside to allow Dalvenjah her turn. He picked up his drink and turned back to watch her stance. That was the moment when, after three nights of playing darts with the dragon, he suddenly realized her advantage. "Hey! Whoa! You're way too close to the target."

"You told me to stand behind the line," she protested.

As a matter of fact, her hind paws were behind the line. But that was not at all the restriction it was meant to be to a mortal player. Dragons were built on the vertical; when Dalvenjah leaned over to throw, her three feet of neck put her nose halfway to the target, her throwing hand not far behind.

"You throw from behind the line," Allan told her sternly. "Or else I'll pay off my debt in light beer."

Dalvenjah frowned fiercely, but Allan knew that he had won when she laid back her ears. Dragons did not drink light beer, not when they preferred mead to beer anyway. Dalvenjah stepped back until she was well behind the line, then threw her darts.

The disgusting thing was that it made no difference.

Allan stepped up to take his own turn, and was rewarded for his diligence with a triple nineteen. A single seventeen followed; the lower side of the board was kind to him. Dalvenjah lifted her head and looked around, her ears twitching with consternation.

"Someone comes," she said.

Allan launched his final dart. It was straight on target toward the double seventeen when it hit the wire and bounced back. The wayward dart crashed through the very middle of Vajerral's fortress, scattering blocks, before it finally stuck in the carpet.

"I was robbed!" Allan declared.

"Kor derivash!" Vajerral added, equally annoyed. That had been a most exceptional castle.

"Someone is outside," Dalvenjah repeated.

Her warning was followed almost immediately by a light rapping at the back door. Allan stood for a moment, then quickly waved the dragons to their customary hiding place in the bathtub. He waited until they were well under cover, then hurried to the back door.

"Who's there?" he asked cautiously.

"A friend," a woman's light voice, almost that of a young girl, responded softly.

That seemed to answer a number of questions in itself, although not very clearly. It suggested someone who knew what was going on here, and someone who was sympathetic to their cause. He unlocked the door and opened it just enough to peer out into the night.

What he saw standing outside should have surprised him, but it did not. He had lost the ability to be surprised some weeks earlier. Standing on the back porch was a young female centaur. She was considerably smaller and more delicate in appearance than he had always imagined centaurs to be, standing no taller than himself with a skinny, long-legged body that was small even for a pony. The coat of her equine part was light grey, but her full tail and long, thick hair, almost in appearance like a waist-length mane, were the purest white. Her upper half was lightly tanned, with small, very shapely breasts. Allan noticed that right away.

"Just a moment," he said politely, then turned to shout over his shoulder. "Dalvenjah! It's for you."

Night was settling deep, dark and cold over the forest as they followed the little centaur uphill from the lake, deeper into the woods. Allan followed obediently, trying not to be cold. He understood only vaguely what was going on. The grey centaur had introduced herself as Daphne, inviting Dalvenjah to a hasty meeting in the woods with the leaders of the faerie people. Dalvenjah seemed to understand, at least a good deal better than he did. What he did not know was whether these were old friends of the dragon's or strangers, and whether they had come to offer help or to ask it.

They climbed quickly to the top of a small, steep hill, where Daphne stopped and asked them to wait, then looked about expectantly. Dalvenjah simply sat back on her tail to wait. Allan followed her cue to stand just behind her right shoulder, what seemed to him the proper place for an apprentice. The clearing on the hilltop was small, hardly justifying the word, the tall, dark pines of the forest drawing in tightly all around. There was just enough of a break in the foliage overhead for a small amount of the golden light of the waxing moon to filter through.

A pale, frosty mist began to creep through the trees, warning of the arrival of the faerie folk, as if they did not dare to travel without the concealment of their magic. They came hesitantly, some stalking slowly and cautiously while others darted from shadow to shadow. The long legs of faerie centaurs stepped with the light, furtive touch of deer. Slender elfin forms flitted between the shadows, and smaller, stocky shapes lumbered awkwardly as they tried to race from one bit of concealment to another. Then they paused at the edge of the shadows, peering out of the darkness at the dragon with large, bright eyes that were at the same time apprehensive, beseeching and almost suspicious. Allan could not guess whether they were fearful of Dalvenjah because she was a dragon, or because she commanded magic that was obvious even to him to be far in excess of their own. Or had they simply been in hiding for so long that it had become a part of their nature?

A few of the elusive figures began to move forward, one representative of each of the types that Allan could see. Daphne retreated as a male centaur, subtly older but not much larger, stepped up to take her place facing the dragon. The centaurs seemed to be the brave ones of this lot, and this bold move on the part of the first seemed to reassure the others somewhat. The tallest of the elfin folk, an almost incredibly slender woman small enough to walk under his outstretched arm, joined the centaur. Three others came from different directions.

"Sorceress, we're so very glad that you've come," the elder centaur said, daring to take her hand. "We've awaited this for a thousand years."

"What have you been waiting for?" Dalvenjah asked patiently. "What is it you expect that I can do for you?"

"You can open a gate and let us leave this place," one of the gnarled, dwarvish figures declared in an atrocious Irish accent. The bearded little figure in rough leather did not match Allan's image of a leprechaun in Jiminy Cricket coattails and shoes with bright brass buckles. It seemed that the wee folk had fallen on hard times, especially if they were reduced to begging help from an errant dragon.

"You are the native faerie folk of this world," Dalvenjah concluded, looking at them thoughtfully. "What is left of you, at least. I have only sensed your presence since I returned to the mountains. What has happened?"

"This was never any world for the faerie folk," the elder centaur began. "We were never strong, just a strange, scattered people. But in the younger days of this world, before the waxing of mortal folk and the building of the first of their great cities, we knew a long age of peace. Even when men began to thrive and expand, the world was still a wide and empty place. Most of us withdrew farther into the wild. Others of us tried for a time to share this world with men. They betrayed us, and then they assigned the blame to us in their stories and legends.''

The centaurs had a real grievance on this point, for others who were gathered near enough to hear grumbled their agreement with this complaint.

''More disastrous to us was the growing mortal influence, the greater damage that they never intended,'' the elfin woman added deftly, a rather obvious effort to keep the subject on a more congenial note. ''There was never any great magic in this world, and the mortals never understood magic at all. They increased, making a world of their own that had no place for magic, and the magic has been going out of this world ever since. Our people diminished. We retreated farther and farther across the lands of the old world, until our backs were to the sea and we had nowhere else to go. Then the last of our great sorcerers commanded what was left of their magic to open the gates into other faerie realms.''

''But men were right behind us,'' the centaur continued the tale. ''They took the gates from us, making them into places of worship to their simple gods before other men came and destroyed the gates in fear and ignorance. But the Exiles were trapped, for the magic to open even the least of gates had been lost to us. We retreated across the great sea to this new land, and we have hidden ourselves so well in these mountains that not even the woodcrafty mortals native to these lands learned of us. We hoped to rest, hidden deep in these mountains, perhaps to regain enough of our lost magic to open a final gate and save what remains of our races. And then they came again.''

''So what it amounts to is that we'd like for you to open us a way out of here, and let us go,'' the dwarf concluded, repeating his request. He acted gruff and impatient, as if eager to be gone, and yet Allan realized that he was almost frantic with fear that Dalvenjah would refuse. He could hardly imagine why the dragon would deny them.

But something about this had bothered Allan from the start, and now he was beginning to understand what. He stepped up close behind the dragon and laid his hand gently on the shoulder of her wing. "Dalvenjah, you can't do this. There must be another way."

She turned to stare at him, honestly surprised. "Why ever not? Why should you be opposed to their leaving your world?"

"Why, they belong in this world," he protested, still confused about how to put what he meant into words. "If they leave, the magic will go out of this world forever. There must be some way to bring the magic back, so that they can stay."

The elder centaur frowned and shook his head sadly. "This is the place we belong; you are right about that. But the magic began to go out of this world a very long time ago, and I don't know if all the dragons in existence could ever bring it back. Besides, your people never did want or understand magic. First you learned to fear it, and then you dismissed it for things that you could understand and control. There will always be exceptions like yourself, but your people just don't want magic back."

"Too upsetting to the status quo," the dwarf added, gruffly sympathetic. "It would be difficult to get everyone to give up machines for magic."

"That was never the problem," Dalvenjah said. "There are worlds I have seen, mortal worlds, where machines and magic work as one, and scientists are also sorcerers."

"I just think that there must be some way," Allan protested weakly. "You say that there are mortal worlds where magic is known, so why can't we at least try, as long as people like myself and my niece Jenny are willing to try? I don't want to see this happen."

"Neither do we," the elfin woman agreed. "We've spent three thousand years seeking an alternative. Now we must go. Our time has run out."

"No, no. There is simply no more time," Dalvenjah acceded, and looked at them each in turn. "How soon can you have all of your people gathered here? And just how many are we talking about?"

She lifted her head to look around. Only then did Allan notice what she seemed to have been aware of for some time.

Scores of the faerie folk of every type were gathering all through the forest surrounding the hilltop.

"We are here already," the elfin woman explained. "Of the elfin folk, not more than four thousand. Perhaps half again as many centaurs; they are the least dependent upon their native magic, and so they have been the slowest to fade."

"There are less than a thousand of us," the dwarf added.

Allan was startled when some beast suddenly pushed at him from behind. Turning quickly, he was surprised to find a small, white unicorn looking up at him with immense dark eyes. It was smaller than he would have thought a unicorn should be, no longer than a small pony, but very slender and narrow of chest, its golden horn hardly twelve inches long. It just stood there for a long moment, staring up at him with big, sad eyes like a lonely puppy. Then it nosed him a second time, as if encouraging him to some action.

Allan was hopelessly confused, unable to imagine what a unicorn wanted from him. He turned back to the others, looking at them questioningly, and was again surprised to see that they were watching him with very startled and curious expressions. Then he remembered something about unicorns and their eccentric behavior, and he began to blush furiously. He turned away, trying his best to ignore the beast. That soft nose continued to poke him in the middle of the back, and he reached back to swat it away.

"Yes, we've also got a couple hundred unicorns," the dwarf added, one brow cocked wryly. "The poor beasties have had no one to entertain them in ever so long. You just never encounter a person of those qualities any more."

Dalvenjah only looked confused; the reference was beyond her experience. She turned back to the gathering of faerie folk. "When will you be ready to go through? Not tonight, I imagine."

"No, but we will be ready this time tomorrow night," the centaur assured her. "Daphne will stay with you. She is the strongest of our young magicians. There are things that she can tell you of this world and its magic that you may find useful."

Walking back to the cabin, Allan was still bothered by the thought that there must be some way to restore magic to his world and permit the faerie folk to remain. He suspected that his interests were purely selfish, knowing that the return of strong magic to his world was his only hope of finding magic of his own. And he suspected that Dalvenjah was even more certain of his true motive than he was.

Privately, he had to admit that it was easiest and best to allow the faerie folk to retreat into a world where they belonged. There really was no place for them here, and he was not certain that there ever could be. Nothing would change when they did go; the world as it was would never notice any difference. But something very important would be lost forever. As important as magic was to Dalvenjah, as much as it was an essential part of her very existence, he could not accept that she should so casually allow the magic to disappear completely from an entire world.

At the moment, however, he felt thoroughly annoyed with Dalvenjah Foxfire and her refusal to even consider alternatives. He was also quite annoyed with a certain unicorn that was following him through the woods like a loyal puppy.

A short distance behind, Dalvenjah was walking beside Daphne. The young centaur had been very instructive in her own way, without realizing it. If she was the best, most capable and powerful sorceress left to the faerie people of this world, then they were a sadly diminished folk indeed. Allan, barely trained and mortal, could have taken half a dozen just like her in a contest of magic. Dalvenjah kept that carefully to herself, however. Daphne was very familiar with the subtleties of the magic that was particular to this world, both the common magic and the faerie magic, although both were tame and simple things compared to dragon magic.

"I will be of no use to you in your fight with the evil dragon," Daphne said. "At the best I might be able to teach you how to more easily make use of the common magic of this world. There are not such reserves of common magic here as you might be used to, but you probably know that already. The golden light of a full moon would serve you better."

"I had thought of that," Dalvenjah admitted. She was finding it difficult to walk upright as much as she had this night. But she was too proud to pace on all fours in front of other faerie folk, even ones as rustic and diminished as these. All

dragons were proud, but Dalvenjah was also young enough to
consider herself quite worldly. She had, after all, seen the better
part of four dozen worlds.

"I am most concerned about the company you keep,"
Daphne said hesitantly, fearful of criticizing a dragon. "You
know the effect that the mortals of this world have upon faerie
magic."

"Most mortals, perhaps," Dalvenjah said. "Allan is different. His own magic is very strong within him, in addition
to the dragon magic that I have taught him. I do not expect
that his company will make trouble for me."

Allan dreamed that night of centaurs prancing in a circle in
a circus ring while Dalvenjah cracked a long whip over their
heads, and awoke the next morning with a headache. His day
was already off to a bad start. Then he stepped on the unicorn
sleeping curled on the floor as he got out of bed. The day was
getting worse.

"How about breakfast?" he asked as he finished dressing.
"What do unicorns eat? Grape Nuts?"

Clover swished her long tail, looking up at him with large,
anxious eyes. Communication was established, as far as he
could tell.

He opened the door slowly and peered out into the hall.
Dalvenjah's door was still closed, and he did not hear Vajerral
stirring about downstairs. He was rather surprised that his little
encounter with the sleeping unicorn had not awakened the
sharp-eared dragons. Since they never had to dress first, they
were usually out before he was in the morning.

He descended the stairs and crossed the den to the kitchen,
motioning for Clover to keep quiet. He was not yet certain just
how intelligent this unicorn was; she made no effort to speak,
but she seemed to understand most of what he said without the
need for magic to interpret. He hesitated when he saw something large and dark standing motionless in the front room.
Then he realized that it was Daphne, her legs braced and her
arms folded over her breasts as she slept standing up. He sighed,
realizing that he should have guessed. This place was turning
into a damned menagerie.

He hurried on to the kitchen, leaving Daphne where she

stood. He preferred not to be bothered with the centaur just yet; one problem at a time, and the first problem was preparing something for breakfast appropriate for this diverse crowd. Were centaurs vegetarians? Did dragons eat unicorns? What would Rex and Marie say when they arrived later that afternoon? He turned to Clover.

"First things first," he said. "Do you need to go out?"

Clover only stood there, looking up at him with immense dark eyes, hopelessly enamored. No hope there. Allan went to open the back door, trusting that she would go out before anything untoward happened. Then he paused, and stepped out on the back deck for a closer look. Every unicorn left in the world must be gathered about the house. They began to draw closer when they saw him, stepping out from the trees and the dawn shadows, two hundred pairs of big eyes looking up at him with complete adoration.

He rolled his eyes and sighed. "Oh, enough!"

Just then Dalvenjah came up softly behind him and put her hands gently on his shoulders. "So it's hard to be a sex symbol."

"Now don't you start," he told her. "This is impossible. What am I going to do?"

"I have no idea what these silly beasts really want," Dalvenjah said. "But I suspect that we will have to send you through first tonight and let them follow you, or else they will never go."

Dalvenjah spent the day in conference with Daphne, discussing the native magic of this world and the days of dominance of the faerie folk. Allan found the lost history of his world interesting enough, but the faerie magic persisted in eluding him. That surprised him, considering how quickly he had been mastering the dragon magic from the start. Dalvenjah explained to him that the native magic of his world was diminished and elusive, while her presence made dragon magic readily available to him. That, to Allan, was the whole point. Dalvenjah would pack up her magic and take it home with her when she left. Anything he learned from Daphne was his to keep.

Allan had private plans of his own. If he could even begin to master the common magic, then he could begin teaching it to others. Jenny was a natural first choice. The more people who were using magic, the stronger it would become. He would not need the faerie folk to restore magic to this world, but he could use Dalvenjah's help. It annoyed him that she continued to politely ignore his hopes and plans. Daphne did her best, but her magic remained largely beyond his skill. As she pointed out, there simply was so little magic left for a beginner to work with.

"How long is it likely to take to send everyone through?" Allan asked as he cooked their dinner that evening. Cooking the right thing was more a problem than ever. Centaurs, as it turned out, were vegetarians, while dragons simply were not into veggies at all. As a compromise, he was preparing tacos. Beef and bean.

"That depends upon how organized they are," Dalvenjah said as she chopped onions. "It could take half an hour or half a night. Why do you ask?"

"I was wondering if we could possibly be done with this before Marie arrives."

"Oh." Dalvenjah sniffed loudly and wiped her eyes. "I do understand your wishes in this matter, but there is nothing I can do. Keeping them here will only do them even more harm, and I cannot allow that."

"I understand," Allan assured her, although he did not sound happy. "At best, I can see that we could only ask them to return after the real problem has been solved. I just wanted to know if there was some way to do that, if there was something I can do."

"Not you, no. All the mortal folk of this world would have to want magic. But I am not a part of that magic, and I cannot say." She paused again to wipe her eyes on the back of her hand. "Kallah deshay! Damned onions!"

Allan really did understand, but he felt no better for it. Something very sad was going to happen that night, something that he regretted deeply and wished desperately to be able to avoid. But this was hardly half as sad as when Dalvenjah would go through the Way Between the Worlds herself, never to return.

He expected that Rex and his sister would arrive before the time came, but they were later than usual that evening. Darkness fell early, and a centaur messenger came sooner than they had expected to say that the faerie folk had assembled. Daphne had told Dalvenjah earlier that the centaurs wished to confer with her, and the dragon had gone on ahead immediately after dinner with no word of what it was about. Allan hurried along with Daphne, while Vajerral winged back and forth through the trees. Allan's devoted unicorn trotted faithfully behind.

"Where are they going?" Allan asked. He loved to listen to Dalvenjah's tales of other worlds, of the fanciful and exciting worlds of the immortal folk and the mortal worlds that sounded comfortably like his own.

"We will be going to join the Exiles of this world who left in the days before the gates were lost to us," Daphne explained, her breath silver in the frosty air. "We kept a piece of the stone of the Great Gate, and the magic that lingers within it was enough to show Dalvenjah the way."

That was interesting to know. A thousand years and a half a world away, but they never went anywhere without their piece of the rock. "What sort of world is it?"

"A faerie world," Daphne explained. "Like Dalvenjah's world, but one for folk more like ourselves. Beyond that I cannot say. No one who went has ever come back."

By that time they were more than halfway from the cabin to the hilltop where the gate was to be opened, and already they could see the flicker of red and golden light through the trees. Allan had never thought that Dalvenjah would open the gate without him, but obviously she had. Allan paused and looked back, noticing the headlights of a car coming up the drive to the cabin, knowing that even more trouble was on its way. Then he turned and hurried with Daphne up the hill.

The faerie folk were just starting through when they arrived. The gate itself was as Dalvenjah had described it to him, a dark opening into nowhere that was rimmed with fire. The only difference was that this one was not up in the air but touching the ground, the line of its lower edge scorching the dry winter grass of the hilltop. The lower edge was bent, so that perhaps five or even six centaurs could have entered walking abreast, although the emigrants would have to leap over the line of fire as it hissed and spat, burning its way into the cold ground. A gentle but steady wind poured out of the opening, and its breath was warm and sweet with the scents of a woodland spring.

There were hundreds, even thousands of them, but they were so carefully organized that they would surely pass through quickly. A group of armed centaurs was passing through first, no doubt to assure that they were not walking blindly into trouble. The larger body of the various types of elfin folk followed next, then the ordered ranks of dwarves close behind. The main host of the centaurs, the second largest group of the folk, brought up the rear, all the way down the hill to the cold shores of the lake. They seemed almost to be forming a final fierce rear guard against a world that had long ago turned hostile to their kind.

"Where are the unicorns?" Allan asked.

"They are there, with the centaurs," Daphne explained, pointing down toward the lake. "I think that you must stay here, keeping your distance until they are through, or there may be trouble. They are dear creatures, but hopelessly devoted to the instincts of their strange magic."

"What is the real cause of their fascination with me? I would like to know that, before they go."

She winked at him flirtatiously and took a deep breath, expanding her breasts seductively. "That situation can be repaired, you realize."

"Don't prevaricate." He found her curiously transparent, something he had not expected from a faerie creature, and had been sidestepping her teasing advances all day.

Daphne looked rather uncomfortable. "They find strength and comfort for the magic of their own spirit in virgins, although it escapes me how such a situation came to be. Your being so strong in magic, and the rare combination of a mortal virgin who commands faerie magic so strongly, makes it infinitely worse."

"Oh, I see," Allan said thoughtfully, then glanced over his shoulder at the devoted unicorn standing behind him. "You'll probably have to take Clover here to the gate, when the time comes. She won't leave on her own."

"The others will take her through," Daphne said. "I will be coming back, you know, if only for a time. Dalvenjah will fight her battle and depart in a matter of days, and I must go before then."

She hurried off down the slope for a final word with her own people. Allan stood for a time, watching as the vanguard of the centaurs began to move into the Way Between the Worlds. Then the elfin folk gathered up themselves and their meager possessions and began to file through into the depth of darkness. He wondered what it was like to take this passage into other worlds, knowing that he would never have that chance. Then he turned, seeing that Marie and Rex were hurrying up the hill to join him, while Jenny waved her arms to attract Vajerral's attention.

They suddenly stopped short when they saw clearly what was standing beside him. Clover turned her head and took one long, appraising look at Marie, who seemed rather confused. Then she snorted disdainfully and turned away.

"The faerie folk of our world have appealed to Dalvenjah to open a Way for them to flee into a kinder world," Allan explained before they asked.

"You don't look happy about it," Rex observed.

"I'm not happy about it," he said. "Something older and nobler than ourselves is disappearing from our world forever at this very moment. But I guess that I have to agree to the necessity of it."

As they watched, all the many small kindreds of the elfin folk stepped through the ring of fire into the passage between the worlds, tall, strong centaurs standing ready to help lift them or their bundled possessions over the line of flame. Even as they passed, the winged folk, strange, pale beings of elusive grace, continued to swoop one by one through the upper portion of the gate, disappearing with luminous streaks of light into the thick darkness. Then the dwarves began to file stoutly into the darkness, and the clans of the faerie centaurs gathered close behind as they prepared for their own crossing. Marie and Rex drew back cautiously as one of the largest of the male centaur warriors appeared out of the shadows of the trees to collect Clover.

"Can't we do something to stop this?" Marie asked, growing more anxious with concern with each passing moment. Rex was obviously eager to do something himself, but he accepted Allan's judgment that this had to be.

They might have stood there watching half an hour or half the night, they were so completely enthralled with every lingering sight of the faerie folk. As diminished as they had become, the magic of their very nature was still sufficient to captivate the mortal heart and mind when they drew together in such numbers. It seemed that the magic of the world departed with them, pouring through the gate like a pale mist. Eventually there came a time when the last of the centaurs disappeared into the darkness, and Dalvenjah allowed the Way Between the Worlds to begin to close behind them.

Marie frowned with regret. "I feel like Peter Pan just flew through the window without me."

They returned to the cabin soon after, tired and very cold, surprised to find that it was nearly midnight. Jenny and Vajerral were done in, and it was all they could do to crawl into bed. But Dalvenjah was still out somewhere with Daphne, so Allan went to set up the cot in his room in order to surrender his bed to her. He trusted that Daphne would be able to prop herself up wherever she pleased. Rex and Marie did not yet know that they were going to have another little visitor, and Allan did not want to be the one to tell them.

Allan had the good fortune of being there to see his sister's face when Dalvenjah walked through the door with Daphne close behind. It was a no-win situation, either way she looked at it. On the one hand, there was a horse in the house—albeit a very small one—stomping around the carpet on small hooves. On the other hand, there was half a naked girl standing there in the middle of the room. A very young, shapely half of a naked girl, with small but pert breasts. That awoke her jealousy where Rex was concerned, and her motherly outrage for Allan to see such . . . such things.

Rex was almost panting. "Wow! Great gams!"

Marie afforded him a brief look of disgust, deciding that she had nothing to worry about as long as his sense of humor remained firmly in effect. She fumbled for words, trying hard and not very effectively to be subtle. "Ah, I thought you sent them all away."

"Plans have changed," Dalvenjah declared, obviously very pleased with herself and the state of all the worlds of faerie. "Not all of the centaurs have gone away. They say that as long as there are a few mortals like Allan and Jenny, with friends like the two of you, then perhaps it is just a little too soon to give up on this world altogether."

Marie looked like she had been hit by a stick. "I simply do not understand."

"The magic has been going out of our world for a long time," Allan explained quickly, so delighted that he could have jumped up and danced the polka with every dragon in existence. "I was trying to think of ways to keep it from disappearing altogether."

"Allan and Jenny are both wizards," Dalvenjah added, sitting back on her tail. "It will take much time and much work, but if enough mortals like them are willing to learn the magic of this world, and enough people like the two of you can accept it into your lives, then perhaps the magic of this world will become stronger and not disappear."

"The faerie folk are not willing to remain," Daphne warned. "Only some of the centaurs will stay for a time to do what we can, now that we have the promise from Dalvenjah that she will return every year and give our people some way to come and go. There are some mortals who have been our friends even to this day. Some of them can be taught magic, although teaching it has been against our laws until now. Others, including the two of you, can help us in many other ways. Most of all, you can find the most promising students for us. But for right now, there is something that you alone might do for us."

"Me?" Rex was plainly surprised. "What can I do?"

"We need a place in the wilderness where we can live in peace, unknown to all mortals but those who are our friends," she explained, with the courtesy to be embarrassed. "Ah, you might know that quite a lot of the property about here is for sale. Cheap."

Jenny was especially delighted to meet Daphne the next morning, and to learn that not all of the centaurs had departed. Daphne impressed her nearly as much as Dalvenjah had. Marie

learned just how impressed Jenny was when she stepped outside
to call the two little ones in for breakfast, and saw Jenny playing
with the dragonet down by the lake and wearing nothing but
a grin. Now Marie was not strictly opposed to nudity, except
that it was early in the morning and still quite a bit below
freezing in the shadows of the forest and not much warmer in
the sun. Jenny could come back later in the spring and expose
herself to nature all she wanted, for all Marie cared. But not
at this time of year.

She was not satisfied by Jenny's explanation that magic kept
her quite as warm as she needed to be. That might be fine for
dragons and centaurs, but what would people think?

She oversaw Jenny's dressing—the girl's clothes were predictably full of dust and dry pine needles—then returned to the
cabin and went straight to her room. She returned a few moments later, carrying a scrap of faded red cloth that she tossed
to the young centaur.

"What is this?" Daphne asked, mystified.

"A practical compromise," Marie explained.

Daphne held it out for a closer look, then put it on. It turned
out to be a rather old and thin red tee shirt that was several
sizes too large, especially about the belly, with the words
BABY ON BOARD stenciled in large black letters. The poor
centaur looked so ridiculous in it that even Dalvenjah was
finding it hard not to laugh.

"Oh, take it off!" Marie acquiesced at last. "I can live with
the consequences."

Dalvenjah and Daphne both disappeared immediately after
breakfast, going into the woods to consult with the other centaurs. The contingent turned out to be only half a dozen in all,
and not all that hard to be kept hidden. At the moment they
were trying to decide whether to retreat back to the far north,
where they had remained safely hidden for years, or to remain
where they were, near to their mortal students. In the event
they did stay, Rex and Marie were trying to figure out how to
get hold of the greatest amount of money to buy as much land
as possible to either side of the cabin. Daphne insisted that
their mortal friends in the north could help, selling the thousands of acres of land that had been purchased for them there
over the past century.

Jenny rushed into the house a couple of hours later, bouncing with excitement. But whatever was so important was momentarily forgotten in Marie's outrage. Their earlier argument about a proper state of dress had been settled on Jenny's part by a halfway compromise; the girl was stripped to the waist.

"Listen to me!" Jenny declared as Marie prepared to lead her by the hand to find her missing items of apparel. "Vajerral went down a hole, and it's too deep for her to come back up again."

"What do you mean, she went down a hole?" Marie asked impatiently.

"We found an old mine shaft or something," the girl explained. "We threw in a rock, and we heard it hit right away. We guessed that it must have been no more than twenty feet. I guess it just hit a ledge or something. Vajerral used her magic to let herself down, but it turned out to be a long way and she can't levitate herself that far back up. And she won't go on into the mine because she says that she smells something really mean."

"Where can we find Dalvenjah?" Rex asked.

"I have no idea," Allan admitted.

"We never could find the centaur camp," Jenny added. That had been the object of their morning expedition. "And Dalvenjah can't go down. The hole was barely large enough for Vajerral's wings. Dalvenjah is too long, even if she keeps her wings folded."

"I'll have to go down myself. We can't wait to try to find Dalvenjah," Allan decided. "There's no telling what might have followed the faerie folk into this area and crawled into those mines. We need the rope out of the storeroom, and the guns."

Jenny led the way, with only a minor diversion down to the lake to collect her shirt and jacket. Their expedition that morning had led them rather far afield. The mine shaft was on the far side of the road, climbing well into the steep, boulder-strewn slopes. The shaft itself was in a small, concealed clearing at the base of a large cliff of bare rock, and surrounded by large boulders and trees.

Jenny walked over to the opening of the narrow vertical shaft and looked down into the darkness. "Vajerral! Are you still there?"

"Dye, lyen kahlan," the dragonet called back from a very long way down.

"I'm going to let myself down," Allan said. "Rex, you lower the rope after me. I'll send Vajerral up first. Then I should be able to levitate myself back up to the top, if you can tie your end of the rope to a tree once or twice and let me rest."

"Do you want me to drop a gun down to you with the rope?" Rex asked.

"No, I won't use it," he answered. "I don't like the thought of shooting a gun in a narrow tunnel. No telling where a bullet might bounce. Fire-magic will be safer and more effective down there."

He sat on the edge of the shaft, then pushed himself off. He dropped down the center of the shaft freely for just a moment before he began to use levitation to break his fall, unsure just how far he had to go. He never dared to look up to check his progress, fearful of hitting one of the numerous rocky projections along the side. He was still dropping at a quick pace, and he had already descended much farther than he had anticipated.

At least his landing was not in darkness, for Vajerral had conjured a pale light at the bottom of the shaft. He landed lightly, and Vajerral emerged out of the shadows of the horizontal tunnel bisected by the shaft to leap into his arms. Holding the little dragon close, he leaned back to look straight up. The opening of the shaft was reduced to a tiny circle of blue sky far above.

"Rex!" he shouted. "I don't think the rope is long enough."

Rex was a long moment in answering. "There. I've let out all the rope."

Some trick of the tunnel allowed their voices to carry clearly and easily, as if the distance was only a fraction as far.

"I don't even see it," Allan called back. "Listen, we'll have to find our own way out. This seems to be quite a large mine, so we'll try to find another way out. Have Jenny use all her magic to try to find Dalvenjah."

"You be careful!"

Allan frowned. Something was down here; he could sense

it himself. He suspected that he was going to have a fight on
his hands before he found his way back out. But he had faith
in the dragon magic that Dalvenjah had taught him, and in
Vajerral's bravery.

"You keep the light for me," he told Vajerral as he set her
back on the ground. "I need to be ready to fight for us in an
instant."

"Dye, myn hverinn," Vajerral agreed.

"And keep your ears sharp."

Allan had never been in a mine before, and it really was not
at all like mines he had seen in movies. There were no tracks
for ore carts down the center, no heavy, dark timbers supporting
a crumbling ceiling. It was just a crude, roughly square hole
in the ground, like someone had just started out with a shovel
and got carried away with himself. It was random, completely
unplanned. And it was very confusing. There were branching
ways and sudden pits, some only a few yards long and some
disappearing into the dark. Allan had to trust that he was in
fact following the main way. It was hard to tell. Sometimes
the passage was large enough for a small car, at other times
so narrow that anything much larger than Dalvenjah could not
have pushed through.

At least they had started out in the general direction of the
lake, downslope. And since they did not seem to be going up
or down to any great extent, they would be nearly down to the
lake before they intersected the surface. Allan went slowly,
pausing often to give his magic and Vajerral's sharp ears a
chance to check for movement either behind or ahead. He knew
that something was in these tunnels, but he was unsure just
where it was and he was not certain that he would have to fight
it to get out. He did know that he would be coming back with
Dalvenjah when this was done, but he would prefer to get the
little dragon to safety before the battle began.

He stopped short, aware that several whatevers were approaching rather quickly from behind like animals on the scent.
Allan turned, waving Vajerral on ahead of him, then sent an
extra special fireball down the corridor behind. This fireball
almost had a mind of its own, for it negotiated the turn in the
tunnel about a hundred feet back and kept on going, scorching
the interior of the passage. It exploded upon reaching its in-

tended target. A muffled boom shook the length of the mine, followed by a flurry of howls and screams of rage.

"Keep going, little one," Allan said, urging Vajerral on ahead. "Do you have any idea what these things are?"

"Daesa hven mer alberse," she replied, looking back briefly over her shoulder.

"No one I know, either."

That narrow passage ended unexpectedly in a rather larger chamber, at least in relative terms. It probably was not very much larger than a two-car garage, but Vajerral's magical luminescence barely reached the dark corners of the chamber. They had only reached the far side when the enemy attacked from three different directions, the main party rushing down the tunnel behind while others leaped out from either side.

Allan was at first almost too startled to react. He had been expecting the same little draconic creatures that he and Dalvenjah had fought a few days earlier. These odd little monsters must have followed the faerie folk; he recognized them out of classical mythology, although he could not for the moment think of what they were called. There were none of them much over three feet high. Their legs were like the hind legs of goats, with cloven hooves and covered with thick, curly fur. They were manlike in the upper half, although their mad eyes and excessively sharp noses and chins gave them a decidedly demonic look. Small horns poked through their long, tangled hair.

Then Allan noticed that they bore small bows and arrows. They stopped as soon as they came within sight, chattering in what seemed more like animal sounds than language, glaring at their prey with looks that were cold and hungry, before they bent arrows to their bows. Allan did the only thing he could, hurtling a blast of flame right into the center of their number. He bent to snatch up Vajerral, then turned and ran as fast as he could.

The entrance to the mine and the welcoming light of day was visible as soon as he passed the very next bend in the tunnel. Vajerral was held backwards, her head and neck emerging from under his arm. She began to make a variety of small exclamations that he was presently too busy to catch. Then, to his considerable surprise, she took a deep breath and released a cloud of flame. Allan was waiting for the feel of one of those small arrows in his back at any moment, but he thought that he was too near the entrance to turn and fight now.

He was out into the sunlight an instant later, emerging from a steep, rocky hillside about half a mile along the shore from the cabin. He turned immediately to his right, dodging to one side of the entrance of the mine in case there were any arrows following along behind, hoping to disappear into the nearby bushes before he was seen.

He had only just made it to concealment when more than a dozen of the little goat-men rushed from the entrance of the mine and stood blinking in the bright light of day, their bows drawn. A moment later half a dozen bows snapped, and as many of the goat-men fell, transfixed by long arrows. The rest fled shrieking back into the mine as a dozen centaurs leaped out of the bushes to charge after them. To Allan's surprise, they pursued their enemy right into the mine.

Vajerral made some vague exclamation of excitement, and Allan belatedly remembered to let her down. In the next moment he was turned around by strong hands and kissed very soundly. He was very surprised to find that Dalvenjah had hold of him. He had never been kissed by a dragon before; she was very good at it. She let go of him before he really knew what was going on, and snatched up Vajerral to hug her close.

"You were very brave," Dalvenjah told him.

"Oh, I don't know," Allan fumbled. Now that it was over, he found to his surprise that he really was not very surprised or alarmed at all. It had been just a wizardly sort of thing to do. Right now, he was heartily embarrassed. He had never been kissed by a grateful dragon. "Just what is going on?"

"Jenny showed a lot of good sense," Dalvenjah explained, letting Vajerral down so that the little dragon could go in search of her young friend. "Following your instructions, she called upon all her magic and flew to find me. These creatures are old enemies of the centaurs."

Daphne came trotting out of the mine a moment later, returning an arrow to the quiver on her back. She hurried over to join them. "Satyrs. Allan did not leave that many alive, and the rest took a wrong turn in their panic and are trapped down a blind passage. But we'll have to go through the entire mine and make certain that we really do have them all.''

''Allan and I can help,'' Dalvenjah offered. ''What are those creatures?''

''Oh, just satyrs,'' she explained as she unstrung her bow. Allan remembered the name now. ''They always were mischievous, but they've declined considerably since they came across from the old world with us. Now they are little more than animals, and utterly evil. This last group must have followed us here, no doubt hoping to find a way out. Perhaps they even sensed Allan's magic and thought to make him open a gate for them.''

''I should tell Jenny and Vajerral to find Rex and Marie and say that nothing is wrong,'' Dalvenjah said, and retreated.

''You're really quite a bold fellow, for a mortal,'' Daphne said, as she slipped her bow over her shoulder. Then she surprised him completely by stepping up close and putting her strong arms around him, deliberately nestling her firm breasts against him. ''Are the unicorns still bothering you?''

''Ah, no,'' he stammered, confused. He had never been propositioned by a horse before. Maybe Danny Grehan could fix her up with Mr. Ed.

''They might come back,'' she told him seductively, and kissed him. It seemed to be his morning for being kissed by faeries, and in a variety of ways. He was too surprised and alarmed to protest. She pulled back slightly to look at him with an elusive smile. ''Keep it in mind. The faerie folk can be very different from any lover you have ever known.''

She turned and trotted away, swishing her hindquarters as only a centaur could, and poor Allan could not find his voice in time to explain that he had never known any lover and was unlikely to know the difference. He hated to waste the experience, and was not at all certain how it could be done. At the same time, something deep within him panted and said yes.

Allan felt the powerful hands of the dragon close on his shoulders a second time. Dalvenjah was glaring at the retreating centaur, then turned her head to afford him a very stern look. He could see that she was furious, and trying hard to contain it. ''Do not consider it, Allan.''

"I wasn't," he protested, then remembered that Dalvenjah was a telepath. "Not really."

"It is not a safe thing," she told him in quiet warning. "Most faerie folk are not like the Mindijaran. We are very careful and serious in our affairs, but they can be most irresponsible. Daphne will play games with you most willingly, but she expects that you understand the matter as she does. She will save her love for her own kind. If you love her, you will only be hurt."

"I could never love her," Allan insisted. "I have no intention of accepting her offer."

"See that you do not," Dalvenjah said, her voice conveying a harsh order. Then she looked at him, and forced herself to relax. "I've become extremely fond of you, Allan, perhaps more than I should be. I do not wish to see you hurt. Come, now. We will have to hurry before those brave centaurs come to any trouble in the tunnels."

• Part Six •

The Alliance

ALLAN'S STOCK HAD gone up considerably where Dalvenjah was concerned, as fond as she had been of him before the incident. She knew already that he would willingly face danger at her side, but she was very impressed that he had gone down into the mine alone and without hesitation to protect Vajerral. Dalvenjah was very much like Marie in one respect; their outwardly casual disregard of their respective children actually hid a tremendous love. The Mindijaran were fairly private and independent people, but they were also very expressive in their gratitude.

Allan was actually rather surprised at himself. Not that he had gone to Vajerral's rescue; there had been no choice in that. It surprised him that he had not been afraid; indeed, that it had never occurred to him that he should have been afraid. He was quietly pleased with himself, and very pleased that he had been able to make Dalvenjah so happy.

The problems that Daphne presented were much more difficult to solve. The centaur continued to flirt with him rather atrociously for the rest of the day, and then abruptly lost interest that evening. Allan was left to wonder if Dalvenjah and possibly

Marie as well had had a very long and serious talk with her. He resented Daphne for doing this to him, and he also somewhat resented that Dalvenjah had felt the need to interfere. Being flirted with was a new and fun game for him, but he could not allow matters to go beyond that. He certainly had not needed Dalvenjah's warning that he should never become involved with a faerie. He would miss her friendship enough when she was gone; he certainly did not need to have a centaur to break his heart.

The matter resolved itself further the next morning, when the centaurs announced that they were on their way north at that very moment to arrange to have their former lands sold so that they could buy more land here. They seemed to think that, between their own contribution and what Rex had to offer, they could very well buy the entire region around the lake. Marie was just as pleased to see them—as she phrased it—pack their bare breasts and go. As it happened, only two of the six remaining centaurs were female. Rex teased her that her real complaint was that the male centaurs did not look at all the way they did in drawings, being rather small and elfin in appearance. Of course, the centaurs would be back in several weeks, and they were already planning to have Jenny present herself for magic lessons every weekend and most of the summer.

Marie did have certain misgivings about leaving Jenny unsupervised in the care of centaurs all summer. She believed that she would have to resign herself to her child becoming a nudist.

"It seems to me that I'm going to have to take responsibility for this colony of centaurs," Rex observed when they gathered in the living room that night after dinner, while Allan toasted marshmallows in the fire. Jenny and Vajerral could be heard splashing in the bathtub. "I have to account for buying about half a million more in property than I myself have money for, and I can't just disappear into the woods if things turn bad."

"I'll do my best to cover your tracks, but I'm just not concerned," Marie assured him. That was her business. She had never engaged in creative bookkeeping, but she understood the theory quite well. Sometimes she had to wonder why she was risking a stiff prison term and the ruin of her career for the sake of centaurs, except that she really had no fear of discovery. She gave Allan a very stern look. "Don't you dare involve us in any more of your little schemes."

"What I can't figure out is how he talked Dalvenjah into this one," Rex remarked. "When we arrived Friday night, she was turning her ears away at the very mention of the idea."

"I can't figure it out myself," Allan admitted. "I had given up, when all of a sudden she announced that arrangements had been made."

"I changed my mind," Dalvenjah offered reluctantly. "I had my reasons. Good reasons."

"You don't do anything without reason," Marie observed, staring at the dragon. "We just can't figure out your motives."

"I had two good motives in this," she explained. "For one thing, I very much do not like to see the magic go completely out of a world. The centaurs brought up the idea, observing that they had ready-made mortal students. They do not expect that the faerie people can ever return, only that they might be able to teach mortals to use and preserve the magic. Mortal magic, not faerie magic. They seem to think that maybe you people are finally ready to listen. So all I really did was to agree to check on them at specified times, so that they will have some contact with their own people."

"What was the second reason?"

Dalvenjah made a face of disgust that only a dragon could have made. "You people have corrupted me beyond all hope. I have become inordinately fond of you all, and both Allan and Jenny are especially dear to my heart. Although it is impossible that I could ever return myself, I want to know if Allan will ever be able to find magic of his own."

"Why is that impossible?" Marie demanded.

Dalvenjah stared at her in amazement. "Gee, I never knew you cared."

Marie crossed her arms impatiently. "Is it at all possible to get a straight answer out of you?"

"I have duties and responsibilities," the dragon explained, considering her words carefully. "For all my delight in your company, and my special fondness for Marie not to stand with, this is unfortunately the least of my affairs. Others will have to attend to the centaurs for me. I doubt that I will ever see this world again, and I certainly cannot bring Vajerral back.''

''Oh. Notwithstanding.'' Marie's look of confusion became one of sudden enlightenment. ''I still haven't the slightest idea why.''

''It has much to do with magic. Dragon magic is different from all other magics, for it is powerful and quite dangerous. It disrupts all other magics, especially mortal magic, unless the mortal wizard is strong and well trained. If there is any hope of bringing the magic back into this world, then I and all my kind must stay away.''

Dalvenjah had other reasons, but those were entirely her own and she had no intention of sharing them. But the danger worked in both ways. It was too damaging to the dragon magic to associate too closely with mortals, to go into a world where there was so little magic, and to care for them too much. Mortal love cut too deeply into a dragon's spirit. She had learned to care for these people far more than she should, than she had ever intended. But then Allan had risked himself to save Vajerral, and that had won a depth of gratitude and caring from her that she could not refuse. She enjoyed their friendship, but it was becoming too close. For the sake of her magic, she needed the time and distance necessary to chase him back out of her heart.

Something occurred to Marie, and she glanced at the dragon sternly. ''What do you mean that others will be attending to the centaurs for you? What others? The Good Witch of the West?''

''No, no. By leaving a passage existent but sealed, certain friends of mine, elfin and mortal sorcerers, will be able to come through when they wish. The passage is already open, in fact, in the clearing by the centaur colony.''

''Mortal sorcerers?'' Marie asked, dropping her voice. ''That's all I need. Is the influence of mortal sorcerers likely to lead Jenny to want to go to their worlds and study magic with them? I know what hanging out with centaurs did to her in just one weekend.''

Then she paused, having noticed that tiny footprints were moving by themselves through the thick carpet. The shapes were indistinct, but much too long to have belonged to a dragonet's hind paws. "Jennifer Breivik! What are you up to now? Make yourself visible at once."

The trail of footprints turned around. "Mom! I've got no clothes on."

"That doesn't stop you from running around the countryside wearing only an air of exuberance." Marie knew quite well what Jenny had been doing during her daily expeditions with Vajerral. She could just imagine someone seeing Jenny running through the snow in her birthday suit, and take her away to sell to a freak show. Then Marie would have to pay a dollar to see her own daughter, Jenny the Wolf Girl.

The trail of footprints turned and started on again.

"Hurry up," Marie called after her. "We have to leave for home right away."

"Children that age love to find that they can get away with things they used to fear to consider," Dalvenjah observed softly, mildly amused. "Magic keeps her from being cold and from being seen. It will not harm her, although I must admit that mortals look best in clothes. I've seen Allan often enough to know that."

Marie ignored that remark. Dalvenjah often said things like that for her hearing, just to be annoying., And if it was true, she really had no wish to hear the particulars. She shrugged helplessly. "I don't care what she does when she's alone with the centaurs this summer."

Dalvenjah glanced at her with considerable confusion. So did Allan and Rex, for that matter. Vajerral came waddling out of the bathroom at that moment, bearing a large dry towel. Allan gathered her up and retreated to the one empty chair, where he began rubbing the dampness from her.

"I suspect that she will lose interest as soon as the novelty wears off," Rex offered. "Let her indulge herself while she has dragon magic to protect her, and she should be over it by then."

Marie frowned as she considered the merit in that. "We'll try it your way, although I'm not sure about the logic. Her magic helps protect her, but it also encourages her to think that she can get away with more. Dragon, is there some secret for raising magical children?"

"Nerves of steel," Dalvenjah answered without hesitation.

"We went through the attack of the illeshyan together, and I will always be grateful to Allan for bringing Vajerral alive from the mine. But I would do nothing to discourage her bravery and curiosity; my only comfort is in seeing her learn discretion."

"Will you marry again?" Marie asked suddenly.

Dalvenjah looked up at her. "Never was married. Dragons don't do that, or many other of the faerie folk. When you are immortal, you realize that love seldom lasts forever. You just enjoy what you have, never knowing when or if the time may come to part. Which is fair advice even for mortals. I could ask you the same question."

"Oh, I'll be getting married soon enough," Marie agreed without hesitation. "I am mortal, and I do trust that I've found a love that will outlive me. The time will eventually be right."

Rex had been looking very pleased with himself until she reached that part about "eventually," and then he deflated like a flat tire. Dalvenjah had a hard time trying not to laugh. Then she turned to Allan. "What about you? You have been alone too long. We have enjoyed our time together, and I know that you will dislike being alone more than ever because of it."

"That remains to be seen," Allan said quietly, on the very edge of a self-conscious blush. "Your friendship has been very special to me, and perhaps that's taught me how to accept even more. When the time comes, of course. I'll just have to let come what may."

He looked up in some surprise, as did the rest, when a suitcase came floating out of the kitchen and settled itself near the front door. Marie looked down at the impressions in the carpet. "Jenny, those footprints simply are not big enough for shoes."

"Ah, mom!"

Marie eventually let Jenny have her way, seeking a safe way to possibly break the girl of her newfound fascination with nudism. Jenny had to ride in the back of Rex's sports car, under the immense glass dome. And Marie was willing to bet that, as soon as they began to return to inhabited regions, the girl would begin to wonder what would happen if her magic failed and she was trapped for all the world to see. The nine-year-old mind occupied itself constantly with such fanciful what-ifs. Jenny would be practically desperate once they reached crowded city streets, with her clothes locked in the suitcase.

"After all this, I should be very glad to go home," Dalvenjah remarked as they turned back to the house after seeing the others off. "This is a very strange world, and prone to all manner of trouble."

"Any regrets?" Allan dared to ask.

"Oh, certainly!" the dragon insisted. "All this work, and I am not getting paid by anyone to do it."

The weather turned slightly warmer during the following week. The snow disappeared entirely from the area around the lake, which had previously been free of snow only in the small region that Dalvenjah held in premature springtime by her magic. That was not to say that spring had come, just that winter was beginning to get packed away in time to make way for spring. The days were clear and relatively warm, and the nights at least made an effort to remain above freezing.

Even so, the mood in the cabin that week was a subdued one. For this was the final week of Dalvenjah's recovery. After the others made their last visit that next weekend, she would then turn her attention to the problem of finding and defeating Vorgulremik. she was not exactly distressed by the prospects of a coming battle that might well be her last, mostly because she had no such intentions. She began to devote most of her time to either exercising or practicing for her fight, or else rehearsing in her mind her strategies and tactics. She searched her extensive memory for spells of potent magic and special tricks that sorcerers had employed in the past for the task of defeating evil dragons who were considerably larger than they.

But Allan was depressed when he realized that this was the final full week that he could count on Dalvenjah's company, and her magic. He hardly knew which he was going to miss more, although he really did know deep in his heart that he would give away all the magic at his command if his dragons could stay. That was an equitable trade, since all the magic he had could not tell him how to make them stay, not with both of them longing for home. And with Dalvenjah so busy with her own thoughts, he had entirely too much time to contemplate his own concerns.

He toyed with the idea of asking to go with them, but what would he do? There was certainly no need for principal cellists there. He doubted that he would have much of a future as a sorceress's mortal apprentice in a dragon's world, surrounded no doubt by more than enough immortal mages. He might eventually go to one of the other mortal worlds where magic was practiced and appreciated, but he would still have to leave his dragons, and what was the point in that? He realized that he might just as well stay where he was, practice his cello and try to make a solo career. That had been his goal before Dalvenjah had arrived, and he had been happy enough then. Or, if not happy, at least satisfied. He would just have to be satisfied with the lesser magic that the centaurs could teach him.

That long, miserable week did pass at last and the others returned, earlier than they had ever made that long run from the city, late Friday afternoon. In such company it was easy for them to forget that this would be the last time that they would all be together. Rex, Marie and Jenny would say their farewells Sunday night and return to the city, and the following night Dalvenjah meant to seek out Vorgulremik for their final confrontation. And after that . . . Allan did not know just what she meant to do, but he was certain that she meant to return to her own home as soon as possible. If she was at all able. She was not one to criticize, but he did have the distinct impression that she considered too much contact with mortal folk to be unhealthy for her child.

"It's a great place to visit, but I wouldn't want to come back," she said when he pressed her about it.

Since they usually arrived a little late for dinner, Rex had brought pizza with him when he had collected Marie and Jenny, and the three of them had indulged themselves for most of the last hour. Fortunately he had anticipated the need and had brought more than a dragon's share. One large pizza and half of another were still left, which was nearly enough to have that night and again the next day. Dalvenjah might eat more than a petite mortal girl of just over a hundred pounds, but not as much as one might expect a petite dragon of two hundred and fifty pounds to consume. Dalvenjah had never had anything quite like that particular culinary disaster before she had come to this world, and she hardly knew what to make of it. Vajerral certainly had no doubts. She wolfed down a very surprising portion, "wolf" being a particularly apt description of both the amount she ate and her table manners.

They had just finished dinner and were beginning the process of cleaning the dishes when there came a knock at the front door. It took a few moments for most of them to fully appreciate the special meaning of that otherwise commonplace sound. Dalvenjah understood immediately; she turned and headed out the door and down the hall, and Vajerral, responding to a telepathic command, was very close behind. Allan and Jenny went into action when they saw the dragons disappear, but Rex and Marie simply stood where they were for a moment longer.

"Oh, come on!" Allan said impatiently, turning. "We have to take care of this."

"What do we do?" Rex asked hesitantly, still confused.

"We hope that it's nothing more than the guys in white shirts that ride bicycles," Allan told him. "Or that, whoever it is, they have legitimate if unimportant business knocking on cabin doors in the middle of nowhere and will go away."

"Oh." Rex was hardly his usual quick wit. "But where did the dragons go in such a hurry?"

"To hide. I had told them, back in town, to always hide in the tub."

He paused at the front door for a moment to collect his thoughts, while Jenny moved in close beside him to provide a united front. This was not simple nosiness on her part; they were the two trained magicians, and they possessed a combined magic that could have stopped an armored battalion. If there was any serious trouble, they could hold the fort long enough for Dalvenjah to make an even more formidable appearance.

Allan opened the door on a pair of men who effectively exuded a sense of officialdom, a look that said "cop" even if they were dressed in ordinary if slightly worn business suits rather than uniforms. Or perhaps those rumpled suits were uniform enough. They were not the tall, bull-shouldered plain-clothes troops one often expected, but very ordinary, middle-aged types. They would have looked like bankers or accountants on the street of any city in the daytime. But there, at a cabin in the middle of the wilderness on a cold night, they could not have looked more out of place. Or official.

"Good evening, sir," the taller of the pair said, even sounding official. He brought out the standard little wallet and flipped it open to reveal a badge. "My name is Dave Wallick, and my partner is Don Borelli. . . ."

"Jesus, the cops!" Jenny exclaimed, and slammed the door. Wallick caught it before she had a chance to lock it, forcing his way in. Jenny punched him in the knee, but paused and looked up when she saw that it had no effect. She made a decision, took a quick step back and began the standard windup that both she and Allan used for pitching fireballs, but Allan stopped her.

"Just a moment," he warned.

"Yes, give us a chance," Wallick insisted somewhat apprehensively, as if he understood exactly what that gesture meant. "We're not here to hurt anybody. We need your help."

"I'll help you out the door, you pin-striped skunk!" Jenny declared threateningly. "You got a warrant?"

"We're here in an entirely unofficial capacity," Wallick insisted as he and Borelli continued to try to push their way gently but firmly into the house. "We are not going to do a thing to anyone."

The conversation was interrupted at that moment by the slamming of the bathroom door just inside the hallway, nearly opposite the room from the front door, and everyone glanced expectantly in that direction. What followed next was best described as sheer pandemonium, as unlikely a name as that was to describe something so violent. Pandas were normally gentle, quiet creatures; the cabin could have been packed full of the creatures and they still could not have made half the noise that now ensued. A very large party of rutting hyenas might have come close. Only a dozen elephants pretending to sing baroque opera could have surpassed it.

After what seemed like half an hour of pitched battle, Wallick arrived at last outside the bathroom door and knocked sharply. "Please, Miss. Won't you come out and talk to us?"

"I must insist that you leave my house immediately," Rex said sternly, amid a flood of other orders, insults and a wide variety of threats. Jenny would go into her windup about once every thirty seconds, so that her own side was hampered by trying to keep her from burning down the house and everyone with it.

"And there is no one in there, I tell you!" Marie practically shouted.

"Don't force us to break this door down," Wallick said, concentrating on his one-sided conversation with the dragon he thought to be inside.

"Don't you dare!" Marie roared, so that everyone shut their mouths abruptly to stare at her in surprise.

Marie did not wait to see if she was to be obeyed. When Wallick turned to her to say something, she doubled up her fist and popped him in the jaw with a fearsome punch that caused him to sit down suddenly and by no means either gently or voluntarily. She had in fact been aiming at his nose, so it was just as well for him that she had missed—if not by much. The silence that followed was so profound as to be startling after the previous uproar, and Rex looked as if he was entertaining thoughts of having to flee the country.

Marie did not even care; she stood over the fallen agent with her fists doubled, ready to dish out more. Wallick did his best to ignore her. He rubbed his jaw, moved his mouth experimentally to see if it was still hinged, and rose slowly.

"Now just stay quiet for a moment and listen to me," he said. "Mr. Borelli and myself are with the FBI. We have been working on a special case for the last six weeks, a very unusual case involving dragons of three different sizes. We've managed to get rid of the little ones. Now we have to do something about the big one, and we need your help for that. You help us, and we'll turn our backs and let all of you go your own way as you please. Getting rid of those evil beasts is far more important than harassing these two. We don't even want to arrest them. It's not against the law to be a dragon, and we can't think of a single law that you've broken."

"They are illegal aliens," Borelli offered quietly, but his partner gave him a very stern look.

"Look. This is the deal," Wallick continued. "We have two possibilities and three different answers. First, there are no dragons in your bathroom and we will go away looking like a pair of fools. Fine and dandy. Second, you do have a couple of dragons in there. Either they accept our proposition and come out voluntarily, or they keep their mouths shut and we will still go away and pretend like they never existed.''

"Oh, there are no dragons in there," Rex insisted.

"Then who is in there?" Borelli asked.

"Ah . . . no one," the good doctor declared, for the first time in his life at a loss for a good lie and unsure how to handle such an unexpected situation. "Ah . . . we accidentally locked the door from the outside years ago, and we never have been able to get in.''

"But the door just slammed, not a minute ago," Borelli pointed out.

"Ah . . . just the wind, I'm sure.''

"Oh, this is ridiculous!" Wallick declared. "Listen. I don't have to convince you people. The ones I want to talk to are your dragons. Why don't you just let me make my little speech, and then we'll see what happens?"

The others considered that for a moment, and shrugged as a group.

"All right," Wallick continued. "First, let me explain how we came to believe that there are dragons in this house. As I may have said, we found evidence of three different types of dragons the day after you arrived here—apparently from some other world. We thought at the time that you two had gone back to where you came from. That left us with one big one and lots of little ones. We started hunting down the little ones, and we spread the word with all the area police and the state troopers to keep an eye open for unusual creatures.

"That's how I began to suspect that you were still around, and that you had found help from someone local. You see, we heard a report from a couple of small-town cops who reluctantly admitted to seeing someone stick a creature with a long, golden tail into the back of a van. A van that eluded pursuit by flying away. A van that had a license belonging to a Dr. Rex Barker, who also happened to have a cabin only a few more miles down the same road.

"Then I began to suspect something. I thought to myself that you could not have one of the little dragon-things, since they are too mean to keep. It had to be one or both of the middle-sized dragons. It occurred to me that, since you seem to relate to them just fine, then they might not be evil but could possibly even be here to help. And that the only reason they have not helped so far is that one was injured and recovering. I even thought that we might work together.''

"How does he do it?" Borelli asked, affecting a thick British accent.

"Elementary, old boy," Wallick answered smugly, then turned back to the door. "What do you say, Miss?"

"What makes you think, even if we do have a dragon in the bathroom, that it is miss?" Allan inquired politely.

"Quite a few things here are amiss," Borelli remarked softly.

"Don!" Wallick said impatiently. "I am only guessing, of course."

"An educated guess, or just a hunch?"

"I really can't say," he explained, shrugging. "They are obviously the same type, so it seems very likely to me that the little one is the young and the big one is the mother who hatched it."

"Hatched?" Dalvenjah's muffled but plainly irritated voice drifted through the door.

"Your dragon?" Wallick asked, with some satisfaction.

"Ah . . . of course not!" Rex responded rather lamely. "Just . . . ghosts."

"Talking ghosts?" Wallick paused a moment to consider his next step, and leaned closer to the door. "This is getting us nowhere. Listen. I want for you to be able to trust us. Don and I are going to give our weapons to your friends. Then you can feel safe."

He removed his own pistol from the holster inside his jacket, but Borelli was plainly hesitant. "My gun?"

"Yes, your gun."

"But there's a dragon in there!"

Wallick sighed deeply and made an impatient gesture, and Borelli complied with visible reluctance. They held out their weapons and Jenny, self-appointed guardian of the guns, collected the pair. No one noticed in the confusion of the moment.

"Now, your friends have our guns," Wallick continued, speaking through the door. "Now perhaps you can feel safe enough to come out and talk to us. And I'll tell you what. If you come out but decide that you don't want to work with us, then we'll go away and pretend that we never saw you. All we want to know is if you can help us get rid of that big dragon.''

''Can't we just talk about it through the door?'' Borelli asked nervously.

''Not if she won't answer us,'' Wallick said sternly but softly. ''What's the matter with you? Surely you aren't afraid of these dragons. These people obviously get along with them just fine.''

Borelli only shrugged, and Wallick turned back to the door. ''You will excuse him, I'm sure. Some of his best friends were eaten by dragons. . . . Oh, what can they be doing in there? They can't get out, can they?''

''Can who?'' Allan inquired politely.

''Oh, you're no help,'' he snapped impatiently, and turned back to the door. ''Listen. Don and I are going to go outside for a while so that you can talk this over with your friends.''

''We are?''

''Never mind.''

They all turned expectantly toward the door at the sound of a muffled voice from within, but several long seconds of silence passed before any other sound was heard. And then it was the unmistakable sound of a certain bathroom contrivance being set into operation.

Wallick looked surprised. ''What can they be doing in there?''

Borelli shrugged. ''Since this isn't a drug raid, I'll hazard no guess.''

Just then the door was unlocked and opened slowly, and Dalvenjah poked her head cautiously outside for a look. Borelli and Wallick drew back involuntarily at the first sight of those silver horns emerging. But when she looked out at them with her large, jewel-green eyes, they could see immediately that there was no evil in her but something very wise and caring. Then Vajerral's head emerged in a like manner, only much lower in the crack of the door, glancing up in a blatantly beguiling manner at the two fine figures of authority.

''Great heavens, there were dragons in the bathroom!'' Borelli exclaimed softly. ''I hardly dared to believe it. In fact, I was sort of hoping that it wasn't true.''

Dragons do take a little getting used to, enough so for someone who had no prior acquaintance with their sort. And especially so for someone like the two agents, whose previous experience with dragons had been with evil ones. No one ever thought that this might work both ways, but Dalvenjah had much the same trouble getting used to them. Their appearance was quite bad enough, but their manner was often enough to put off a troll. She did begin to appreciate the fact that she had been blessed by fairly intelligent company so far. Wallick and Borelli were likeable enough, even amusing. But they were abysmally stupid by her own standards. The unfortunate fact remained that Allan, Jenny and even Marie, who were true geniuses by mortal standards, made only slightly above-average dragons in terms of intelligence.

At least the two had made no mention of the centaurs, for as much as they seemed to know about dragons. She was just glad that the centaurs were six days on their way north.

She began by telling her new associates all they wanted to know about dragons and where they all came from, emphasizing that there was not one but several dragon worlds. "Primarily there are four main worlds where dragons come from. Two worlds are of the evil dragons, one of land dragons and one of sky dragons. There is one world of great dragons who are good, and my own world. We are sky dragons and the smallest of any intelligent breed, although not the smallest of all dragons. But we are the only type with a civilization entirely of our own. Wyverns are no larger and some can be quite capable, but most are dull and unambitious. We are necessarily the weakest; our magic is not the strongest but it is by far the most versatile."

"And this Vorgulremik is an evil sky dragon?" Wallick assumed. He and his partner were seated on the sofa, the other mortals arranged in chairs facing them almost like a jury, and with Dalvenjah sitting back on her tail in the very middle of the room.

"He is Morilyekar, a steel dragon, to be precise," Dalvenjah said.

"And you believe that you can defeat him?"

"I can," she said without hesitation. "His magic is great, his strength is greater, but my magic is subtle and I am fast. And I am a Veridan, a trained warrior-sorcerer. I can defeat him, if I am careful. My magic and my intelligence make up for my other lacks.''

"Faster than a speeding bullet,'' Allan remarked.

"More powerful than a locomotive,'' Rex added.

"Smarter than the average bear,'' Marie put in.

Wallick glanced over at her. "You don't like Dalvenjah very well, do you?''

Marie shrugged indifferently. "She's pretty good, for a dragon. We do have quite a lot in common. We're both single parents, trying to make a professional career in spite of having children who are entirely too smart for their own good.''

"Well, let's not get off the track,'' Wallick said. "We have a very good idea where this Vorgulremik is. . . .''

"I have a very good idea where he is as well,'' Dalvenjah interrupted. "I will be able to find him easily enough as I get nearer to his lair. That really is not the help I need.''

"Then what help can we give you?''

She frowned as she considered that. "I never did mean to allow anyone else to become involved in this fight. For one thing, I alone can defeat him. I alone have the power to even harm him. If I fail, then your people must use the type of weapon that you probably would rather not use, if you understand. Nothing else will hurt him.''

"I understand,'' Wallick agreed guardedly.

"But there are two things that some of you can help me to do, when the time comes,'' she continued. "First, you can help me to bring him out of his lair. His own magic may be strongest in the air, but he knows very well that I have no magic that can harm him as long as he stays hidden within some deep hole. I must get him out into the open to fight him.''

"That doesn't sound quite so easy,'' Borelli remarked with some apprehension. "If we have no weapons we can use that can harm him . . .''

"You do not. But your big guns will surely be an annoyance to him, and sting quite a bit as well. Working together, we can easily get him out into the open where I can fight him. Even then . . . perhaps you will find a chance to distract him long enough for me to destroy him. We shall see.''

"Do we need reinforcements?'' Wallick asked.

Dalvenjah laid back her ears as she thought about that for a moment. "I do not want anyone else a part of this. I will take my chances with the two of you, but should others show up uninvited, then I will simply disappear and handle it myself. As for what else we might need . . . more guns?"

"We have those," the agent assured her. "That was our way of dealing with the little monsters. First we would track them down, set up an ambush somewhere in their path, then start shooting. There was no time to reload, not with the little beggars coming at us no matter what, so we always kept five loaded pump-action shotguns for each person. We can spare a few; they're out in the truck right now. But just who is we?"

"Allan is going under any circumstances," she said. "He alone has the ability to lend me magical aid, should I need it. Originally it was just to be my hunt and his."

"I have pretty good magic now!" Jenny declared.

"Yeah, kick ass!" Vajerral added.

Dalvenjah smiled tolerantly. "You might think you do, but you are not yet ready to fight a dragon like that."

"You can count the rest of us in, just the same," Marie announced with an indisputable air of finality, much to everyone's surprise. "We can at least hold a couple of those shotguns and serve as a rear guard."

Wallick looked at her inquiringly. "Is this what you really want?"

"Yes, I think so," she said, and shrugged as if she really could not figure that one out for herself. "Well, me and this dragon have come through too much together for me to miss seeing how things come out."

"That goes for me, too," Rex added soberly. "Besides, I have a dead dog to avenge."

"Very well, but when?"

"Tomorrow night," Dalvenjah said. "I had originally thought to wait until Monday night, but the time will be better just after moonrise tomorrow night. Then the moonlight will be more golden than it will be two nights later. That at least is to my advantage."

Wallick looked at her questioningly. "Why is that?"

"Gold enhances magic," she explained, and frowned. "I have no real gold; that would be a help. I am not sure that golden moonlight is any great help; it works for some, not for others. I hope that it will work for me.''

And so it was decided. Dalvenjah insisted that they retire early that night and get all the rest they could; they would have most of the next day to make all of their final preparations. The two agents had already discovered that, whether they liked it or not, they were now taking orders from a dragon. They were trained to think of themselves as leaders and protectors, on duty to guard others. They found it just a little disconcerting to be delegated to the roles of mere assistants, but Dalvenjah was very much in charge. If she could face Vorgulremik and win, then they were perfectly happy to let her. Or not perfectly happy, for their sense of social responsibility extended to her as well. Perhaps it was best to say that they had no choice. Sorceresses, it seemed, outranked all other public servants.

''Can she really do it?'' Wallick managed to ask Allan privately in the kitchen after all the others had wandered off to bed. The two agents were to be put up in anything they could find to pass as a bed, which left Allan at least to wonder if they were not about to take their eyes off Dalvenjah until the deed was done.

''I really don't know,'' he was forced to admit. ''Why ask me?''

''Because you know her better than anyone in the world . . . quite literally.''

He considered that. ''Actually, I believe that even she does not know for certain. But she means to do her best. What does it matter, from your point of view?''

''I don't want her to try unless she has a very good chance of surviving. Not just winning, but surviving. She tried once, and failed.''

''You know what the alternative is?'' Allan asked soberly. ''She knows her own magic, and she has a very good idea of what our weapons can do. It's not enough to kill Vorgulremik. He's immortal, like she is, only not to the same degree. If she dies—and if Vorgulremik doesn't consume her soul in the process—then she is reborn. Steel dragons are different. You see, you can't kill one of them no matter how much physical harm you do it. Destroy his body completely, but if his spirit survives he can generate a new physical form. She can blast his flesh and spirit with her magic, if she gets the chance. But for us to kill him once and for all . . . she's very sure that nothing short of atomic weapons will do that.''

"Yes, I see," Wallick agreed soberly, and paused only a brief moment to consider that. He shrugged. "Even so, I would not have her sacrifice herself. We have a fairly good idea of where this big dragon is; we could dump a small bomb on him with no more harm than a big, glowing hole in the middle of the wilderness.''

"But Dalvenjah wouldn't have that," Allan insisted. "The wilderness is her home. She would gladly give her life to prevent that. Unlike us, she has the reassurance of knowing exactly where she is going when—or if—she leaves this life.''

"And her little one?"

"I can take Vajerral back where she belongs."

"Yes, but . . .''

"Listen, I know every argument you could possibly think of, and quite a few more besides," Allan said. "One thing I've learned beyond any doubt where Dalvenjah is concerned: I don't have to like her plans, but I know that I am not going to be able to do a thing to stop her.''

Wallick smiled. "Maybe you can't, but I can. Borelli and I could leave right now, look in all the holes where this dragon could be hiding, and have a missile down it by dawn. I can arrange a nuclear strike. We were afraid that it might come to that all along, so the arrangements have been made.''

"Then why don't you?"

He shrugged, this time helplessly. "I guess that I don't want to see that happen any more than she does.''

Allan had no answer for that. He frowned, and sighed heavily. "And what happens when this is done? Are you really going to just let her go?''

Wallick smiled again, this time even more satisfied with his arrangements. "Of course. We can't afford to lie, not in our business. Our most effective weapon is our integrity, even if no one knows the truth but ourselves. Do you honestly believe that one of our prime objectives is to hunt down aliens for the purposes of dissection? Even if there is some standing order to that regard, which I doubt, then she's not an alien from outer space in the first place. There is nothing illegal about being a sorceress, a dragon or an unwed mother, even if she is all three. Why do you think we've decided not to report in until this is over?''

"I can't imagine."

"Simple. In our business, you sometimes have to be judge and jury in the split second of a decision. When you can only do one thing at a time, you have to decide what is most important. Can the average cop insist upon finishing writing out a ticket for speeding and watch a murderer get away? It's a matter of priority, and right now it's much more important to get rid of an evil dragon than to capture a harmless one. Of course, she is an illegal alien, as my short associate has pointed out, and she will be treated as such.''

"What?" Allan demanded with considerable alarm.

"Of course,'' Wallick insisted, grinning even more. "And the standard practice for dealing with illegal aliens is to show them back to their own border. Go get your rest, son. That golden lady is going to need all the help you have to give her tomorrow night.''

• Part Seven •

The Battle

"YOU'VE GOT TO be kidding!" Marie exclaimed after the small convoy of vehicles came to a stop on the hilltop that overlooked the ancient, deserted mansion—the place where Dalvenjah knew the steel dragon Vorgulremik to be. The place was half in ruins, big and dark in the fading twilight, evil and very threatening. Was it mere coincidence, or did evil creatures really care that much about having the proper professional atmosphere?

"He is in there?" Wallick asked, waiting as Dalvenjah stepped down out of the side door of the van. She was again wearing her harness with its useless sword and knives. She had to fight Vorgulremik not as a Veridan warrior, but as one dragon to another.

"He is," she said with indisputable certainty. "Can you not smell him, even from here?"

Wallick sniffed rather loudly. "Well, no. What does he smell like?"

"Metallic," she replied, almost absently. "Not unlike a copper coin that has been left on a stone to get hot in the sunlight."

"Oh, I see," Wallick said uncertainly, a sentiment that the others shared. Lacking a dragon's keen nose, they had certainly never thought that a penny had any smell at all, hot or cold.

"All the halls must be filled with his foul reek," Rex quoted, his lighter mood undaunted even in the face of dragonslaying.

Dalvenjah stepped out from between the van and Rex's car, which had barely made the ride up the back road, and stood for some time staring down into the valley at the ruined mansion. It was obviously very old and bigger than it looked to her eyes, since her kind built somewhat larger than human folk for practical reasons. The palace of Versailles was certainly older and just a bit larger, but so was her own little stone cabin in the mountains. Then again, a dragon's castle is her home; no dark, damp cave for this lady! But she could still appreciate just how large this place had to be, if a hundred feet of Morilyekar was hidden somewhere inside.

"What is this place?" she asked suddenly, breaking the long moment of brooding silence. She had seemed unaware that Wallick had come up quietly behind her, but she addressed him directly.

"This is the old Roundpick Mansion, humorously referred to as Charleston Estates by the locals," he answered, giving her a dull, textbook explanation. "Roundpick made his fortune—and quite a considerable amount—during the time we call the Roaring Twenties, half a century or so ago now. But he lost most of it during the hard times a decade later, and the mansion has been deserted since. No one else with the money to keep it has ever wanted to live in this area."

"He must have been the bootlegging king of the west," Rex remarked.

"No, actually he was the major supplier of flapper dresses and accessories west of the Mississippi."

"Flapper?" Dalvenjah repeated, looking over her shoulder at her wings.

"Not quite that."

"Any idea where he would be inside?" she asked.

Wallick only shook his head. "Not at all. I know the story about this place, but nothing more. What will you do now?"

"We have to get him out. I cannot fight him inside."

"Hmm, I was afraid of that," the agent said thoughtfully.

"I have done it before," she replied ambiguously. She turned to walk back to the vehicles. "He knows that he is safe as long as he remains in there, so he must be provoked. For once it is a shame that I am female."

"How is that?" Rex asked.

She looked up at him. "It is why the full name of my folk comes out as 'faerie dragon' in your language. We are not at all like other dragons. We are alike in form, but we also bear live young rather than hatch a brood, and we have breasts. We are as much faerie as we are dragon."

"I can appreciate that."

"Yes. Well, with other dragons, the males of their kind experience a type of battle rage, a mindless, purely instinctive response to any challenge from another male of any type. But females of most types are very level-headed, cold and calculating. They must be, to protect their broods, and so they hardly ever know a true battle rage. Faerie dragons are not like that. It takes a lot to provoke a male of our kind to a true battle rage. But the others tend to forget that. If I was a male, Vorgulremik would have already been out here in a rage to drive me away. But I am female, and he knows that he must be very cautious with me. We will have to provoke him in another way."

"By going in after him?" Wallick concluded.

"There is no other way," she said. "Allan and you two will come with me. The others will be given guns and left to protect the vehicles. That will give us a base to return to. Once Vorgulremik comes out, it will be entirely my fight."

"Our fight," Allan corrected her firmly.

She turned to look at him fondly. "That is kind, but . . ."

"But nothing," he interrupted her impatiently. "You know damned well that you can't handle this alone. You tried that once before, and he has gotten stronger while you are only just back to the point where you were. You know yourself that the only way you can do this is to have me there to distract him. If I can do that, you will have the chance you need."

"That is true," she admitted reluctantly, although she conceded quickly enough to show that she had already considered this . . . and had come to the same conclusion.

"I certainly have the power," he continued. "In fact, you

could help yourself even more if you will just give me my inner name and make a true sorcerer out of me, if only for this fight.''

"No," she said, almost sharply, and looked away. "Allan, that is just not possible."

"It is possible," he insisted. "According to you, that's exactly how it's done. I don't care if you leave for your own world right away and take all the magic with you. You need all the help I have to give, and I can give even more if I am a real sorcerer."

"No, it's not that," she insisted, almost pleading. But she still could not look at him. "Allan . . . I had not thought that it would come to this. It is not a matter of cannot or will not. Once you are a true sorcerer, you will remain that forever. But you cannot afford the price."

"What?" he demanded apprehensively. "Is there something I don't know?"

"You do know, if you consider it," she said. When he still looked confused, she sighed and continued. "Allan, I have told you that you are using my magic, dragon magic, not mortal magic. If I give you your inner name and shield it against your enemies, then it will be the inner name that would have been yours if you had been a faerie dragon and immortal. I know your true inner name, your mortal name, but that one I cannot give you. And if I give you this name, then you will become what it describes, dragon and immortal. Once done, it cannot be undone, for your name will be shielded even against me. Dragon you would become, forever and ever."

"But . . ." Allan hesitated, stunned by this discovery. "But you never told me."

"I never meant to keep anything from you," she insisted almost desperately, turning away in shame. "I knew that you had strong magic, but I never knew that it was in you to learn so quickly. I never thought that it would go this far, but that I would be gone before you had learned very much at all."

"But what can I do?" he asked himself aloud.

"What indeed can you do?" she asked in turn. "Dragons really are not built to play the cello, and I have seen that your world has no real use for a sorcerer. You may help me—or not—as you wish. But it will have to be with the powers you already have.''

Allan did not reply but stood with his head down, lost within his own thoughts. Dalvenjah hazarded one quick glance at him over her shoulder, but then she turned and walked away, back toward the hilltop. Perhaps she was fearful of his silent accusations. Perhaps she was even afraid that he wanted magic at any price. She glanced once at Marie, wondering why that devil's advocate had remained silent, but Marie did not seem to have an argument at hand. She might have been pleased to hear that her brother could not keep his magic, but instead she looked sad and thoughtful, as if she regretted for the both of them.

''Well, let's get on with this,'' Wallick said, breaking the silence, as he walked around to the back of the late sheriff's truck. ''Everyone line up and take a gun. And don't be afraid to use it, either. You'll also need to take all the ammunition you can carry, although these monsters do hold quite a few shells.''

''How does this work?'' Marie asked. She was the first in line, and she plainly had her doubts about the weapon now in her hands.

''I can show you,'' Rex said, taking his own.

''It's really very simple,'' Wallick insisted, glancing in their direction as he unconsciously handed a third to Jenny. He paused and did a startled double-take at the skinny little girl holding a shotgun that was nearly as long as she was tall. ''Hey, just a minute . . . !''

''Oh, let her have it,'' Marie told him. ''As strange as this may seem, I would rather that she had it. In this place, it seems the lesser of two evils. Besides, she might actually know what she's doing.''

''I always know what I'm doing,'' Jenny remarked tartly. ''This is a long-range weapon. If anything comes too close, I'd rather trust to my own magic.''

''If anything comes that close, you will have already been within range of its flame,'' Dalvenjah pointed out. ''Trust the gun. Fly if you can do so, but don't let yourself be caught in mid-air. Remember that he can fly much faster than you can. Otherwise, look for the nearest trees and run like hell.''

Wallick walked over to where Allan stood by himself, brooding on his own thoughts. "Don't you want a gun?"

Allan shook his head without hesitation. "No, my magic is stronger and I need to have my hands free to pitch fireballs."

"Fireballs?" Borelli asked, breaking his own apprehensive silence for the first time in several minutes. "Say, Dave! Isn't that what the girls used to call you?"

Wallick turned to glare at him menacingly. "You say that again and we'll use you for bait!"

Vajerral was left, with great reluctance on her own part, with those who would remain to hold the fort, such as it was. Following Dalvenjah's lead, the others made their way boldly down the steep hillside toward the mansion. She was at first worried that Allan was in no frame of mind to have any part in this fight, that he was too preoccupied with his own dismay at learning that he could never be a full sorcerer.

But he seemed to put that aside as they made their way toward the deteriorating mansion, concentrating entirely on the task at hand. She could sense his alertness, his deliberate concentration on the magic he knew and on tensing his powers for battle. And she approved of him all the more. She could never hope for a better apprentice. The shame was that he would always be the apprentice, never the master. He had always told her that the memories made it all worthwhile. She hoped that he had been telling the complete truth, for memories would be all he would have left when this night was through.

There was no question about knocking. The doors were not only open but ripped from their hinges and thrown aside. Now even Dalvenjah wondered at Vorgulremik's decision to make his den in a human home, even one this big. He had squeezed in like an eagle locked inside a parakeet's cage, so tight a fit through the wide double doors that the razor-sharp spines along the edges of his wings had cut deep grooves in the doorframe. There was similar damage to the very center of the top frame.

"The old bastard hit his head," Dalvenjah remarked when she saw that.

She alone seemed unimpressed. Allan began to understand that his idea of dragons had been blunted by his awareness of what a fine, intelligent lady he knew Dalvenjah to be, and to appreciate that some types really were the big, mean monsters that he had been brought up to believe in. Or not to believe in, as the case may be.

They stepped inside cautiously, trying to remain as silent as possible. Deserted mansion though this place may appear on the outside, the necessary props, scattered antiques wrapped in dusty sheets, were missing. If such things had indeed been left when the place was abandoned, which really was not very likely, then they had long since been picked over down to the smallest stick of furnishing. Even the lighting fixtures were gone, and there were gaping holes where such items as what might have been a large marble fireplace had been removed. The place was not just deserted, but scavenged.

"Cold," Allan remarked. "Can these steel dragons handle the cold?"

"They have to sleep a lot, to save their energy," Dalvenjah explained. "Then they will burn that energy quickly to keep themselves warm."

Borelli stood for a moment just inside the doorway, blowing out big, warm breaths that he delighted in seeing turn to white mist. "Hey, look! I'm a dragon!"

"As hard as he is to kill, Vorgulremik is still very much alive in the same terms both you and I know," Dalvenjah continued, ignoring him. Wallick was looking as if he contemplated taking a bat to his partner. "He can still feel hunger and cold—which he no doubt does. And he can certainly feel pain. Enough to encourage him into a fine rage."

"So how do we invite him outside for a fight without getting him thoroughly pissed off?" Wallick asked as he looked around.

"That's just the trick," Dalvenjah said. "We want him enraged, or he will not come outside and fight . . . and make the other mistakes that he must make if I am to defeat him. And we also have to survive his rage long enough to get ourselves outside."

"Ah, you did say that before," Wallick agreed. "Any ideas?"

"We play that as it comes," she said, checking her harness to insure that her weapons were secure. "The first thing is to find out just where he is hiding. We will start here. I will go to the right and look in that direction. Allan will go to the left.

You two stay right here and make sure that we have a way open.''

Borelli looked rather dismayed at that order. The "stay here" suited him just fine, but he had his doubts about how they could keep the way open if a steel dragon wanted to go through this door. Wallick was smart enough to realize that their major function in standing rear guard was to stay out of the way. He was also impressed by what a matched pair she and Allan had become, each one sneaking off in opposite directions to perform the unenviable task of finding a very big and nasty monster. Dalvenjah also seemed to have the same high opinion of her protégé. She spelled everything out in no uncertain terms to the two agents, but she had not bothered to remind Allan that, if he should find Vorgulremik, he should inform her immediately and not try to enrage the monster himself.

The two magicians came sneaking back at almost the same moment. Dalvenjah had a very interesting approach to sneaking, dropping down to all fours even though she plainly detested walking on her bare hands and feet through the deep, soft dust that carpeted the floor. But Dalvenjah was almost too sneaky for her own good. Borelli looked up suddenly and saw the shadow of a vast dragon's head against the far wall. He considered the matter only briefly; all he knew was that Dalvenjah had not gone in that direction, and the shadow suggested a head far too large to be her own. He brought up his powerful shotgun and fired, the blast echoing through the entire mansion.

Fortunately faerie dragons had tremendously swift reflexes, so that she was able to duck her head out of the way as the tight spread of pellets blasted a gaping hole in the wall just inches above her head. She looked up, startled, at the hole that went completely through the plaster wall into the next room, opening a round port nearly large enough for her to poke her head through. Then she turned swiftly to glare accusingly at the erring agent, her ears laid back.

"Asshole!" She declared. Borelli only shrugged helplessly.

Allan came around the corner at that moment to see what was going on. If Vorgulremik had been unaware of his visitors before, there was no question about it now. He shook his head to indicate that he had found nothing. Their search of the ground floor had proven itself fruitless, which left a basement and an entire upstairs yet to search. The basement, deep and damp, seemed to be the most likely place for a dragon; she sent Allan in that direction. She already knew that Vorgulremik was in a large room upstairs, having become aware of him when she had passed directly beneath him earlier.

A vast banistered staircase led the way upstairs, immediately across the entrance room from the front door. It was very wide, more than large enough to accommodate the bulk of a steel dragon, but in such an advanced state of decay that it could have hardly supported his weight. Even Dalvenjah had to take the steps cautiously, pausing a moment halfway up to peer down into the darkness through a break in the boards, revealed where someone had pulled up the carpet. Wallick and Borelli stood at the ruined doorway and watched with equal parts of awe and amazement as she turned unhesitatingly to her right at the top of the steps and disappeared into the darkness.

At least the ancient halls were not dark to her eyes, only dim and deeply shadowed. She paused a moment in the vacant passage, sensing the rising of the moon at that very moment far to the west. This world had such a cold, distant moon compared to the one she knew, as if it was withering away through want of magic. But it did have some magic to spare, for she sensed a new strength and excitement, small though it was, as golden moonlight flooded over the cold, wooded mountains. She felt curiously at home, and she knew that to be to her advantage. Vorgulremik was out of his element, an exile in an unfamiliar land.

On the other hand, this was also a mortal land. Mortals were no danger to him; he could even strengthen himself upon their souls. Mortal souls only weakened her own by their contact, chipping away at her spirit to expose her innermost self, wounded and vulnerable. She was the one in danger by remaining here. She had to fight him now—and win—for if she stayed here a day longer she might lose herself and never be able to leave.

And Vorgulremik knew her danger, surely. Why else would he have remained in this place, except for the hope that she would grow too weak to fight him, the greatest of all Morilyekarin? She was the only faerie dragon alive who possessed the strength and cunning to destroy him. If he could rid himself of her, then he could likely make himself free in any world he chose. For if she could not defeat him here and now, only the greatest sorcerers of the silver dragons might have the power to destroy him.

That went both ways, of course. Vorgulremik alone among the Morilyekarin possessed the strength and cunning to destroy her. What he lacked was a good, adept apprentice to support him in the coming fight.

Well, she thought, this was not solving the problem. She resumed her stealthy advance down the hall, where deep scorings in the oak flooring spoke of his coming and going. A wide bank of windows at the very top of the stairs had been ripped out, providing Vorgulremik a way to come and go without having to trust to the decayed stairs or the too-small door frame. She was almost surprised that Vorgulremik had not come out to meet her, knowing as he must that their final battle was inevitable. That meant only one thing. He knew her new weakness and he planned to use it against her. She began bracing herself for that attack upon her innermost self.

She found him in a large, secluded room well along the north wing of the upper floor of the mansion. It was a place that he had adapted to his own needs, blocking out the windows of the outer wall with a barrier of stones that he had laboriously transported inside. Immense fireplaces at either end burned brightly with magical flames, warming this den that he had made for himself. He had even begun a new hoard of gold, a source of pleasure and reassurance in this strange world as well as a reserve of strength for his own magic, even though it barely made him a pitiful handful.

Vorgulremik himself lay stretched at his ease in the center of the room, reposed in a bed of pine boughs and old mattresses that he had gathered for his leisure. His eyes glittered silver in the magical firelight as he regarded her almost with detached interest, and her own jeweled eyes gleamed bright green in response. The golden light flickered with a metallic sheen from his knife-edged scales and spines, just as it did from her own golden scales and silver horns. And yet, Dalvenjah noted with some hope, he was not yet so large as he might have been, hardly any larger than the last time they had fought, and so hardly any stronger. Too much of his own power had been given into securing his den and making it into a fortress.

"Greetings, Dalvenjah Foxfire," he said with casual amusement, his deep, rumbling voice speaking in her own language.

"Greetings, Vorgulremik Bluesmoke," she responded, dipping her head in a half-formal gesture. "We meet again."

"One last time," he agreed. "I should almost ask why you are here."

"Did you give me any choice?"

Vorgulremik shifted himself to a more alert position. "Perhaps none, considering who and what we are. But I still wonder, especially now. You have already lost once. Now I am stronger than I was once, and you are less. Do you hardly dare to call yourself a dragon? You are a tiny one even by the standards of your own stunted kind."

"My strength is measured by what I can do, not by my size," she told him.

"So?" he asked. "Perhaps I did not mean it quite like that. You are less than you once were. I asked if you still dare to call yourself a dragon. Once I would not have questioned that, but you have allowed yourself to diminish until you are hardly more than the mortals that have surrounded you these past weeks. You needed their help? You would have done better for yourself on your own. You have allowed yourself to care for them, to understand them, and now you have grown small and weak, as they are."

"I am all that I ever was," Dalvenjah declared proudly.

"Then prove it!" Vorgulremik roared, and he spoke the words of command.

Dalvenjah had seen this test coming, and she had prepared herself as best she could. Even so, it was almost too much for her. Vorgulremik was right, of course, although she had not been about to admit it. Her close association with mortals these past few weeks, her concern for them and her growing fondness for them, had resulted in a weakness within herself, a flaw in the hidden armor that guarded her inner name. Vorgulremik sought to exploit that weakness, to tear away that armor and redefine her inner name in purely mortal terms. She would have remained a sorceress, but mortal and human and much less than what she had always been.

Dalvenjah struggled under that assault, fighting as she had never fought before. And she very nearly lost. It was dangerous for immortal folk to have much dealings with mortals. Mortality was an insidious disease that could eat away subtly but completely at everything that set the faerie folk apart. Her magic was no less for what had been happening, but the defenses that guarded her inner name were weakened to the point that Vorgulremik nearly broke her inner shell and stripped it away.

Exerting a supreme effort, she tightened her defenses under his attack and fought back with a powerful blast of her own magic. The breaking of his own spell combined with her assault nearly stunned the larger dragon, hurtling him out of his bed and throwing him violently against the stone wall that cracked and tumbled around him. Now there was no question about whether or not he was properly enraged. He pulled himself out of the pile of rubble and looked about with murderous intent. But Dalvenjah was already gone.

Although she was young, she still knew which side was up. One did not have to be a genius to know that when you have something that big and that mean and that mad coming up close behind you, you need to run like hell. Operating under such solid logic, she did just that. The unfortunate part was that Wallick and Borelli, attracted by the sounds of the dragons' struggle, were making their way cautiously up the stairs. They paused at the sound of something coming in their direction in a hurry and raised their guns. It was fair to say that they could not have been more surprised when Dalvenjah whipped around the corner and hurtled down the stairs directly toward them, moving so fast that they could hardly tell whether she was flying or still on the ground. And since she was moving so fast, there was also no real question about whether or not she would be able to stop.

The three of them hit in an explosion of bodies. The only thing that saved the two agents from serious injury was the fact that Dalvenjah did her best to avoid hurting them. She dived headfirst between their legs, knocking them off balance so that they came down on top of her. That did her no harm, but it was considerably more than the rotting boards could take, and the stairs parted to dump all three into some dark hole beneath, all to the sound of two guns going off one after the other.

That double crack at least had the effect of slowing Vorgulremik down for the moment. He paused at the top of the stairs for a careful look around the room before he began to descend slowly. At that moment a small door on the right side of the stairs opened soundlessly and the two agents hurried off to find themselves a good place to hide, never once looking back at the vast dragon who, by some stroke of fortune, was looking in the other direction at that moment.

Then Vorgulremik found the hole in the stairs and poked his great, armored head inside for a look. All that earned him was a powerful crack across the nose from Dalvenjah's tail. He reared back in pain and alarm, and his smaller adversary seized the opportunity to leap straight up out of the hole and make a wild dash out the front door. Vorgulremik sent a blast of flame after her, but it was already too late. Faerie dragons could put a racehorse to shame when it came to speed, especially in an emergency, and she threw herself into the air the moment she was out the door. By this time the steel dragon was in a fine rage, stamping and thrashing his powerful tail in his fury.

That was exactly the wrong thing to do. The stairs could stand no more, and now the entire upper half of the structure surrendered under his considerable weight. He disappeared into the darkness with a startled noise and a small jet of flame, landing with a tremendous crash inside the stairwell. That floor gave way as well, and a moment later he found himself in the basement. There followed several seconds of thrashing and thumping, and then Allan himself shot out of the hole inches ahead of another blast of flames. Lacking wings to catch on the door frame, he flew straight out the front door.

A long moment of dead silence passed before Vorgulremik began the process of pulling himself laboriously out of the pit. He emerged headfirst, lifting himself up almost the full length of his great neck, periscope fashion, for a careful look around before he dared to drag the rest of his bulk out of the hole. There was certainly no loitering here, for he had inadvertently set fire to the place.

Allan joined Dalvenjah with the others at the top of the hill only a few moments later. They watched in silence as Vorgulremik pulled his massive form through the door of the mansion, then spread his immense wings and lifted himself straight up until he was perched like some vast raven atop the roof. He and Dalvenjah stood for several long seconds, simply staring balefully at one another. Already they could see flickering yellow light through the broken windows of the old house as its dry wooden structure was consumed by greedy flames. As they watched, Wallick and Borelli emerged at last from around the corner of the building but remained where they were, only too aware that Vorgulremik would see them in an instant if they stepped out of their present concealment.

"Now what?" Allan asked.

"Now we play chase, to see how the game is going to turn, and who is the stronger," she said, and turned to him abruptly. "If I fail, I will see that you get my magic before he does. Then you must save yourself at all costs. You cannot fight him, but you can get the others to safety. And you will then be the only one who can open a Way Between the Worlds and take Vajerral home. Do not fail me in that. You must take Vajerral home."

"I'll remember," he promised her. "But you watch out for yourself. You can beat him."

"That is what I intend to prove," she said, smiling. "Alyesh thyarnan, de'lyr ledhar."

"Ahl shayn'vhas, de'lyr ledhar," he told her in turn. "I'll do what I can to help."

"What can you do?" Marie asked.

"I can certainly be a distraction."

"Just be sure that you distract him, not me," Dalvenjah said just before she leaped back into the air with powerful thrusts of her wings.

Vorgulremik stood upright when he saw her take to the sky. He really was not built for that stance, for his arms and legs were proportionally shorter than her own. He lifted his head high on his powerful neck and roared a challenge that echoed back and forth through the hills like a blast of thunder, and Dalvenjah answered him with her own soprano bark. The challenge offered and accepted, he thrust himself off the top of the burning mansion with a kick that was powerful enough to cause a portion of the roof to collapse beneath his legs.

They circled each other warily for two full turns before the faerie dragon suddenly darted in. Then she broke and dropped low for a quick dash into the forest, a blatant invitation to a chase that he accepted eagerly. The object of the game remained simple at this point, each attempting to make the other act in desperation, without caution or careful planning, and thereby make a fatal mistake.

At least Dalvenjah had three major advantages relating to her size. She could fly beneath the canopy of the forest, so long as she was careful about it. Because she had proportionally more powerful lift-magic in relation to her small size, she was much faster than any true dragon and far more maneuverable. And she could flame or toss fireballs just as far, but at the same distance she made a much smaller target. She ducked under the cover of the forest at a speed that Vorgulremik found difficult to equal, forcing him to do his best to track her from above.

That was his first mistake. She deliberately allowed him to move ahead, then thrust herself upward with a tremendous push from her lift-magic and, cautious of his swordlike spines, leaped onto the middle of his back. Holding on as best she could, she played a sustained flame up and down along his back and neck. She could do him little harm this way, since his scales were almost as proof against fire as her own thick, golden scales, but it did hurt. He jerked and bucked, and Dalvenjah was forced to let go after a few seconds or risk harm on his spines.

Dalvenjah separated and dived away, having to dodge fireballs launched by her irate adversary. Even more than he was annoyed by the brief pain, he was enraged—and very disturbed—that she had gotten the best of him so quickly and easily. She seemed to be trying to repeat the trick, returning to the protection of the forest, but this time he did not hesitate to follow her in. He was so intent upon preventing her from repeating her first ploy that he failed to consider the consequences. She angled sharply to flash between two large trees, and Vorgulremik had to stop in a hurry to avoid breaking his wings against their thick trunks.

Fuming at being fooled again, Vorgulremik made his way to the nearest clearing and returned to the open air . . . and Dalvenjah was on him yet again. She took him firmly around the neck and held on tight, using the large, thick plates of her belly to protect her from the shorter spines just behind his head as she directed a blast of flames into his face. Even this did him no real harm, so long as he kept his eyes tightly closed. But while he was blinded, she was using the full thrust of her lift-magic to force him down. She abandoned her reluctant mount at the very last moment before he crashed headlong into the trees. He tried to recover and failed, and he was finally forced to fold his wings straight up above his head to prevent breaking them against the thicker branches as he dropped down into the foliage.

He should have been thoroughly enraged by the time he pulled himself out of the wreckage of a large tree. But Dalvenjah had done her part too well; he was now beyond rage, and beginning to feel a little desperate. An offensive battle had done him no good, for he was taking all the lumps. Now he needed to go on the defensive, at least until he could take control of this battle away from the faerie dragon.

Stepping out into a large clearing, he lifted his head high and spoke words of command. He summoned clouds out of the sky itself, and they came to his call. Not a thick, dark sheet of clouds to blanket out the moon, for he was as dependent upon its golden glow as his tiny adversary was. Instead he called forth smaller banks of clouds, roiling, billowy forms that he could use for dodging and evading. But for the moment Dalvenjah would not allow him to retreat to the cover it offered, keeping him pinned to the ground with her flames. They exchanged fireballs, but she had the advantage of being small and swift in flight while he was vast and slow on the ground. He was struck time and again, twice alone full in the face, barely saving his vulnerable eyes by blinking. Again he knew that he could not win this way, and he spoke new words of command to the sky.

Great spears of lightning suddenly leaped down from the sky, forcing the faerie dragon to break off her attack and run. Then one powerful bolt caught her squarely in the back, doing her no lasting harm but stunning her just long enough to hurtle her from the sky. She saved herself only at the last moment, turning her fall into a swift glide that arched back up toward the sky. But then she was forced to evade yet again as Vorgulremik was upon her, having won his way into the air during her fall. Now she was forced to seek safety of the clouds that he had summoned for his own protection. She was still weak and dizzy from the lightning strike and she could not yet put together an effective counterthrust.

And Vorgulremik pursued her relentlessly, finally able to turn this fight to his own favor. She attempted to hide in the clouds, but none were large enough to allow her to lose her adversary. The two dragons had magic enough to sense each other's movements, but that was less effective than a bat's sonar. And all dragons depended upon magical enhancement to allow them to see well enough even in full darkness. The fight had become a chase, and Dalvenjah did not yet know how to end it.

Vorgulremik was moving in toward his prey yet again when another fireball struck him in the face, this time stinging his eyes before he was able to blink them shut. He brought himself to a hover, his eyes tightly closed as he waited for his vision to clear. But he did not need to see to recognize his latest mistake. He had not considered Dalvenjah's mortal apprentice to be any manner of a threat, nor even a possible contestant in this battle. Knowing that she needed his help, Allan had flown up to the level of the clouds and had simply waited until the steel dragon came within range of his fireballs. As he waited, Vorgulremik was struck again and again. Then, seeing no hope for it, he simply closed his vast wings and dropped straight down.

This was the chance that Dalvenjah had been waiting for. She turned and shot straight toward him, gathering speed rapidly before her entire form began to glow and then transformed into a spear of flame. This was her ultimate weapon of magic, the only thing she had that was capable of destroying him. But he saw her coming and brought himself out of his fall quickly, twisting around in an unsteady hover so that he could defend himself with fireballs. Realizing that she could never come in for a strike as long as he was ready for her, she broke off her attack and allowed her flames to withdraw, returning to her dragon form.

Encouraged, Vorgulremik resumed the chase. This time Dalvenjah had a very good head start on him, so that she returned to the clouds well ahead of him. Only then did she look back, and she saw to her alarm that he had turned and was streaking away in almost the opposite direction. Too late she realized his ploy, to her horror. His game had been spoiled by Allan once already. He knew that he could not afford to have his attention divided, and so he was going back to finish off her friends so that he would then be able to concentrate on her alone. Summoning all of her strength and speed, she shot after him, but she realized all the same that she was too late.

Fortunately Allan saw him coming in plenty of time, and guessed what he must be plotting. He dropped back to the ground as quickly as he could, directing the others to gather in the small space enclosed by their three vehicles. He turned just in time to say the proper words of command, accompanied by some helpful gestures, and a transparent shield of force snapped up around them at the very last moment to deflect the first fireball. Two more fireballs were turned away harmlessly. Then Vorgulremik himself dropped down to hover barely his own wingspan away, directing the full force of his flames against Allan's shield.

It was a very uneven contest of magic, for Vorgulremik was Dalvenjah's equal and more than a match for her new apprentice. Allan quickly began to feel the strain. Then Jenny and Vajerral added all the magic they had to offer to the effort of keeping the shield up, while Rex, Marie and the two agents began a steady barrage with their powerful shotguns. The shield, which turned the flames effectively, seemed to have no effect upon the tight blasts of pellets from the guns, but Vorgulremik flinched under their sting. Still he refused to break off, seeing perhaps the best chance that he was likely to get.

The matter was decided suddenly with Dalvenjah's arrival at the scene. She hit him with fireballs squarely in the back three times before he could ignore her no longer. He broke off and twisted his head around to send a fireball of his own in her direction, forcing her to break off. The two dragons climbed back into the sky with long, sweeping strokes of their powerful wings. Allan relaxed his magical shield but remained ready against the possibility that this was yet another trick.

"That was close," Rex commented.

"She is tiring," Allan said, mostly to himself. "This can't go on much longer."

"Go to her," Wallick told him. "She needs your help if she is going to win this fight."

Allan turned to him. "I must. Load your guns and get into the woods. You are all too vulnerable out in the open like this."

"And you?" Marie asked anxiously.

"I can watch out for myself," he insisted. "I'm faster than he is, and smaller than either one of them."

He leaped back into the air, leaving them to do as he directed. He had seen already that Dalvenjah was subtly keeping their battle to this general area, always focusing back on the burning mansion and the open hilltop. That way he could keep himself to the very center of the battle, making himself available to protect the other mortals at the same time that he was always ready to dash forward and lend his support to Dalvenjah.

The matter was decided quickly. Dalvenjah dodged back into the clouds, then switched back abruptly to meet Vorgulremik head-on. They were still too far apart for their own flames to be effective, and so they resorted to yet another type of magic. The sky around them exploded into sheets and arrows of fiery lightning, but this time Dalvenjah was getting the worst of it. She suffered no more strikes than he did, but she was small and tired and each blast weakened her all the more. Stunned nearly senseless by a final, violent blow, she nearly tumbled from the sky. She never saw Vorgulremik coming until his great, powerful hands closed about her, plucking her from the air.

Allan had already been on his way to offer what help he could, and he saw what happened. He was nearing the end of his own strength; wingless, the effort of flying tired him all the more. But he knew that he had to act immediately if he was to save Dalvenjah's life, or at least prevent Vorgulremik from feasting upon her immortal spirit and adding her magic to his own. The only thing that had saved her this long was that the steel dragon was nearly exhausted himself, and he paused only a moment to catch his breath and savor his victory.

Summoning his remaining strength, Allan shot forward and his own form began to glow, changing from the blue of lift-magic to fiery golden, and then he disappeared within a shaft of flame. He knew that he lacked the magic to make this work properly. He could not kill Vorgulremik or even harm him greatly, but he could do some damage, perhaps enough to force the steel dragon to release Dalvenjah. He struck Vorgulremik in the very middle of the back and deflected off the armored ridges, and the dragon's scales split and smoked from that contact.

More than anything, Vorgulremik was taken by complete surprise by that sudden attack. He arched his back and roared in pain, but he did not release his prisoner. Allan maintained his fiery form by supreme effort and turned back, striking the steel dragon's thick arm just above the wrist. This time he did let go, and Dalvenjah tumbled free.

She fell and fell, doing nothing to save herself, and Allan feared that she was unconscious or even dead, crushed lifeless in that powerful grip. He shot to her side before transforming back to his true form. Seeing that the ground was rushing up quickly, he reached forward and took Dalvenjah by the straps of her harness, then pulled back with all of his strength. He had his doubts about his ability to save her from this fall, but he had to try. At least he was able to slow her somewhat, and after a moment he felt her respond and make an effort to control her own flight. Even that was beyond her, but she was able to get her wings out and resume a plummeting glide that Allan was then able to control through his own flight.

With Vorgulremik removed to nurse his own wounds, Allan knew that they had a few minutes at least. He directed their path back toward the hilltop and, by a tremendous effort on both their parts, was able to get her landed in the dry grass without further injury. There she lay, lifeless except for her labored breathing, lacking the strength even to fold away her wings. Vajerral peered into her face anxiously, but it was Marie who brought her a soft drink and something to eat from the van. Allan was too spent to take care of himself, so that the two agents had to lower him to the ground.

"Is that the end?" Rex asked as he bent over Allan in a professional manner.

"I don't know," Allan admitted, then waved the doctor away. "No, I'm just tired. Go see about her."

"I am well," Dalvenjah said faintly, lifting her head with some effort and blinking. She did not look all that well; Rex and Marie had to practically lift her into a seated position, but she did seem to recover somewhat once she had a drink and a few bites from the sandwich.

"Where is he?" she asked at last.

"Oh, he's sitting down there on the step of his burning house, panting like a dog who has been chasing too many sticks," Wallick reported, leaving his reluctant partner to watch the steel dragon. "I don't know quite what Allan did to him, but it did seem to hurt him quite a lot. You could see the smoke coming from his back for quite some time. The two of you might be exhausted, but he's hurt. So how do things stand from that?"

"I don't know," Dalvenjah admitted, shaking her head sadly. "I could finish him quickly if I had the magic. But my magic is gone for now, and I can find no more."

Marie was startled by her own idea, and she looked down at the rings she wore. The rings that she had received from James Donner so many years before, a man now long dead except in her memories. Then, with a sudden resolve, she pulled off the rings, handing the larger to Dalvenjah and the smaller to her own brother.

"Here," she said. "I remember what you said about gold enhancing your magic. It's not much, but maybe this will be enough to see you through."

Dalvenjah hardly knew what to say, then thought that she should best say nothing. She slipped the ring on her own hand, seeming to gain strength from every moment of contact, and smiled. "Alyesh thyarnan."

"Will that do it?" Wallick asked.

"I think so," she said. "Vorgulremik has no gold. If we act quickly, we can defeat him before he regains his strength."

"Can you really do it?" the agent insisted. "It seems to me that you've taken the worst so far."

"Nonsense!" Dalvenjah declared. "I am just tired; the gold is curing that in rapid order. Vorgulremik is hurt, thanks to Allan. And he has no one to help him."

"I guess you know best," Wallick reluctantly agreed. He glanced quickly over his shoulder, then continued softly. "I'm sorry about Don. We've been through a lot already, and this is just about too much for both of us. All of you are extraordinary people. I know that we're supposed to be above average ourselves when it comes to handling unusual or extreme situations, but you people seem to thrive on this sort of thing.''

"Think nothing of it," Dalvenjah assured him. In fact, neither she nor Allan had the slightest idea of what he was talking about, but they could guess easily enough. Borelli must have just about hit his limit during Vorgulremik's attack on their group.

"One more time," Dalvenjah told Allan. "Now, before he gets any stronger."

"Right behind you," he agreed.

Dalvenjah spread her wings and leaped into the night sky, seemingly well recovered from her ordeal. The small amount of gold that she had received from Marie did very little to augment her magic, but it had permitted her to recover her strength, both physically and magically, very quickly. Allan was still rather surprised to find that she had come to no harm during those long moments that Vorgulremik had had hold of her. She sprang into the air with renewed vigor, hurtling herself forward with powerful strokes of her wings while the misty blue light of her lift-magic thrust her to tremendous speeds.

She circled wide around the edge of the valley before dropping down toward the burning mansion, now nearly consumed in ravenous flames. Vorgulremik saw her coming and glanced up at her almost wearily, as if resigning himself to playing out this game to the bitter end. Did he sense her renewed strength, knowing at the same time that his own remained low? Did his battle rage permit him to withdraw defeated but alive, or did he even recognize the possibility that he might lose if he continued their fight? Either way, whether by choice or urged against his will by his very nature, he could not flee. He had run from her once, and found that running only prolonged their contest. And he was far from finished here; hurt and exhausted, he still had at least an even chance of winning.

He watched as Dalvenjah shot past, then spread his wings and heaved his own massive form into the sky with long, weary strokes of his wings. His scorched back no longer smoked, and he also seemed to regain much of his strength once he was back in the sky. Circling one another widely, the two dragons began their long, spiralling climb back toward the clouds, their chosen battleground.

Dalvenjah saw Allan signalling to her silently as he unobtrusively rejoined her in the sky, and she altered her course to head toward him as he hid himself in one of the larger banks of clouds. Vorgulremik followed her in casual pursuit, but he stopped short, backwinging to a startled hover, as she reemerged out of both ends of the cloud simultaneously. He blinked once and then again, until at last he understood. One was the real faerie dragon, and the other was her mortal apprentice wrapped in a strong illusion. But which was which? Appearance did not tell him. And when he tried to sense their individual magic, he found that they felt exactly the same. Allan had no magic of his own but was using Dalvenjah's, and so his magic felt to the senses exactly the same. The fact remained that he could not begin to tell which was real, and which was fake.

Reacting in that moment of indecision, both faerie dragons turned and headed directly toward him. Their forms began to glow with golden light, and then transformed into shafts of shooting flame. Now Vorgulremik's dilemma became acute. Both were dangerous, but only one had the power to destroy him. And he still did not know which one. He wasted precious moments trying to think his slow way through this problem, so lost was he in confusion. By then it was almost too late. He abruptly dropped his head low and dived straight down, letting gravity aid his magic in giving him the speed to escape. He did not possess this magic himself, and his adversaries were much faster than himself in their fiery forms. But they could not hold it for long.

One arrow of flame altered course, shooting down suddenly to intercept him. It seemed to be the faster, so therefore he assumed it to be the real Dalvenjah and fled from it, climbing yet again. But now the other streaked in with the same lightning dart, blatantly steering him back around as he tried to flee the prescribed area of the combat for the open sky. Now the first came up below him, forcing him to labor with all of his strength to gain height.

Higher and higher they climbed, until the burning mansion was nothing more than a point of light far below and the clouds

that the steel dragon had summoned began to thin in the icy
air. Then the two fiery forms slowed and transformed back to
their physical shapes, although they once again became two
Dalvenjahs. Still fresh even after that ordeal, they continued
to harass the larger dragon like two sparrows after a cat. Such
was Vorgulremik's state by then that he responded to their
attack. He knew that he was being herded and played with,
but he lacked the wit in his present confusion and agitation to
see his way through this problem.

But then desperation itself showed him the answer, and he
saw his one chance to counter this ploy of deception. Concentrating his magic as he had earlier, he called forth lightning
and directed it at one of the two faerie dragons whom he selected
more or less at random. It struck her full in the back before
she could shield herself with her own magic, momentarily
stunning her so that she nearly fell from the sky. But she
recovered in the next moment and looped away quickly to
recover. But Vorgulremik knew. Her apprentice might have
shielded himself from that blast, but no mortal, no matter what
magic he possessed, could have survived that last blast without
any protection. He now kept a careful eye on the one he knew
to be false, diving after that one.

The answer to this game was simple. If he could destroy the
false dragon, then he could concentrate his full energies on
defeating the real one as well. Now the false Dalvenjah turned
and ran from him, although the illusion remained as vivid as
ever. He wondered at that, knowing it to be a great drain of
magic. But he had failed to consider their own counterploy.
The first faerie dragon now rejoined that one and they flew
together so tightly that they could have reached out and joined
hands. They began a spectacular aerial dance, spiralling in and
out around each other until he no longer had the slightest idea
of which was which. Then they parted and shot away, each
disappearing into a separate bank of clouds.

Vorgulremik slowed almost to a hover. He watched and
waited patiently, ready to attack the first of the two to show
itself. Then one Dalvenjah darted out of the clouds behind him,
beginning the run that would lead to fiery transformation. But
the steel dragon was ready. Lightning lanced down out of the
sky to strike the tiny figure again and again, until golden scales

were singed and smoking and delicate wings were rent by gaping tears. Then, just before she tumbled helpless from the sky, he dived forward to grasp the faerie dragon out of the sky, crushing the life out of her as his spirit consumed her own. His powerful claws closed upon . . . nothing.

After first one dragon and then two, he was not prepared for the illusion of none at all. In the next moment Allan's flaming form shot down out of the sky to strike him squarely in the middle of the back, his former injuries exploding in new agony. He lifted his head to scream in pain and anguish, only to stare in silent disbelief as a second, far greater shaft of flame hurtled down to impact against his exposed chest.

The explosion of flame and magic filled the night sky, illuminating steely grey clouds momentarily gold, blue, and red in that brilliant flare. There was a misty, almost glowing quality to those flames, so great was the magic that Dalvenjah summoned to destroy her enemy. Then that tremendous flare of light and power died away in an instant, and the blackened, withered form of Vorgulremik tumbled lifelessly through the clouds that now seemed almost to draw away before it, dissolving back into the air with the death of the power that had summoned them. Blasted in body and utterly destroyed in spirit, the greatest of all Morilyekarin fell burning from the sky, a trail of thick, oily smoke marking his final passage.

· Part Eight ·

The Parting

DALVENJAH AND ALLAN descended together from the night sky, landing gently in the soft grass where the others stood looking out from near the edge of the hilltop. The ancient mansion was now fully enwrapped in flames that leaped up in eager shafts of fire as the old, dry timbers were consumed like paper. Vorgulremik's blasted remains had fallen into the woods perhaps a quarter of a mile to the right. A thick column of dark, heavy smoke still rose in the bright golden moonlight like an epitaph to the ending of an evil existence. Dalvenjah turned her head to glance a final time in that direction, seemingly disinterested. Then the others ran up to join them.

"You really did it!" Rex exclaimed. "The two of you destroyed him!"

"He really is gone?" Wallick asked guardedly. "For good?"

"Yes, he is gone."

Dalvenjah hardly seemed to care. The mortals fell silent, sensing something about her they did not understand. She did not seem tired or in any pain from her exertions, and certainly none the worse for wear. But she seemed neither excited, pleased, sad nor dejected. Indeed, she seemed almost to be waiting for something new to begin, something else to seize her attention and carry her away to other worlds. But Allan stared at her, and he realized with a sudden shock of sadness and dejection the one thought that occupied her mind at that moment, a distant smell of pine resin, the feel of a cutting wind over the ridges and a great, dark place she called home.

She turned then, as if hearing his thoughts, and nodded slowly. "Allan, will you help me please to open a Way Between the Worlds before our magic fades away?"

Before the magic fades away. Allan had to swallow dry tears, but he nodded sharply and stepped forward to take the hand she offered. The others retreated quickly back to the circle formed by the parked vehicles, waiting anxiously, never saying a word of comment on the suddenness of this departure. The pair turned and faced out into the night and a hazy blue mist of magic enveloped them as they called forth their magic. The dry grass was stirred by a sudden breeze that curled about their motionless forms, as if the wind itself was seeking something. The golden light of the rising moon seemed brighter than ever.

They focused their magic in a sudden thrust, the blue glimmer that surrounded them flaring into a sharp, bright light in the union of their magic. A brilliant white spark of light sprang into existence in the air above them, just beyond the edge of the hill, as they concentrated their full powers upon tearing open a rift in the substance of space itself. The curtain between the universes parted reluctantly, only a pinpoint at first, but gave suddenly under their unrelenting force. Great waves of magic mist flowed out in expanding circles from that point, and then the passage opened wide. They could all see down the length of the tunnel through the sky into the distant night of another world, and a cold wind poured out from the opening to stir the dry grass that carpeted the hilltop.

Dalvenjah turned to Allan, daring a half-smile of appreciation and reassurance as she searched his face to read some clue to his thoughts. But he only released her hand and turned away, unable to look at her. She stood for a long moment, watching him sadly. Did he think that she did not share his hurt and sorrow at the thought of this parting? If anything, her burden was the greater for having to make that decision. But her initial confrontation with Vorgulremik, there within his very den, had taught her an important lesson. Mortality was indeed contagious, if one dared to care for mortals on their own terms. Just as Allan was himself infected with her immortality.

The time to go was now, while she still could go and have any hope of ever being again the person she was before.

She checked the fit of her weapons in her harness, then turned and walked quickly back to where the others continued to wait in the shelter of the circled vehicles. Jenny and Vajerral sat together by the front wheel of the van, looking up at her with large, pleading eyes that asked if their time really had to end so soon. Then Wallick, gathering his courage first, stepped forward to meet her, extending his hand.

"I'm sorry that you want to go so soon, but it really is best," he said. "They must have seen that last explosion all the way back to the city. And with the old place still burning like that, someone will be along to investigate any time now."

She perked her ears, cocking her head inquisitively as she regarded him. "So you really will let me go home without a fuss?"

"We made you a promise, and you've earned it," he said. "I also think, as great and beautiful as you are, that there really is no longer any place in our world for dragons and magic. It's better that you go now."

"And your world will never know?"

He shrugged, unconcerned. "That's not for me to decide. We have that great, smoking carcass to show the world, and lots of little ones besides. But what can we say about dragons and their beauty from that, except that they're gone again? I thank you, for everyone, for all that you've done for us. And I at least will never forget you."

"Farewell, then."

She turned and walked over to where Jenny and Vajerral still sat together in the grass beside the van. She dropped her head well down so that she would be on a level with the girl, and Jenny, accepting that invitation, leaped up suddenly and hugged her firmly around the neck.

"I don't want you to ever leave!" she exclaimed, weeping aloud. "You dragons are the most wonderful thing in the whole world! Please don't go away so soon."

"I think you know why we must," Dalvenjah told her gently, holding her back so that they could see eye to eye.

"Yes, I guess," Jenny agreed, pausing to wipe her eyes on the bottom of her sweater. "Will I ever see you again?"

Dalvenjah shook her head in regret. "We may yet meet again, in another world and time. But never again in this one."

Jenny wept again, and hugged the sorceress tightly about her long neck. After a moment Marie walked over and gently laid a hand on the shoulder of her wing.

"I hate to admit it, but I am sorry to see you go so soon," Marie said. "As far as monsters go, you are something. Do you really have to go tonight?"

Dalvenjah smiled and nodded. "I wish to converse, confer, and otherwise hobnob with my fellow wizards. And this world is no place to raise a child, you must admit."

"I guess so," Marie smiled in return, sharing their private joke.

Dalvenjah glanced down, and quickly removed the ring from her hand. She held it out. "I suppose that you will be wanting this back."

Marie only shook her head, a firm, decisive gesture. "No, why don't you keep that to remember us by? I think it's time I let Rex get me a new one anyway."

Rex looked up at her in some surprise, then sniffed loudly and wiped his nose on his sleeve. "You mean that?"

"Of course I mean that," Marie said impatiently. "But you are going to have to shape up. I know who put leaves on my tree, but you're going to be on your own from now on."

Then she held out her hands to him, and he took her in his arms and they kissed, quickly but tenderly. Dalvenjah, looking on, smiled with warm satisfaction and was privately glad that she had waited long enough to see how their story was going to end. Jenny, observing from a safe distance, looked impressed and very relieved.

But all was not well, not by any means, and some stories might not have a happy ending. Dalvenjah turned and looked over her shoulder. Allan still stood alone in the darkness, a lonely and dejected figure, refusing to speak to her. Or perhaps just waiting for her to come to him. She smiled with tenderness and regret. However his story ended, she knew that she could delay this no longer. But she also knew in her heart what she must do.

Marie laid her hand gently on the faerie dragon's shoulder yet again. "I don't suppose that you have any magic words that will make him happy?"

"Perhaps I do," Dalvenjah remarked with just a note of decisiveness.

She walked out into the night, approaching him slowly and silently from behind. Still he would not speak nor even turn to look at her. She waited patiently for a long moment, wondering if he would ask. Or even if he knew what he wanted well enough to ask for it. She knew what she wanted.

"Lye assanda min," she told him softly. "I love you. Take your new inner name, and come home with me. I need you."

He turned and looked at her in open surprise. Such a turn of events, such a conclusion of their own thoughts and feelings and understanding, had obviously never occurred to him. But he needed hardly more than a moment to examine it all and decide what he really wanted. He reached out to take up her hands in his, smiling and yet on the verge of tears all at once.

"Of course I will," he promised her. " Lye assanda min, kas. On iydahs. Forever."

They stood for just a moment longer, before Dalvenjah stepped back until they were holding hands at arm's length. The others watched cautiously from the cover of the vehicles. Allan knew that she was allowing him a last moment for hesitation and regret, for once done it could never be reversed. And yet he knew in his heart that he had no regrets, not for the person that he had been or might yet have been, for all his hard work in pursuit of his dream, not even for those he left behind. New worlds awaited him, a new life altogether. His one regret was that circumstances could not have been quicker in bringing them together, through all the long years that he had needed her. And Dalvenjah read his heart, and knew that he was ready.

A soft, blue glow surrounded them again, as it had before when they had worked their magic together. The breeze died, and the night fell deeply silent as if in anticipation. The others, watching from the circle of the parked vehicles, looked on in silence. Then Dalvenjah said the words that defined his new inner name in a soft, clear voice.

"Desh'radhah hyena'ghenshye khavan."

Allan heard his inner name, the definition of his new inner essence, and it entered him and became his own. His entire form began to glow in a brilliant white light, so bright that it was blinding, and yet he could still be seen as a black silhouette within that bright flare of pure light. Then that black form flowed and shifted, and shaped itself into a new, larger likeness. Then the light faded quickly after a last sharp flare, and he stood revealed in the golden moonlight. Vajerral cried out some word of approval and delight, echoed by Jenny, although the others could only stare in awe and wonder.

Dalvenjah released his hands and took a single step back to regard him fully. Allan bent his own long neck to look at himself as best he could. He was at least a third again as large as she was, emphasizing well for the first time the fact that Dalvenjah really was very small for her kind. His scales were a deeper, almost burnished gold; his silver horns were longer and heavier, and the massive muscles that stood bunched over his double shoulders gave him an almost barrel-chested appearance in comparison. But he still possessed the same elfin beauty and grace, evoking the same sense of joy and wonder to mortal eyes.

Then Dalvenjah laid one hand on his cheek, gently but firmly forcing him to look up at her. His first reaction to her was one of hesitation, almost fear. But she did not leave him to wonder long; she leaned forward and they kissed, deeply and with the passion that they had never known existed. Vajerral made another sharp sound of approval, voicing her own delight, while Marie wept for joy.

And so it was that the dream that Dalvenjah had hardly dared to dream was proven true, and they both found new happiness when daring to take what they desired.

They parted and turned to watch as Jenny ran up to join them, weeping herself as she bore the ungainly burden of the cello case. She presented it to Allan without a word, and he accepted it, smiling down at her before she turned and ran back to rejoin the others. And it remained a mystery thereafter just who had hidden his cello in the back of the van, as if anticipating just such a need, or who had sent the child to fetch it. Dalvenjah herself had not known for certain that this was how their story would end. Marie kept that secret to herself, but she always wondered if she had worked her own magic that day. She had always professed to know what was best for her little brother, even if it turned out to be a dragon.

But the time had come to part. Dalvenjah glanced over her shoulder at the Way Between the Worlds, then looked to her mate. Allan spread his broad wings experimentally, looking back over his own shoulder, then turned to her and nodded. Vajerral had already leaped into the air and was darting back and forth over the vehicles like some oversized bat. Dalvenjah went first, and Allan lifted himself into the sky with the combined thrust of lift-magic and long, broad strokes of his wings. The dragons circled once wide around the hilltop, Allan with the cello held against his chest, lining up for their passage into a new world, as the mortals watched in wonder and joy.

They went together into the night, and the Way Between the Worlds closed behind them.

CLASSIC SCIENCE FICTION AND FANTASY

___DUNE Frank Herbert 0-441-17266-0/$4.95
The bestselling novel of an awesome world where gods and
adventurers clash, mile-long sandworms rule the desert, and
the ancient dream of immortality comes true.

___STRANGER IN A STRANGE LAND Robert A. Heinlein
0-441-79034-8/$4.95
From the *New York Times* bestselling author—the science
fiction masterpiece of a man from Mars who teaches
humankind the art of grokking, watersharing and love.

___THE ONCE AND FUTURE KING T.H. White
0-441-62740-4/$5.50
The world's greatest fantasy classic! A magical epic of King
Arthur in Camelot, romance, wizardry and war. By the author
of *The Book of Merlyn*.

___THE LEFT HAND OF DARKNESS Ursula K. LeGuin
0-441-47812-3/$3.95
Winner of the Hugo and Nebula awards for best science fiction
novel of the year. "SF masterpiece!"—*Newsweek* "A Jewel of
a story."—Frank Herbert

___MAN IN A HIGH CASTLE Philip K. Dick 0-441-51809-5/$3.95
"Philip K. Dick's best novel, a masterfully detailed alternate
world peopled by superbly realized characters."
                                        —Harry Harrison